Dislocation

Diana Duncan

Copyright 2025 Diana Duncan

Dedication

to Peter, Angela, Melissa, Emily, and Olivia.

International Edition

National Library of New Zealand

ISBN: 978-0-473-75773-1

1

'Can you *please* hurry up,' said the woman waiting behind Libby Prescott in the aisle of the plane shortly bound from Sydney to Christchurch. Libby, who was looking for her book in her hand luggage, glanced over her shoulder in a deliberately dismissive manner and thought about whether to respond. She *could* say in a wounded voice, 'I *do* apologise. I'm a little disorganised I'm afraid; you see I'm going home to my father's funeral.' *That* would make the woman feel bad. But since one thing she was learning with age was that it was always better to say nothing rather than something in most circumstances, and since the woman in question had the uncompromising face of a high country farmer's wife, she simply made a performance of looking for her pashmina shawl before leisurely putting her case in the overhead compartment, and muttering 'fuck you' under her breath as she turned away and smiled at the bleary eyed toddler leaning over the seat behind.

She had felt a weary sense of déjà vu while waiting to board. She had caught this flight many times after flying overnight from Hong Kong and her fellow travellers on this leg of the trip never seemed to change. There was the usual assortment of young backpackers nodding wearily into their headphones, several older women with crisp short bobbed hair and sensible walking shoes, and only a couple of 'suits' or travellers who looked as though they might be off on business. A young couple had spread some toys out on the floor for their toddler and now watched him with an indifference that suggested they had been travelling for some time, and when a delay to the flight was announced a young woman, breastfeeding her baby under a baby blue blanket covered with white lambs, slowly put her head back on the seat and closed her eyes as if it was all too much for her. A frail elderly couple waited patiently to board first, the woman in a wheelchair; as Libby watched them the man leaned over and rearranged his wife's shawl over her shoulders and she smiled up at him with the radiance of a child. Ever since she left Hong Kong Libby had felt tears threatening and now she looked quickly away.

Gosh she was being feeble! But she was so exhausted: her flight had landed late, so she had missed her connection and had been waiting in the transit lounge for hours. And flying always put her in such a *state*. All those years of travel; yet she still felt an uneasy premonition every time she boarded a flight, as though this time her luck might finally have run out. Even the rituals she had developed over the years – carrying a fashionable bag (of late a leather tasselled backpack) putting her sky blue pashmina in her hand luggage, and using the Mont Blanc pen Tom had given her for her fortieth birthday to fill out the customs forms – hadn't eased her anxiety on this trip.

She caught sight of herself in the window of a Duty Free shop as she walked to the gate and shook her head at her reflection. Unless you are a real beauty, age does you no favours, she thought. In some ways she was lucky; at least she had inherited her mother's broad forehead and wide mouth, and her eyes, Tom once told her after a few drinks, were stunning; the colour of a cold, cold sea. But now they were bruised by tiredness and her thick brown hair was a mess. She ruffled it half-heartedly as the staff checked her boarding pass. It would just have to do.

She knew she should be thankful that her father, Sam, had died peacefully in his sleep, but she still regretted that she hadn't been there with him as she often was at that time of year.

Last winter, he had suddenly looked like a very old man. Always slim, he had lost a shocking amount of weight, and although his pure white hair was still combed back carefully from his forehead, his nose, once so aquiline, now dominated his whole face and gave him a hawk-like appearance. And something in his demeanour had changed too. His eyes were glazed and creamy with cataracts. It was as though a light had been switched off somewhere inside.

He spent more and more time in his garden and Libby, watching him one day as she made lunch, wondered what he was thinking about as he leaned thoughtfully on his garden rake outside the kitchen window. Maybe he was dreaming about the time he spent in colonial India when he was young and lived in a world of polo, tiffin and summer sojourns to the hill towns. She suspected that the past had become far more real to him than the present. Now his winters were interrupted by the annual visits of his bossy expat daughter, and annoying grandchildren who lived in their own world of laptops and ear buds; and mobile phones which they kept in their laps even at meal times.

Last year was the first year she had visited on her own. They sat up late the night she arrived, watching a one day cricket match between Pakistan and New Zealand. Sam, ready for bed, was dressed in his pyjamas, his plaid slippers, and, incongruously, a faded Japanese kimono she had given him years ago.

'Shall we go to the doctor while I'm here?' she said, choosing her moment carefully, as she handed him a cup of tea. 'You should get regular check-ups at your age.'

'What on earth for?' he responded, not even looking away from the screen. 'Who was it said "Death is an old man's friend"? I'm not interested in playing for time. If you'll pardon the pun,' he added.

'Well, it's your funeral,' Libby said.

They both laughed. 'I'll run you a bath,' he said. 'The Paki bowling is ruddy hopeless. You should get to bed.' 'Ruddy' was the only swear word he ever used in front of women. 'Probably on the take,' he grumbled as he went into the bathroom.

'Your generation is so racist Dad,' said Libby. 'You can't say things like that nowadays.'

But now she wished she hadn't let him change the subject so easily.

She felt the usual mixed feelings at the thought of seeing her siblings together again. She had lived away for so long that she often felt like an outsider. They had their sprawling houses and solid accoutrements of old school friends, merino wool jumpers and cushions that lay flattened and untidy on tired sofas at the end of the evening when the families went to bed. *She* was used to the expat life, with an apartment filled with Chinese lacquer chests and exotic Asian furniture that – in the early days when she had full time help – was polished daily by her Filipino helper, who arranged the cushions meticulously on the sofas every night like props in a play. She knew she would get over these feelings of estrangement after a few weeks, but each time the culture shock surprised her and she felt all the irrational hostility that foreigners often experience when they visit a new country.

And she hated the way she always regressed. She became the baby of the family once again, always struggling to be heard, somehow always on the back foot, even though she had left years ago and been independent and survived without them all. We never escape our childhood or our place in the family, she thought. It is pathetic.

Her sister Charlotte met her at the airport.

'Gosh, you took ages to come through.'

People found it hard to believe they were sisters. Charlotte's thick chestnut hair was pulled back in a bandana, emphasising her high cheekbones, short top lip and aristocratic nose, like her father's. She was wearing an extravagantly embroidered jacket with a long flowing dress underneath. The jacket was covered in exotic animals and birds, cheetahs and peacocks, elephants and parrots with beaded eyes and sequined ears or tails. The top button was missing and her collar had a stain, as pale as a baby's breath, on it, but she was piled high with charm and her carelessness with her clothes had always been a part of her persona.

'You look fabulous,' said Libby.

'You look exhausted.'

'Thanks.'

'I mean washed-out with all that travelling.'

'I told you not to bother picking me up,' said Libby. 'It's crazy coming out at this time of night.'

'Well, how did you think you'd get home?'

'Taxi of course.'

'You're not in Asia now you know,' said Charlotte. 'You'd be lucky to find one so late at night. And if you did find one, it would be quite likely to be driven by a serial rapist. The city isn't safe anymore. I haven't even had time to make up the bed for you at Dad's house. Are you sure you want to stay there? Alone?'

'Still exaggerating I see, and yes, it's fine. You've got a house full.'

Charlotte was such a drama queen. Everyday problems in the household – a disappointing date for one of her girls, a lost dog, or an imagined slight from a friend – were elevated to the same status as catastrophic world events. Although a part of Libby admired the energy it took to live with this degree of passion she preferred to be an occasional observer, rather than a participant, in the circus Charlotte called everyday life.

Yes it would be peaceful staying at home, although after the funeral Libby supposed they would have to clear the house out and put it on the market. That is, if some of the more valuable pieces hadn't been spirited away already. Her other sister, Tilda, would have made sure that *her* personal favourites were well gone. No doubt the antique silver serving spoons from India, Rose's art deco brooches that were now back in vogue, and the hand mirror with the faded embroidered back that Tilda had always loved, would be long gone before the family assembled to observe the 'Lottery Clause' in Sam's will. And nobody, not even Charlotte, would dare to ask where these had mysteriously vanished to. They had learned over the years that where Tilda was concerned it was always better to leave well alone.

At this time of night the wide avenue they drove along was deserted, the streets and houses empty, like a city under curfew. She and Charlotte fell silent, frozen like subjects in a still life painting. Only the occasional car lights flashed past them, coming and going in the darkness. Above, Libby heard the low throb of a plane and saw the steady heartbeat of its lights as it came in to land. The houses on either side rose and fell behind them in a cacophony of adjectives in her mind: 'neat,' 'tidy,' 'residential,' 'uniform'. They were mainly low wooden bungalows with doors for mouths and windows for eyes. Chimneys were everywhere, like exclamation marks against the skyline. Inside the houses she imagined sleeping couples, curled together or as remote as planets in their beds, mouths open, snoring, their books open on the bedside table, beside half-eaten apples and reading glasses. She pictured the children, safe in their bedrooms down the hallway, snuffling and turning like puppies in their sleep.

Then, with a wild rush of homesickness, she thought of the contrast to Hong Kong, where night was like day, and where the bars were so crowded at all hours that they spilled people onto the streets where they gathered like theatre goers in an interval. In Soho, the pedestrian escalator that glided from the heart of the city up to the residential area halfway up the peak was always crammed with giggling office girls in miniature skirts and breathtakingly high heels, delivery boys with jeans hanging off their bottoms clutching cardboard boxes and iPhones, and 'suits' with their heads down who strode up and down the escalator like athletes on a treadmill. On the narrow streets and lanes every night of the week, the young professionals wandered along looking for somewhere to eat, confident, brash, and trailing behind them the scent of wealth and sex and success. You could almost smell the trace of Dior and Gucci and stale beer and late, late nights every night of the week. Unlike this city, Hong Kong was an insomniac. It never slept.

After Charlotte left Libby went into the living room and sat on the faded velvet armchair facing the fireplace. It was deafeningly quiet and she realised with surprise that she had never been alone in the house before. She half expected her father to come out of the bathroom in his old striped winceyette pyjamas and cross the living room door on his way to the bedroom. Although she bought him new pyjamas each year for his birthday, she suspected she would find several pairs still unwrapped in his chest of drawers. In winter he wore the same old outfits most days: the pale blue or grey cashmere sweaters with the frayed cuffs, fawn or black corduroy trousers, faded gabardine shirts, and lace-up brown shoes that he polished carefully every morning. She went through to his bedroom and switched on the light. She opened the wardrobe. It was as cold as a chapel inside. A couple of tweed jackets, three or four pairs of trousers, a knitted vest that he never wore. Since Rose had died his life had become as simple as a monk's, his clothes arranged neatly each night on the occasional chair placed in the corner of the room. A lump rose in her throat and she swallowed. Her mother, Rose, had died four years ago and her memory was now a tender one, easier to live with, when she returned home each year. She knew there would be no hot water bottle in her bed tonight, wrapped like a gift inside her pyjamas, no fruit cake in the dented tin on the kitchen table, no full-blown roses from a winter garden extravagantly packed into a crystal vase on her bedside table.

Last year when she visited she and Sam had settled into an easy pattern as though they had lived together for years. They both loved watching rugby or cricket on the TV; Libby had learned to enjoy the banter of the commentators, the thrill of the catch, the grinding physicality of the rugby scrum, and Sam said one night – high praise indeed – that she was as informed about the rules as 'any chap'. It was often after midnight before they got to bed.

It was obvious that he was happier now she was here on her own. When the girls were young, she could tell they made him feel his age; they were like young goddesses, brash and confident and hogging all the attention. Suddenly his life was full of teenage tantrums, gleaming lipsticks and perfume bottles and cleansers that lay all over his bathroom. Denim jeans with savage slashes like wounds were draped on kitchen chairs; he tripped over their scruffy boots as he came through his *own* front door; they left doors open and lights on and never sat at the table to eat meals. He was ambushed everywhere he went by their loud voices, side-lined by a vernacular as strange to him as a foreign language. Driven out of his living room, he would retreat into the garden and tend his roses, finding comfort in the daily routines of pruning and mulching, clipping and digging, patiently waiting out the time until he could be alone again.

She wandered through to the kitchen. His presence was still everywhere. The place was full of him, all the daily bric-a-brac of his life on display. In fact, the house was still, in essence, her mother's. Men changed little in a home when a wife died. The Old Staffordshire bowl, 'Chinese Rose', lay on the mantelpiece, the insipid watercolours of North Canterbury landscapes swamped by embossed gold frames smothered the living room walls and the crystal French bonbon dish, once filled with fresh lemons each week, was now empty and had been pushed to the back of the sideboard behind a couple of old newspapers. On his tallboy his white handkerchief still lay neatly folded and his coins lay in the cut glass bowl that had been there for as long as she could remember. Her father was remarkably careless about his loose change and she and her brother Edward had regularly taken money from the bowl, half crowns in those days, never more. The son of a wealthy North Canterbury farmer who had lost his farms in the Great Depression, her father had inherited some extravagant habits from his mother. One of these had been his love of beautiful houses.

'She was profligate,' he told Libby one night when she asked him about his childhood. 'She bought and sold second houses as often as other women buy and discard shoes. My poor father had to live by himself all week out on the farm while she flounced around town moving us from one home to another when the mood took her.' When the children were young Sam would sometimes point out his old family homes to them as they drove around the city on Sunday drives. Two of them were extensive mansions, now restored, with sweeping circular driveways and Range Rovers parked outside. Another one had been turned into apartments. Its once grand driveway was covered in weeds and the original harmony of its façade ruined over the years by cheap extensions and extravagant windows. 'It's a travesty,' he muttered every time they passed. 'Ruddy nouveau riche.'

So it was Sam, who loved looking at property, not Rose, who'd found their holiday house, Belle Maison at Akaroa, where, for many years, the family spent every summer holiday.

When a dog barked somewhere along the street Libby went to the window and pulled the curtains back. The animal was bored, judging by the plaintive repetitiveness of the sound. There was a light on in the house across the road and she imagined a woman, like her, frozen in a nightly ritual of insomnia, reading or mindlessly watching television.

This country was so far from the rest of the world. In the suburbs you always had the sense you were missing out on something; the occasional street lights, the dog barking, the empty roads and the pitch-black nights made you feel as though you were alone, as far away from the centre of the universe as it was possible to be. And yet, even after all these years away, something still settled inside her when she arrived back. The sky outside the window was so familiar – vast and beautiful – and even on a cloudy night there was a great world above of shifting clouds and stars and space. Although it looked as though rain was threatening, the night had a glorious translucency about it, the air as clear as glass. Charlotte said a hot nor-wester had blown across the plains that day.

'But a southerly change is forecast for tomorrow,' she added, 'so dress warmly.'

One day soon, Libby promised herself, she would drive over to Banks Peninsula. She would choose a sunny morning and walk down the hill to the seafront, around the promenade, out on the wharf to check the local fishing catch and past the light house on the point. She might even go over to stay at Belle Maison and offer to tidy it up. It would need a good sorting out after all these years. She smiled to herself. Clearing up and throwing out was her forte. She loved creating order out of chaos. It would be especially rewarding now that her own life was so messy. She was better at managing houses than she was relationships, she thought grimly.

Tom told her he had fallen in love with someone else just weeks before Sam died. Libby embroidered the story to make it more entertaining when Charlotte asked about it, because that's what you did in the family when dealing with matters close to the heart. Exaggeration was recognised as an art form, as if a story well told somehow made things less painful.

'He said he felt *remorseful*' she said, as Charlotte made her a cup of tea before she left that night.

'What a ridiculous word,' Charlotte said. 'It's so inadequate.'

'He said he wanted another chance at happiness,' said Libby. 'I told him that was a hackneyed cliché. He said he was in love with Amy, a young local barrister from his chambers. "She understands me. I've been so lonely", he said.'

'Oh *bring* on the violins,' said Charlotte. 'What is it with men? They're pathetic.'

Libby shook her head. '"And *I* don't understand you?" I said. "After 30 years of marriage I understand you better than anyone! And I understand *her* type too. I could write her CV with my eyes closed. I'll bet she's bright, ambitious, loves older successful men and will use you to further her career at the Bar."'

'Good on you,' said Charlotte. 'What did he say to that?'

'He shook his head at me, as though he was puzzled by my unreasonable attitude and said it was disappointing that I'd become so cynical and world weary. And he is right, in some ways,' Libby continued, running her finger around the top of the chipped mug Charlotte had handed her. 'As I've grown older I *have* become more cynical; but then maybe that's just another word for wise. And anyway, it's like my occasional smoking habit, or my obsession with wearing cashmere. I am too set in my ways to change.'

She might have added, she should have seen this coming. Tom had always worked excessively hard; it was a quality she admired. So she'd tried not to complain when he'd returned early from their summer holidays, leaving her alone with the children. It was the expatriate way of life after all and how could she grumble when every second year they were able to do something exotic like renting a handsome villa in Tuscany or tastefully restored country houses in the Dordogne where they spent glossy indulgent summers lying round pools overlooking hills as soft as crushed velvet. In the morning she walked into the nearby villages, just like a local, with a basket slung over her arm, and shopped in the weekly market for cheeses and peaches and fresh breads.

But maybe they had lost an edge over the years spent living like that; maybe they had become spoilt and lost the resilience you need to keep a long marriage going. After the children left home they should have changed direction and found new projects and hobbies together. She was as much to blame as Tom. She had worked hard to be promoted in the international school she worked in and had more time to spend the hours needed to get into senior management once the girls had gone.

'You mustn't blame yourself,' said Charlotte, banging the cups down angrily on the kitchen bench as she washed up. 'Marriage is like a bloody garden isn't it? You have to be always weeding and watering it. It all becomes a complete bore. And,' she added as an afterthought. 'Let's face it. Tom has never got over 9/11 has he? You should take that into account!'

'There is some truth in that,' said Libby. 'And then Mum said you always pay for your happiness. Remember? She said you should never get complacent and she hated it when people said they were "blessed". So I've always been apprehensive if

I'm too happy. I'm scared the Gods will come and take me down a peg. Maybe I asked for it and Amy is my nemesis.'

'That's nonsense. Hubris has never been your thing. Tilda's if anybody's. Honestly, you do go on. That's the trouble with teaching literature for too many years.'

'Do you think I'm still in shock?' said Libby. 'I seem to live through every day in a sort of daze. If I was younger and more confident I would probably think up some sort of devious plan to get Tom back, but I feel ancient and uncertain of myself now and I just don't have the imagination, let alone the energy. And it's always so demeaning somehow when older women try to win back their adulterous husbands from a younger woman, when they really should just tell them to fuck off. And friends can be so cruel. Loyalty is so passé nowadays. It's quite tedious to stick with the injured party. I've seen it happen with loads of my friends. People don't have the balls to bear grudges on behalf of their friends anymore. It's no fun. And,' she added dramatically, 'I feel as though I'm carrying round a wet clump of clay in my stomach. And my chest hurts. Perhaps it's just heartburn.'

'Heart*ache* more like it,' said Charlotte brusquely, but when Libby saw her out she ruffled her hair gently, the strongest expression of affection in their family, and said, 'You know I will bear a grudge against Tom on your behalf for as long as you like, don't you. Years. Or decades. Even though he's my favourite brother-in-law. And you'll get through this. But please don't give up on him yet. Maybe you should talk to a counsellor. Half my friends rush off to them every five minutes; I could get you loads of recommendations.' Then, thoughtfully, 'I know one who is *very* handsome. Like a movie star.'

Libby laughed. 'As if I'd like that. Get me someone who is just above average and I might consider it. I've always felt threatened by good looks.'

'See, that's another problem you could sort out,' said Charlotte, opening the back door and shivering in the cold air. 'You lack confidence. And you know what I think. Tom is fundamentally such a good man. And look at the life you'd be giving up if you left him. Half of Tilda's problem with you is that she's always been madly envious of you and Tom and your expat life. Of course, having lived in Hong Kong myself I tried to tell her it wasn't as glamorous as she thinks, although of course I was lying through my teeth. We all know, in our hearts, that there's no place quite like it and you never recover from living there. But thankfully I don't do envy and anyway, I – sadly – just didn't have the resilience to survive there.'

'It's true that you are never envious of anyone,' said Libby. 'I've always admired that quality in you. And maybe I do need to speak to someone; just to make sense of things. Do you remember how happy Tom and I were at first? Tom always tells the girls it was love at first sight, although in reality we were both blind drunk, so I'm not sure that phrase is apposite!'

'Yes, men always look so much more attractive when you've had a few drinks,' said Charlotte.

'In fact; we all do.'

***

Libby met Tom when she was teaching English at an international school in Hong Kong in the early seventies. She was appearing in a local production of *The Importance of Being Ernest* – bullied into playing the role of Gwendolen Fairfax by the director, her head of Drama – who found herself in a fix when she realised that the talent pool she had to draw from in this colonial backwater wasn't all she imagined it might be.

'Amateur actresses are such a painful lot,' Brenda complained. 'They all think they have a leading role in them and get terribly offended when you don't give them the main part.

And if they do get the main part they instantly become prima donnas and want to run the show. I am confident you won't be like that,' she said, looking at Libby hopefully. 'A little bird told me you've dabbled in some theatre.'

Libby doubted her limited experience and moderate talent would extend to playing a leading role, but it was impossible to say no to someone as desperate and persistent as Brenda, and anyway, once she had learned her lines, she found to her surprise that she enjoyed the camaraderie to be found working with a small cast and in particular the after-show drinks they shared in the backstage bar each night after rehearsals.

She was introduced to Tom at the first night party. One of her flatmates had been at Oxford with him. Tom was tall and lanky with thick brown hair which looked as though he only occasionally ran a comb through it and an attractive rakish smile. He was leaning on the bar in a pub in Central; one of the few drinking establishments around in those days and popular with expatriates as it was decked out like a classic English pub with dark wood furnishings, football posters on the wall and a bar wide enough to dance on. Although the pub was smoky and the lighting dim she could see that he had the sort of eyes she liked; they crinkled up and almost disappeared when he laughed.

'You were very good as Gwendolen,' he said. 'I enjoyed your performance immensely.'

'Really?' said Libby. 'I noticed that Paul sniggered through most of the first act and didn't reappear after the interval. Rumour has it that he was in the downstairs bar. Were you with him?'

He didn't even have the grace to look disconcerted. 'Not my favourite play actually,' he confessed. 'But I did like your take on the accent.'

'What do you mean?' said Libby indignantly. 'That Wilde can only be done in Received Pronunciation?'

'Of course not!' he said hastily. 'The play is all about Performance anyway. People pretending to be someone they are not. It certainly doesn't need the actors to use artificial accents as well.'

Libby said, smiling, 'I *am* pretty hopeless in the part. Let's be honest about it. The play itself is not really my thing either. I've always thought Wilde overrated.'

'Not at all,' Tom said gallantly. 'It's true to say I was very moved by your performance; I'm not exaggerating when I say I'd travel thousands of miles to see you on stage again. Fortunately,' he added with perfect comic timing, 'I live in the Mid-Levels so that won't be necessary. In fact I think I'll come again tomorrow night.'

Libby laughed. 'Come again any time you like. I like a man with stamina. Three acts of Wilde. You'll need it!'

Tom raised his eyebrows as though they had just shared a risqué joke. And he did come to see the play the next night, as promised, waiting for Libby afterwards at 'the stage door' as he called it, drawing out the three words as though he was referring to a film title, although Libby suspected there was irony involved as there were only two flimsy metal doors that opened onto the shabby laneway outside from their cramped communal dressing rooms. When he told their daughters the story years later, as one of a series of their favourite bedtime tales that they loved hearing over and over again, he exaggerated it and said he sent twelve red roses to the theatre every night until the season finished.

'The roses were crimson and still dripping with the morning dew,' he boasted. 'I picked them myself from the botanical gardens as I walked to the theatre. Your mother was a huge hit. Queues of eligible young men, every one of them handsome enough to be a prince, waited at the stage door each night to pay her homage.'

'But Daddy there are no roses in the gardens,' said Abbie always the literal one. 'And it's bad to pick flowers in public places.'

And Cleo added innocently, 'Can you call it a season if it is only four nights long?'

'There was one secret hidden corner of the gardens that had two rose bushes in it in those days,' Tom said, warming to his theme. 'It was tended by an old Chinese gentleman and he was growing the roses in memory of his wife, whom he had been married to since he was a very young man in Shanghai. They had escaped the Communist regime there and suffered many hardships over the years, but he told me she had always been hardworking and true to him and when he became very rich after being poor for many years he knew he had her to thank for it. I often asked him about his life and stopped to talk to him as I walked through the gardens to work on winter mornings and he told me that I would know I had fallen in love when I wanted to take some of his beautiful red roses to my girlfriend. Then one day he wasn't there when I walked past the rose bushes, nor the days after. The rose bushes started to bow down under the heavy weight of the flowers because nobody was pruning them. And that,' he said triumphantly, 'is why I filled Libby's dressing room with hundreds of roses each night. I knew the old man, my friend, would want me to take as many roses as I could carry to my girlfriend when I finally fell in love.'

'Oh well that's ok then isn't it Daddy,' said Cleo. '*That's* not stealing.'

'You fill their head with such nonsense,' Libby said to him after they tucked the girls into bed. 'But it is beautiful nonsense.'

And it was true that Tom did send her red roses each night and it was true that they were crimson; although not dripping with morning dew. Their reflection in the make-up mirrors brightened up the drabness of the dressing room and the other cast members declared themselves dazzled by such an excessive gesture.

And Libby knew that she and Tom looked good together. Falling in love made her beautiful. She had inherited some of her mother's mannerisms and had a way of putting her head to one side when she was listening to him that Tom found enchanting. That summer was – for both of them they agreed later – a time when they felt that they were close to the essence of life, right at its very centre.

'Are you sure about this?' said Rose doubtfully when Libby told her she wanted to marry Tom. 'With *his* background?'

'Most mothers would be happy to have their daughters marry someone from a privileged background,' said Libby. 'I don't understand what you've got against the English. Why are you so prejudiced?'

'It's so easy to be taken in by their wonderfully cultured voices,' said Rose. '*I* know all about that.'

'What are you talking about?' said Libby, exasperated. 'Honestly Mum; that is ridiculous.'

'It's just that you always rush into things,' Rose continued, unabashed. 'Think of those ridiculous shoes you're always buying.'

'You're overexcited, Mum,' said Libby, watching as Rose made a performance of wiping the bench down and putting the dishes away in Libby's untidy kitchen cupboard in her tiny Hong Kong apartment. 'You just want me to marry a good old Kiwi boy. I don't know how Dad puts up with your bossiness.'

'Oh he likes me taking charge,' said Rose complacently. 'He's become as meek as a lamb since he retired.'

'That's true,' Libby said. Now, when she visited her parents, Sam spent much of the day in his garden, tending his roses, or making the odd foray to the TAB to place a bet. Travelling abroad was something he did only reluctantly.

'You can't know a man properly after such a short time,' Rose continued. 'And do you really want to live in Hong Kong permanently? And don't worry. I've known plenty of people like him in my time. Those *Oxbridge* types. They are just not like us when it boils down to it. You only have to think of Sebastian Flyte.'

'Are you joking? What on earth does *he* have to do with Tom? He's a character in a novel for God's sake. A novel! Fiction, Mum. That means the characters are not real people.'

'I know that. I know that,' said Rose. 'There's no need to be smart.'

But she looked flustered and Libby couldn't resist adding sarcastically, but with an amused smile.

'Mum. May I remind you? You thought *Flashman* was a real person.'

Thank goodness, she thought. Her parents would soon be safely in Greece, where they had rented a village house for a month. Libby spent a week there with them and was moved by the beauty and simplicity of the island. The house was a steep walk up from the town and was set above a rocky bay. It was crumbling with age, painted cream and covered with sturdy vines of wisteria. Weathered wooden benches and a sturdy table were set out in the small courtyard overlooking the sea over the sloping orange tiled roofs tops of the traditional village houses below.

Molyvos, a small town on the island of Lesvos, was set under the protection of a vast 12th century Byzantine fortress. In the morning they sat in cafés watching as the drama of the morning ritual unfolded; the fishermen noisily unloading their boxes of sardines and mackerels to waiting pick-up trucks so they could be hurried off to the markets in Mytilene or sold to other towns and villages around the island.

At night they wandered down to the village under the canopy of wisterias that lined the main street and dined in simple tavernas, set off the cobbled lanes and overlooking the coast of Turkey. Libby could see it from her bedroom window; like a huge animal slumbering on the horizon. She thought about Tom constantly and tried to call him each night from the village post office, but even if she got through to him the line was usually bad and crackled and spluttered so loudly that she couldn't hear half of what he said.

Sam and Rose seemed so content there together that Libby wondered whether they should stay there forever; living a simple life away from family and friends. She cried bitterly when she left them. She had never been good at saying goodbye.

Libby hated preparing for bed in her father's wretched bathroom. She splashed her face quickly, too tired to unpack her toilet bag. Sam's toothbrush and toothpaste still lay on the wooden ledge above the basin, and a pink flannel with 'Nonna' embroidered on it, given some years ago to her mother by Libby's Filipino helper, rested on the side of the bath. It was the little things that caused so much pain; the muddy shoes outside the kitchen door, the silver hairbrush on the tallboy, the bathrobe hanging behind the door. The towels were so old they were only held together by threads in places.

They should all have looked after him better. Men were hopeless on their own. And *she* should have been there when he died. If she'd been in the next room she might have heard him cry out. It was too awful to think of him being alone. If she hadn't been brooding over her own life, wondering what to do next and where to go and whether she was so deeply hurt because she still loved Tom, or whether she just feared loneliness, she would have been here, visiting her father as she always did during the hot, long humid days of a Hong Kong summer. She had let him down.

2

The next day she woke early to the sound of rain splattering lazily on the corrugated iron roof. She turned over, snuggled back under the covers, and thought of all the days over the years when she had awoken in this house to that same sound. With it belonged the clatter of plates and cups as her mother prepared breakfast, the clunk of the fridge being opened and closed, the static of the radio and the snap as her father shook the pages of the newspaper into place.

She stared absentmindedly at the ceiling. A leak must have developed somewhere in the cavity between the rafters and the roof and a dirty brown stain was spreading slowly across it and down one corner of the wall. She half closed her eyes to try to detect a form to it. She had done the same thing with light and shadows on the ceiling when she was a child, lying in bed on summer mornings when she had been told it was too early to get up. The stain definitely had the profile of a hawk nosed person, but if she closed her eyes even further, it became an exaggeratedly large-bosomed woman with tiny feet. 'Bosom.' How she and Edward used to giggle whenever they heard that word. Nobody used it nowadays. She sighed and looked at her watch. Only 6.30 a.m. but already the room with its flimsy, unlined curtains was flooded with the crisp early morning light.

The rain had stopped. The curtains slouched against the wall. The whole house should have been renovated years ago; it was a mess now with its faded oriental carpets overlapping one another in the living room, the half-closed venetian blinds, the musty scent of neglected cupboards and out-of-date food.

The year before Libby had decided, on an unseasonably fine day two weeks into her annual visit, that she would give the house a facelift. She would start by replacing the faded quilt spread on her father's bed with a duvet. On his golf day, with the whole morning free, she stripped the bed, changed the sheets and arranged the new duvet inside the crisp white 1000 thread count duvet cover she had bought. She stood, hands on hips, the sun falling on her shoulders through the open window, and smiled to herself. That looked so much better. She placed the bedspread, neatly folded, on top of the battered metal rubbish tin standing outside the front gate awaiting the weekly collection. Unfortunately for her, Sam returned home early. If he had arrived a little later it would have been a fait accompli. In fact, she thought sourly to herself in retrospect, being a man, he probably wouldn't have even noticed the change. He had played a poor round and his temper was not improved by the sight of several young men carelessly tossing his bedspread from one to another and into the back of a smelly old garbage truck. Startled by his angry shouting, they listened sympathetically and had retrieved it for him just as Libby came out to see what all the fuss was about. Crestfallen, she could feel their disapproval, even though she smiled at them in what she imagined was a conspiratorial way. Apparently immune to her charms, they hoisted themselves up on the back of the truck, and one of them, covered from head to foot in tattoos, saluted her father sympathetically as they took off.

'It was rather presumptuous of you,' Tom said carefully when he called that night.

'I should have known better than to expect any appreciation from the family,' she continued, ignoring him. 'And then to add insult to injury, Dad made me put the quilt back!'

'If you'd heard the way Dad carried on about it you'd think I'd dismantled his whole jolly bed and put it out to be taken away,' she complained later to Charlotte.

'Serves you right,' said Charlotte. 'You are a typical teacher. So bossy. In fact, you're a control freak.'

'Ruddy cheek,' said Sam, when she tried to justify herself to him. 'How would you like it if someone threw your bedding out?'

She smiled wryly to herself as she got out of bed. Now she could put the bedspread in the rubbish with impunity.

She pulled the curtain back and looked out. The roses lining the driveway – her father's pride and joy – were sodden from the previous night's rain. Rusty brown blooms hung in tatters from the branches. She imagined they must need dead-heading, but had only a vague idea of what this meant. She would Google it and tackle it later in the week. Over the road a furtive-looking neighbour, clad only in a t-shirt and underpants, dashed out to get his newspaper. He glanced over her way and she quickly stepped back from the window.

She shook her head. Her mind kept returning to the phone call she had received just as she was about to climb into bed. It was Tom, sounded uncharacteristically glum. He was the last person she wanted to hear from. She was cool to him and answered in monosyllables as he asked about her journey. 'Why on earth are you calling?' she said eventually. 'As though nothing had happened.'

'Well I feel a little left out,' he said. 'I loved your father too you know.'

'Oh my God. Everything is about you isn't it?' said Libby. 'How you dare call me on the eve of my father's funeral and talk about yourself and your loss! It's my loss, not yours and you should have been here with me. But you're not and that makes it even sadder for me. I'm going now, before I start to cry.'

Now she was so upset she wouldn't be able to sleep. She wandered through to the kitchen and found some teabags. There was some milk in the fridge, some hard cheddar cheese, old butter the colour of custard on a white plate, but no bread.

The temperature had dropped suddenly and she watched the rain beating down on the corrugated iron roof of the carport outside. The weather reminded her of dull winter afternoon drives to Sumner for afternoon tea, when they were kids. Despite threats from Sam that he would stop the car and leave them on the footpath to make their own way home, she, Tilda, Edward and Charlotte would squabble incessantly in the back seat. Sumner was usually deserted apart from a few brave people, usually dog owners, walking along the esplanade. In her memories, the weather was always cold and blustery and the water an icy green under a weak sun. Although she knew that café life and better roads had transformed the Sumner she remembered, childhood memories were always fixed in a time and place; there was no room in them for redemption.

Charlotte, as always, was late to pick her up the next morning and Libby was waiting impatiently outside for her when she finally arrived. They were to view Sam's body at the crematorium before the funeral the following day.

'I'm not that keen on doing this. Seeing Dad I mean,' Libby said. 'I'd prefer to remember him the way he was the last time I was here.'

'One of the lucky escapes you had living overseas. You didn't have to see him at the end.'

'Hang on! I was only here a few months ago. It's not as though he had a terminal illness or anything.'

'That's true but it was hard going keeping his spirits up. He'd even stopped popping in to the TAB. Old men get so grumpy, don't they?'

'It wasn't that easy living away all these years you know,' Libby replied. 'I missed the family. We had no real support system. Especially when the girls were young.'

'You had a maid!'

'We call them helpers now,' Libby said, shaking her head reprovingly. 'We've moved on since you were there. That doesn't make up for it anyway. But let's not get in to that. I still think it's a weird thing to do don't you? "Viewing the body". It sounds like a movie title.'

'I don't know why Edward and Tilda didn't ask me when they went to see Dad yesterday,' said Charlotte. 'They said they'd called me and there was no answer, but I was home most of the day.'

'Maybe they did.'

'Rubbish,' she said. 'They've got my mobile number anyway. They just wanted to leave me out.'

'Why on earth would they do that?'

'Whenever Tilda comes down from Wellington they start to cut me out. They pal up. It used to be you and Edward. After you left it became Tilda and Edward.'

'Well, I'm here now,' said Libby. She squeezed Charlotte's shoulder. 'Thank goodness I've got someone to go with. I need your moral support.'

'Sorry. I'm just tired. Edward was good, though. He helped me to choose the clothes to lay Dad out in: your tie, Tilda's shirt, and my underpants. Well not *mine* exactly, but the ones I gave him for Christmas.'

'Last Christmas I hope. Not the Christmas before…'

Charlotte giggled. 'Yes, I know what you mean. Most of his old undies were long overdue to be used as dusters.'

'What a practical world we used to live in. Old undies used as dusters. No one would dream of doing that nowadays. Surely Dad deserved a brand new pair to be buried in?'

'Waste not; want not,' Charlotte said. 'His generation was full of those clichés. The tie was one of the rugby ties Tom gave him over the years. He loved showing them off. Not that he wore them very often of course. Mum was always trying to throw them out.'

'Thanks!'

'Don't worry. He never let her. But you know what it's like. When you stop working ties just hang about in the wardrobe making a mess. I'm sure somebody was helping themselves to them though, because when I went to choose one for him to wear there were only a couple left. I wouldn't be surprised if it was Hugo.'

'You're probably right. He loves a freebie.'

'Don't let Tilda hear you say that!'

They were silent for a moment. It surprised everyone in the family how Tilda, an independent woman who successfully ran her own small editing company, put up with her husband Hugo. Full of the confidence of the self-made man he had a home-spun philosophy about life that made her siblings cringe at his naiveté. But theirs was – on the face of it – a close marriage and if you offended Hugo by disagreeing with him, you offended Tilda.

Libby laughed. 'You're right. Now let's concentrate. Do you actually know where the funeral home is?'

They were driving somewhere out near the airport. The inner city was behind them now and on both sides of the road were bald fields, recently mowed of a crop, the stubble left to die off before the next planting. They drove past a golf course deserted apart from a lone player who was leaning into the wind as he strode across the greens.

'Now how could that possibly be considered fun?' said Charlotte crossly. 'And where on earth *is* this place?'

'Have you got a map?'

'All these roads look the same. It should be on our right somewhere.'

Libby pulled down the sun visor and looked at herself in the small mirror on it. She sighed. 'Do you ever get sick of having to be the sort of person people expect you to be? And never really working out who you actually are.'

'What?'

'Oh you know. Having to say the right thing and be the right thing and do the right thing all the time. Just playing the part.'

Charlotte was hunched forward over the wheel, trying to see through the rain.

'You always choose the oddest times to get into these conversations.' She looked at Libby and shook her head. 'It's a little bit late to be thinking this at our age, isn't it? I know what you mean, though,' she added, looking in the car mirror and fluffing her hair up. 'I don't even know how to be *me* anymore. I've been role playing for so many years now: devoted mother, capable divorcée, thoughtful daughter. Like you, I'm not sure who I am anymore and even who I was to begin with. But from memory I think I was a real character and lots of fun when I was younger. Wasn't I?'

'You were,' Libby reassured her. 'You still are. Sometimes. I liked the way I lived life when I was young,' she said. 'I think I lived it with some style; it was like a performance. I liked to stand back and look at myself from the outside. It was exciting. Now all the edges are blurred. Then, even if you were behaving badly it was ok. It was part of life's drama. At our age you become irrelevant.'

'You've lost me.'

'Oh you know! We lose that ability to play a part; nobody cares what we are anyway. We're always in the background; we've lost our allure.'

'That's awful.'

'I know. But not all people are like that. Some people manage to make a drama of their lives and get people's attention, even when they're older.' She paused, and raised her eyebrows at Charlotte. 'Come to think of it, *you're* like that. I envy you.'

'I'm not sure that's a compliment.' Charlotte laughed. She had a low chuckle, like a lawn mower heard in the distance on a summer's day. Suddenly Libby's mood lifted. Everything was brighter, although nothing had changed and the rain still poured down. She noticed that Charlotte's hands on the wheel were covered with brown age spots. 'We're suddenly old, aren't we,' she said. 'When on earth did that creep up on us?'

There were orchards on either side of the road now and soggy leaves from a recent storm splattered up against the wheels as they passed.

'I wish we could just keep driving.'

'Well we *can't*. We have to get through this. No escape. This doesn't look familiar. I thought it was nearer town,' Charlotte said in that way she had, as though any inconvenience to her was always somebody else's fault.

'Have you got the address, a phone number?' said Libby.

'No. It should be simple to find. Why isn't it better signposted? Imagine cars full of mourners after a funeral trying to find the bloody place, driving round and round with all their lights on. It's ridiculous.'

Above them the clouds, spread across the sky like ugly wounds, darkened, and an even heavier rain began to fall. It was savage, rushing down the windscreen in a torrent.

'Look at the time,' Charlotte said. 'We're twenty minutes late and they've got a funeral on later apparently so the director, Mr. Farrell, said we *must* be there on time for the viewing. It's a crazy place to have a crematorium anyway. Out here in the middle of nowhere.'

'There's a signpost,' Libby said. 'Slow down.'

The crematorium lay just off the main road. It had a sweeping driveway lined with sodden white rose bushes and rows of modest headstones. Some were stained and worn by the weather, while others, belonging to the more recently departed, stretched out like lines of pale teeth towards the rows of pencil pines surrounding the graveyard. Through the rain Libby glimpsed a couple of tall chimneys and some low unassuming rendered buildings as grey as wet sand.

'Such stark chimneys,' said Charlotte. 'Talk about rubbing it in!'

'Just what I was thinking. Thank goodness Dad's being buried in a good old-fashioned graveyard. He would hate being out here.'

'Although it is near his favourite golf course I suppose.'

And, of course, they didn't have an umbrella.

The wind bit like a terrier as Libby opened the car door. They found Mr. Farrell waiting for them just inside the lobby. He wore a shiny grey suit that had been poorly ironed one too many times and pulled nervously on his tie when he spoke, like a man fighting for breath. He greeted them with exaggerated gravitas, then said 'follow me,' in a dramatic manner and strode off ahead of them.

'Follow Doctor Death,' Charlotte said, nudging Libby.

The foyer they passed through was decorated like a boutique hotel; a giant palm stood in the corner of a discreet waiting area furnished with four leather armchairs and a glass topped coffee table laid out with brochures and booklets. On the wall behind were two large photographs framed in black. The ubiquitous photo of Lake Tekapo had been taken in summer when the wild lupins grew in waving carpets of pink and purple on the hillsides and the tiny chapel beside the lake was dwarfed by water, mountains and sky. The other photo was a more intimate one. Two small boys sat fishing on a jetty in Queenstown. They were both intent on threading bait onto their fishing lines; the whole scene was one composed of mirror images. The boys, one Maori, one Pakeha, were in the foreground and the lake, the mountains and the clear blue sky touched with only the faintest of smoky clouds spread out in a theatrical backdrop.

'Such *soothing* photographs,' Libby said addressing Mr. Farrell's back as they hurried after him.

Charlotte nudged her and made a face. '*Soothing*? What are you like!' and they both began to giggle like schoolgirls.

'He looks very peaceful,' Mr. Farrell said sternly as he ushered them into a room at the end of a hallway.

'What a stupid thing to say,' Charlotte said after he had closed the door, leaving them alone in the chapel. 'Of course he'd look peaceful He died in his *sleep*. What could be more peaceful that that?'

A silken sheet lay over their father's body. It reminded Libby of their mother's wedding dress which had been made of the same sort of diaphanous material. For a moment she wondered whether it had been cut up for the purpose, but then she remembered that their mother's wedding dress was hanging safely in a dry-cleaning bag in the back bedroom at her father's house. She had put it there herself.

***

Every year Charlotte had a family party at her house, set on a generous lifestyle block on the outskirts of the city. It had been an Indian summer the year after Rose died and with daylight saving, the sun was still shining even though it was early evening. The poplar trees on the boundary of the property were just beginning to change colour and there was a slight chill in the air, a hint of the winter to come. While they kept an eye on their children, Libby's nieces and nephews lay carelessly around the lawn on scattered rugs, while some of them played tennis on the lawn court beside the house. Cries of 'Good shot,' and 'what a fluke', and 'definitely out!' floated across to the older generation who lounged in old wicker chairs on the terrace, watching lazily. Libby and her nephew were stacking the dishwasher after an early dinner when she saw Charlotte's oldest granddaughter appear on the lawn. She was dressed in a billowing cream gown that dragged behind her on the ground as she ran.

'My God!' said Libby, shocked. 'Surely that isn't Mum's wedding dress?'

Rose's wedding dress was made of Indian silk, with a flowing skirt and a delicate bodice embroidered by hand and studded with pearls. Whenever Libby stayed at her parents' house she got it out of the camphor wood box at the foot of their bed and laid it out on Rose's bed so that they could admire it. She loved fine materials and she and Rose had the same conversation every year. Libby would exclaim how slim her mother must have been then, and how neither she nor Charlotte nor Tilda could have ever hoped to struggle into the dress. Rose would smile in agreement and tell Libby to feel how delicate the silk was and tell her you could never find such fine material nowadays, even if you travelled to India.

Charlotte, coming into the kitchen laden with plates, had been instantly on the defensive.

'It was in the camphor wood chest when I cleared it out after Mum died, so I put it in the dressing up box. What else was there to do with it? Nobody would ever wear it again.'

'That's not the point,' said Libby. 'It has sentimental value.'

'I'll get it dry-cleaned,' Charlotte said.'

'No. *I'll* get it dry-cleaned,' said Libby. She put the dress into a plastic bag she found in one of the kitchen drawers. The next day she took it into the Chinese dry-cleaners around the corner, told him not to worry; that she knew the lace, as yellow now as old butter, could never be restored to its original colour, and asked him to deliver it to her father's house when it was done. *That* was where it belonged.

Sam looked as elegant in death as he had in life. A photo of him taken in the 30's always sat on the sideboard and Rose had said he looked just like a film star, dressed in tennis whites, his hair swept back, sporting a neat moustache, and a cigarette dangling from his fingers. 'Class will out,' Rose had said one day as she dusted it.

'You're such a snob, Mum,' Libby had said.

Now, dressed in his best and with his pure white hair brushed off his forehead, he was still a fine-looking man. They stood looking down at him.

'Why on earth did you choose the Baa-Baas' tie?' Libby said finally. 'It's an English club.'

'Then why did Tom give it to him? They all looked the same to me. Maybe Tom should have made the effort to be here. Then *he* could have chosen it.'

'You're right. He should be here. But I don't happen to want him here. Not under these circumstances.'

'You're right. He doesn't deserve to be here. Nobody cheats on our sister like that and gets to come to our father's funeral. Even if Dad did love him.' She paused and then added. 'Maybe even more than us.'

'I'll ignore that,' said Libby. 'You all have a soft spot for Tom. You'll just have to get over it. His shirt is well ironed.'

'I did it.'

'And his tie is nicely knotted.'

'Immi did that. It made me cry to watch her. She adored him so much. And Daisy brushed his hair. I got Joe to polish his shoes. He's never polished a pair of shoes in his life!' Charlotte leant over and straightened Sam's tie, smoothing it down gently, like a baby's bib. Libby felt tears rush into her eyes.

'I wish my girls could be here,' she said.

She thought of the last family wedding she had attended; her nephew's. As usual Tom had been unable to go, but her three girls had managed to get off work to go with her. As they all got dressed for the wedding her father had gone on and on about what he should wear. Should he wear a jumper under his jacket? Would the weather change during the day? If they went out for lunch should he wear a tie? Perhaps it would be better if he didn't go. He was beginning to feel unwell. Libby tried to be patient; old age had robbed him of his confidence.

'Bossy ruddy lot you are,' he'd grumbled, as they helped him to dress.

As they went out the door Abbie said, 'Wait, Grandpa,' and straightened his tie for him. 'There,' she said. 'You look fabulous. You sexy old devil. All the women will be after you.'

Daisy straightened it again just before they went into the church.

'Don't fuss, Daisy,' Sam said.

'Don't fuss,' Libby said, 'He doesn't like it.'

'He *does* like it Mum. That's the whole point,' Abbie whispered to her. 'Old people miss out on being touched.'

'Oh, sorry, Dr. Freud,' Libby replied, but she thought guiltily of how seldom she touched her children now they were grown up and she took Sam's arm as they walked into the church.

'I think we'd better go,' Charlotte said. 'Mr. Farrell will be getting anxious.'

'I don't like leaving Dad alone,' Libby said, suddenly tearful.

Charlotte put her arm around her. 'Don't be too sad. He'd had enough of all this.' She looked around her dismissively as if the whole world was contained in the unremarkable room. 'And how lucky was he to go in his sleep like that.'

'I still wish one of us had been with him,' Libby said stubbornly.

An old-fashioned clock on the wall opposite suddenly chimed the hour.

'But Mr. Farrell is right. He *does* look happy,' said Libby.' When you think about it, all he really wanted to do was to die himself, after Mum went.'

'I don't get that, do you?' Charlotte said, as they walked out to the car. 'They were so unhappy together for so many years. That's what I remember anyway. Our happy childhood and then years of arguments and Dad drinking too much and then Mum going away for ages. But then, finally, peace.'

'I don't understand it either,' said Libby. 'But their generation was so full of secrets and they never shared anything very meaningful with us, if you think about it. And we never asked.'

'Mind you, I think my children share *too* much with me,' said Charlotte glumly. '*Too* much information! I really don't want to know by text every few minutes how their day is going and how they hate work and how angry they are at everyone when they have PMT. I spend my nights lying awake worrying about them and then when I call them in the morning they're as happy as Larry. It's crazy. They're adults, for goodness sake!' She nudged Libby, who was gazing out the window. 'I've always wondered who on earth "Larry" was. Have you? And why was he happy?'

'Yes I've always wondered that too,' said Libby. 'Another one of life's little mysteries. And by the way, while I'm here I'll go over to Akaroa and clear out the house. That will be a project for me. I'll sort out all the old photographs and stuff.'

'Do you really want to do that?' said Charlotte, doubtfully. 'All that history tucked away in those cupboards. We could just get some cleaners and removalists in for some of the furniture and chuck the rest. Let sleeping dogs lie I always say.'

3

'I've written a sonnet for Dad,' Libby announced when the family got together that night to finalise plans for the funeral. 'I wrote it on the plane.' She wanted to be a part of the service this time. At Rose's funeral she had felt excluded as all the planning had been done before she arrived back. But then it came with the territory anyway, when you were the youngest and had lived away for so many years.

She knew the sonnet lacked some authenticity, but in essence it was true. Her parents had been happy at the beginning and devoted to one another at the end. That's what mattered. Not the bits in between. If she made a collage in her mind of her memories of those last years when both Rose and Sam were alive; it was all smiles and small kindnesses and an increasing dependence on one another.

'Really?' was Tilda's half-hearted response when she said she'd like to read it during the service. 'I wasn't aware that you wrote poetry. Should we hear it first do you think? To see if it's ok. You know Dad hated anything too sentimental.'

'Well Dad's unlikely to be around for this particular occasion, isn't he,' said Edward. He was pouring them all drinks and stopped what he was doing to frown at her. 'So does it really matter? And with any luck he'll be too busy up there enjoying a round of golf or making Mum a cup of tea to worry about what's said about him when he's gone. After all Matilda; Libby's hardly asking if she can deliver the Gettysburg Address! Fourteen lines sounds good to me. Dad always liked brevity and I bet he'd like it better than the patronising sermon we'll get on God and death from that boring minister who kept turning up at the house after Mum died.'

'Yes, he was a shocker,' Charlotte agreed. 'Anything Libby wrote would have to be more palatable than one of his soliloquys. Always about himself. But I take Matilda's point. Dad would like something pretty simple. Nothing gushy.'

'It's not gushy,' Libby protested.

'So, let her read her sonnet,' said Edward. 'Trust her. She's the English teacher after all. What do the rest of us know about literary appreciation? Speaking for myself, nothing.'

'You're always speaking for yourself,' Tilda snapped. 'And you and Charlotte only call me Matilda when you want to bully me. It's childish. Maybe we can find an appropriate poem for you to read out Libby. What about "Remember Me"?'

'I didn't take any part in Mum's funeral,' said Libby. Her voice was all shaky the way it always got when she was upset. She took a deep breath. 'None of you stopped to think that I might feel left out. And that's not really an appropriate sonnet to read at Dad's funeral anyway Tilda. Do you even understand what it's about? It's a lover's sonnet.'

Before Tilda could reply, Edward, so often her knight in shining armour, stepped in. 'So that's settled,' he said briskly. 'A sonnet from Libby. Done.'

'That's fine then, 'said Charlotte. 'All organised. And don't sulk Matilda; sorry, Tilda. You still get to do the eulogy.'

The next morning threatening clouds floated across a frigid metal grey sky and by the time the family gathered outside Sam's old school chapel for the service, the weather had closed in and the stream running through the school grounds was sprinkled with rain drops. As the coffin was carried across the small bridge spanning the stream outside the chapel, and then placed in the hearse waiting at the school entrance, the heavens opened.

Once inside the school hall where they were to have refreshments, Libby pulled her coat around her and shivered.

'It sure is funereal weather isn't it,' Cleo announced, always one for stating the obvious. She had surprised Libby by flying over from Sydney that morning and had gone straight from the airport to the service. 'I hope there's some decent food. Those egg sandwiches look pretty sad.'

'Trust you to think of food before anything else,' said Tilda sharply. 'You know you have to watch your weight when you live in those colleges on campus. All that binge drinking.'

Libby looked at her and shook her head in disbelief. 'I can't believe you just said that.'

'Yes, what planet do you come from Tilda,' snapped Charlotte. 'There's nothing better than a healthy young woman with a healthy appetite.'

'Yes, *thanks* for that Tilda,' said Cleo. 'I'm not proud of my weight, but it's better than being anorexic isn't it. Or so my lovely Mum is always telling me. You read beautifully Mum,' she added. 'That was the best part of the service. Everybody loved your sonnet.'

'Well not everybody,' said Tilda unkindly. 'Nancy didn't like it.'

'Well she *wouldn't,* would she?' Charlotte said, frowning at her.

Nancy, Rose's younger sister, was always highly critical of anything the family did. Divorced after a brief disastrous wartime marriage, she bitterly resented the fact that she had to rely on her older sister in so many ways. Rose was unfailingly forgiving of her ill temper, explaining to the girls when they grew up that divorce in those days was such a stigma that your social life was limited to family outings and that all Nancy's fine intellect and promise had been wasted because of one youthful mistake.

'You should have seen her face when you read it,' Tilda continued, adding insult to injury. 'She was smirking.'

'Don't listen to her Libby,' said Charlotte firmly. 'Mum and Dad would have loved it. You should frame it,' she said, thrusting the Order of Service at Tilda.

> When we remember what a life it's been,
> The roses that Sam gathered on the way
> And all the love and laughter he has seen
> The family he tended day by day.
> When we remember him and gentle days long past,
> His love for Rose as solid as a tree
> His children's children, branches reaching forth,
> The waves of life as constant as the sea.
> Then all the legacy of love he leaves behind,
> The daily little kindnesses we knew
> Fall sweetly like soft roses on our hearts
> And give us strength to see the long night through.
> While in the garden, talking of the past
> He wanders with our mother, home at last.

'Personally, I would have preferred a Shakespearean sonnet,' Nancy said as she suddenly pushed her way into the group, clutching a cup of tea in one hand and a well-laden plate in another. 'No offence Libby, but I wouldn't give up your day job.'

'When somebody says that you know they are going to say something offensive,' said Charlotte tartly. 'Anyway, I loved the extended image of the garden and Dad and his roses and his enduring love for Mum.'

Nancy turned on her. 'Well some of us knew, better didn't we? And you children chose to be blind to everything that went on. Why sugar-coat the truth I always say; even if you are speaking of the dead.'

'Oh Nancy just *shut up*!' said Rose's best friend Mabel who had flown in from Auckland for the occasion. 'We all know why you can't stand to think of other people being happy. Particularly Rose and Sam. But they were. And you never stood a chance. More fool you.'

'What the hell was that all about?' asked Cleo later, when they had adjourned to Charlotte's for drinks.

'No idea,' said Libby. 'No idea at all.'

But she smiled conspiratorially at Charlotte as she said it.

Of course, they knew.

***

Libby had kept the secret about Rose and Max to herself for years now. Rose told her one year when she was staying because she said she didn't want Libby to make the same mistake she had. She guessed that Libby had fallen in love with someone else; she knew all the signs, she said, when she came into Libby's bedroom and sat on the end of her bed one night.

'What's going on?' she asked.

'Nothing,' said Libby. 'Why?' She turned off the light and turned her face to the wall.

'I'm not stupid you know,' Rose said. 'You lie in bed writing letters under the covers every night, Tom never phones, you're miserable and distracted with the girls. It's *never* worth all the pain,' she added. 'I should know. I just don't want you to repeat the mistakes I made. *Talk* to me! It might help.'

Libby turned over and looked up at her. 'I'm so ashamed,' she said. 'And so lonely. I would never have believed it's possible to be so lonely in a marriage.'

40

Rose sat down on the bed, and then leaned over and stroked her hair.

'We're none of us perfect,' she said. 'Do you remember that year when I went away?' And Rose began to tell her story, so Libby never had to tell her how she and Tom had drifted apart and he was always working and didn't seem interested in her anymore and how someone came along who *was*. It was all such a cliché anyway.

Rose told Libby that she left home to be with Sam's best friend Max in the late autumn so when she arrived in England, it was early summer. It had been a late spring and the daffodils blooming in buttery masses beneath the trees in the park reminded her far too much of Christchurch. The leaves on the trees were a sharp new green, dazzling under clear spring skies that might be unclouded in the morning but glazed over with showers in the afternoon. In the early days she told herself that she was just on a long holiday. It was exciting to live from day to day and to be like one of the romantic couples she saw every weekend on the communal green outside her kitchen window. She and Max would go down to join them after lunch, lying on the wooden benches reading to one another or sprawling on the grass on a picnic rug and dozing in the fresh sunshine.

The summer that year was unusually warm and at first Rose was very, very happy. But when a long damp autumn arrived and she paced restlessly through nearby streets in the late afternoon while she waited for Max to return from work, she began to miss her children with an intensity that sickened her. She tortured herself by imagining what they would be doing each day. Her mother wrote and told her that all the children had been ill with winter flu and Edward had called out for her when he was delirious one night with a high temperature. She wrote that even when he was off school recuperating he had managed to ride his bike at full speed into a gutter flooded after a heavy rainfall and now had five stitches in his head. She added, almost as an afterthought, that Sam had decided not to let out Belle Maison so that he could take the children to Akaroa most weekends. Rose tried to picture them all there; but it was impossible as her day was their night, her autumn their spring. And Nancy would be there, no doubt, the little helper, planning picnics at Okains Bay, inviting people over for the day as if she were the mother, the wife, the caretaker of the house. And Rose had only herself to blame.

And it always seemed to be drizzling in London; streams of rain continually ran down the windows weaving their way through the grime thrown up by the endless traffic passing up and down the street outside. And every Saturday now, Max popped in to 'get something from his rooms.' He didn't look Rose in the eye as he hurried out and she didn't dare ask how long he would be gone. She didn't blame him for not wanting to be with her; she was no company for anyone. Her guilt at leaving the children had now become a physical pain and she found herself rubbing her stomach like a child with a tummy ache. She had even bought herself a hot water bottle and carried that around with her, refilling it as soon as it was anything other than piping hot from the kettle that took forever to boil on the gas ring

One day Max brought home a copy of *A Writer's Diary* by Virginia Woolf. When they were young, he told Rose, the Stephens lived just around the corner in West Central 1 and he talked about the Bloomsbury Group: Virginia, Leonard, Vanessa and Carrington, Lytton Strachey, Duncan Grant and Clive Bell in a tone of familiarity that suggested they may all pop in at any moment.

And now, Max's friends started to do just that. They called in at all hours, lounging on the sofas, sprawling in the chairs, or leaning on mantelpieces. They assumed self-conscious poses as though someone, somewhere, might just be painting their portrait. While they hung around they smoked and drank and talked incessantly in their superior voices about poetry they were writing or poetry they had recently read. Max's best friend from Cambridge, Rupert, had a habit of dropping quotations from his favourite poet WH Auden into every conversation and although Rose was initially impressed by this – his voice was 'heaven' she told Libby – as the winter drew in and he called in more often to see them, she decided he was a show-off, and the enchantment faded. As her homesickness grew so did the early delight she took in listening to their immaculate diction and fiercely intelligent arguments and she started taking to her bed with her hot water bottle and leaving them all to it.

'I'm sick to death of their incessant chatter,' she said, when Max rebuked her for her rudeness. 'They're all in love with their own voices. I'm only there as an audience anyway.'

Now, when she heard the children's voices on the telephone, their sturdy New Zealand accents sounded more real to her than anything she heard around her, and she found a nostalgic charm in their shortened vowels and the way their voices rose at the end of a sentence.

Years later – Rose told Libby – when she read a definitive biography of Vanessa Bell she was shocked by the casual way she and the Bloomsbury group picked up and cast off lovers. And the authorial voice was so approving – as if hearts broken, children neglected and friendships shattered in the pursuit of love were the prices one must pay for leading an intense artistic and creative life.

For there was a puritan streak in Rose (after all she was of Baptist stock, her grandfather arriving in New Zealand on the *Cressy*, one of the first four ships arriving in Canterbury,) and by the time she finished the book she had 'gone off' them all. She couldn't even begin to understand Virginia sleeping with Vanessa's husband, or Clive Bell bringing up Vanessa's daughter with Duncan Grant as his own and – most astounding of all – David Garnett sleeping with his lover's daughter and even marrying her!

Max's friends were also scornful about bourgeois attitudes to love. Soon Rupert took to following Rose into the kitchen when she escaped there to make tea, where he would stand far too close to her in the tiny space so that she had to squeeze past him to get the cups and saucers out of the cupboard. His wife Aileen, a tall willowy brunette with slightly bulbous eyes and a long chiselled nose, was a compulsive flirt with the provocative habit of sweeping her hair behind her ear when she spoke to Max and giggling in a girlish way at anything he said that was remotely funny.

And now, it seemed, every weekend was spent with his friends. The women made Rose feel gauche, with their cut glass English accents and their impossibly milky skins.

One night Aileen recounted intimate stories about her children, describing their antics over the past week in such detail that Rose wept bitterly when she got into bed that that night. When Max asked her what she was crying about he sounded impatient and she turned her back on him and didn't reply.

And daily, she began to find more flaws in his character. He always sought out cheap restaurants, and even on a cold night they always had to catch buses home or even walk, when a taxi was well within his means. Sam, she reflected wistfully, had always had an 'easy come, easy go' attitude to money.

One weekend they were invited to stay at Rupert's country house. It was a stately home close to Charleston, Vanessa and Clive Bell's house in Sussex, but apparently there was little money to go around after the huge death taxes Rupert had to pay when he inherited it from his father, so the heating was inadequate and the bedrooms freezing. When Libby complained to Max he told her she should consider herself lucky as over at

Charleston there was no running water and no heating and the ice froze in the buckets in the kitchen overnight. The village they walked into in the morning was like a picture postcard, with a green surrounded by red-roofed Georgian houses and a church made of stone the same colour as a leaden sky; but suddenly Rose felt a yearning, as sharp as a pain, for the bald tussock covered hills and brazen landscapes of New Zealand.

She began to have the same recurring dream each night where she was standing by a closed window trying to get out. There was no furniture in the room and it had an unpolished wooden floor and white walls. Outside was a tree, succulent with dazzling green leaves that tapped against the window; she longed to climb out onto it. But when she finally managed to force the window and climb out, she slipped on the ledge. She grasped desperately at the leaves as she fell, but they suddenly turned to brittle autumn leaves and crumbled like dry earth in her hands. She never found out what would happen next as she always awoke with a start at this point, and heart pounding, lay still, anxious not to wake Max, until the birds began to sing in the London plane tree outside and she could get up to make a cup of tea.

And slowly, as all jaded lovers do, she began to romanticise the past. She recalled her life with Sam and the children, the day-to-day familiarity of it all, and the carefree summers in Akaroa. She conveniently left Max out of her memories, and instead she recreated in her mind's eye a series of glorious tableaux of cricket games on the oval, games of Scrabble with the children, family meals around the battered oak table, and evenings on the lawn watching the sun set.

Now Max could do nothing right. He was a disloyal friend, a cad, he drank too much and told and retold the same old tedious jokes. The whole Englishness of him, that she once found so irresistible, now became foreign to her, his courtly manners an affectation.

She decided that he was a gentleman in all the wrong senses of the word; not one like Sam, who always opened the door for women, walked on the gutter side of the pavement and sprang to his feet when women entered the room, but the sort of man who sprawled about in private clubs, endlessly debating politics after a few drinks, wore the same tired tweed jacket like an identity bracelet and agreed with everyone by saying, 'indeed.' In short, she told Libby, she decided he was a bore.

One Sunday, near the end, she and Max set out for Greenwich. It was a bitterly cold day and an arctic wind blew off the water as they waited to board the boat. They had argued bitterly that morning: Max couldn't understand why she turned away from him, slipping out of bed and busying herself making a cup of tea in the freezing early-morning kitchen, not willing to make love. How could she tell him that the act now felt like a betrayal?

A young couple walked along the wharf towards them, cuddled together against the cold, and as she watched them they lifted their faces to one another and kissed. The man was wearing a dark olive-green rain jacket and he unzipped it, shrugged it off and wrapped it around the girl. He tucked her long brown hair into the hood of it and she smiled up at him, her face as soft and serene as a Madonna's. On the embankment a young family stopped to look across the river. A boy aged about six or seven swung back and forth on the rails and his sister leaned over them beside him, her hair falling down onto the cobbled pavement. Then she tucked her head under and flipped over the rail in a clumsy somersault. A baby in the pushchair, wrapped up like an untidy parcel in layers of rugs, watched his siblings, spellbound in wonder at their antics, but their mother, an exhausted looking young woman in a long beige overcoat, barely glanced at them and called out 'be careful' in a weary tone, as if she wasn't really bothered either way. The father stood apart from them all, his hands firmly in his pockets as he gazed across the soupy brown water. He had his back firmly to his family and didn't even look around when his wife called out to the children.

Yet Rose found herself envying the woman. The scene reminded her of a winter Sunday the year before when the family was walking along the waterfront in Akaroa. Edward had dashed on ahead and showing off, as usual, attempted a somersault over the railings bordering the sea wall. No doubt he intended to land nimble-footed onto the sand beneath. He misjudged it though, and fell flat on his back on the wet sand; it was as hard as a concrete slab as the tide had only recently gone out and momentarily winded, he lay, uncharacteristically silent, until his breath came back and he bellowed angrily. Suddenly Rose yearned for the fatigue and anxiety of day-to-day motherhood. Her heart felt as raw as a fresh wound and she wondered how she would get through another day.

She told herself that once winter ended she would start to feel better. But then a letter from her mother arrived. It was a blunt letter, responding to Rose's sadness, telling her that she had two choices. She had 'made her bed' and could choose to lie in it or she could get on the next plane home. Her own opinion was clear; she enclosed a money order. The next week, on a morning when Rose had awoken to a sky so heavy that it made her head throb, she got a bus into the city centre and purchased a ticket on the next flight bound for New Zealand. 'I didn't even consider Max,' she told Libby. 'I was too cowardly to say goodbye.'

'It seems to me that most affairs end up the same way,' Rose said as they passed time in the airport café before Libby boarded her flight back to Hong Kong. 'We all end up despising the very things we once loved about people. If we were first attracted to them because they were funny, we tire of their jokes, if we thought them articulate, they become long-winded. If at first we like the fact that they are quiet and thoughtful, they become boring. If they were party loving they become drunks. I'm not presuming to give you advice darling,' she said, leaning over and pushing Libby's hair back from her face, a gesture so familiar that Libby felt a catch in her throat. 'I just want you to think carefully before you do anything drastic.' She sighed. 'And remember that my story is only half of it. Max's version is no doubt completely different. God knows what he must have thought of me by the end of it all!'

'You're right Mum,' said Libby. 'Tom's version of what went wrong is probably different to mine too.'

'So, tell me about it,' said Rose. 'We have time.'

4

'It was such a cool place to be in the early seventies,' said Libby. 'Mad, fast, fun. It was a party town. Well you know how much I loved it, Mum. You did too. But now the glamour has worn off for me. When I think of the indulgent life we used to lead. The afternoons we used to spend lounging around on junks. All drinking like mad. I remember going out one day and we actually laughed when the kids all held hands and jumped off the top deck when we were halfway across the Lamma channel on our way back to Aberdeen. Can you believe it! The water was so choppy and the light was fading and the channel was full of fishing boats and the odd huge container ship and walla-wallas and other junks coming and going. How careless we were. I'm shocked when I look back.'

'No doubt you were all intoxicated so it seemed funny at the time,' said Rose wryly.

Libby nodded. 'I don't know when the magic wore off. I guess I just got bored with the sameness of it all. I needed to work, to be someone other than a mother and Tom's wife. So that's when I went back to teaching. Looking back I wonder whether I got it all wrong. I was in such a hurry to get on with life; I should have spent more time just enjoying those years. I liked my kids being little. And I liked Tom much more when he was worried about where the next case would come from; before he became so successful. And then, of course, I got caught up in my career too. We both just lost our way.'

'We all lose our way in life at times,' Rose said. 'Some of us just get more lost than others. Look at me. I can't even bear to think about what I put you children through. I must have been mad. But in the end that probably makes us better people. Slower to judge. And we *are* lucky you know,' she added. 'Despite our imperfections, we are from a long line of what I would call solid mothers. In the end our children are everything to us. Sadly, I sometimes suspect, to the detriment of our husbands. Time sorts that out though. Look at Sam and me. Now tell me more.'

***

In reality, it took some time for the culture shock to wear off when Libby first arrived in Hong Kong but the memory tends to be selective about the past, and she remembered only that she was in thrall to the city from the minute she arrived.

'To fictionalise our memories is often the only thing that makes them bearable,' Charlotte was fond of telling her. 'I know that from bitter experience.'

To Libby, it was not the sordid, humid, pushy city that Charlotte chose to remember. Libby was enchanted by the very things Charlotte grew to hate: the grey uninspired skyscrapers indigenous to the Hong Kong of the seventies, the tacky resettlement areas and the local Cantonese who thought that yelling at one another was the normal way to converse. But most of all, she loved the overpowering energy of the city. The air was clammy and polluted and had a rotten smell about it. It smelled of hard work, and not enough or too much money. Queens Road Central and Pedder Street were heaving with private cars and mini buses all jostling for a place to drop off or pick up their passengers. Gleaming Mercedes and Rolls Royces driven by sleepy chauffeurs who dozed while they waited parked illegally outside the Peninsula and the Mandarin hotels. There they would drop off or pick up rich Tai Tai's who sweltered uncomfortably in furs in the cold winter months – stored in supermarket cold stores over the summer – and dined out, night and day, in excessive lashings of yellow gold jewellery. Jostling to do business were the rest of the population; workers sleeping perilously in the backs of open trucks, chattering hairdressers cutting the hair of clients who perched on barber's chairs in back alleys, and others who dashed like busy executives from one narrow lane to another with their illegal barrows full of clothes, stereo equipment and toys. They were moved on regularly but without much conviction by the police. In Government House and in the central government offices, civil servants, well paid and with many colonial 'perks' that their local colleagues didn't have, worked steadily but not fanatically to keep this 'borrowed place' efficient.

After they were married Libby and Tom moved into in a huge old apartment on the Peak; it was in an old hospital, divided up after WWII into apartments. Built of red brick it was smothered by an impossibly vivid pink bougainvillea, its branches as gnarled as old men's hands, which climbed up from the gardens below. Wide balconies ran the length of the apartments, which overlooked the harbour. Often the view was hazy, due to the humidity and heat, but in the winter the fogs that smothered the peak reached as far down as their apartment. Then the walls ran with moisture, the oriental carpets fell apart and all their clothes went so mouldy in the wardrobes that Libby started to hang them in the hot cupboard, which was the size of a small bedroom. But the pollution that would afflict the city from the late 90's had not yet arrived and sometimes the days were as clear and clean as glass and the ships in the harbour and the nine hills of Kowloon were as finely defined as a lithograph. It was never tranquil; each day the hum from the central business district ebbed and flowed like the comings and goings of a train but it was a hearty sound and always reminded Libby how alive the city was, and how happy she was to be a part of it.

Tom knew virtually everybody because Hong Kong was a big city but, in many ways, just a village. David, one of his rugby friends and the managing director of one of the big Hongs, held a party for them shortly after they were married.

'I wish we could be more in touch with the real Hong Kong, don't you?' Libby said as they drove up the wooded, windy road to his house further up the peak. It was school holidays and she had spent an idle day shopping and lunching at a club with other legal wives.

'Shoot me if I ever get like them,' she complained. 'They are so boring. I can't imagine myself ever not working. Thank God I've got my teaching; it keeps you down to earth in a place like this.'

'You shouldn't be so critical of them,' said Tom. 'They've got young kids. Maybe that's why they don't work. And you don't realise how lucky you are, having these experiences. This *is* the real Hong Kong. The house David lives in was occupied by Japanese soldiers during the war – he'll tell you all about the fall of Hong Kong if you ask him. He knows his history. His company helps keep this colony as wealthy as it is.'

'But there is no democracy here. The locals don't even get to vote.'

'It's like a benevolent dictatorship. That's true. But it works. We have an efficient civil service, the rule of law, a local population who value education and know they can become wealthy and successful if they work hard. Which they do. What's wrong with that? Look; there'll be Chinese businessmen there tonight who have more money than you could ever imagine. The locals here respect money and success; they don't resent people who have "made it". You can't imagine the hardships some of them have escaped from.'

'You make it sound as though everything's about money. What about freedom?'

'No,' said Tom patiently. 'Only people who live in democracies can afford to have illusions about freedom. People from mainland China can't afford that luxury. Mao said that power comes from the barrel of a gun; you need money to get away from a political system like that if the need arises. None of us really understand China; even the China watchers are guessing most of the time. David's hobby is collecting old Mercedes,' he said, changing the subject as they drove up a long circular drive. 'The way other people might collect stamps.'

'A slight exaggeration on your part,' Libby retorted, still smarting from the lecture he had just given her. 'I can only see four.'

Libby was happy to leave the stifling night behind them as they stepped into the relief of an air-conditioned foyer. It was furnished in a minimalist style with two original (Tom tells her later) Andy Warhols on the walls and grey marble floors scattered with silk Persian rugs.

David was talking to guests in the doorway leading out to the terrace. He was not what Libby expected; not her idea of what a managing director of a major company – whose hobby is collecting old Mercedes – should look like. He was stocky, not particularly tall, and had an unruly mop of fair hair. He looked as though he badly needed a haircut and kept pushing his hair back from his face impatiently as he talked. When he greeted them, he kissed Libby unhurriedly on both cheeks and said, 'Sorry I couldn't make the wedding. Tom told me he considered himself a very lucky man and now I can see why.'

'Then we just exchanged small talk,' Libby told Rose, but right away, there was something there. Was it like that for you? It's as though you've met in another life. An instant recognition.'

'Yes, I felt like that when I met Max. Exactly like that. It's as though you've found somebody from the same tribe. But you wish later that you'd put that down to youth, too much drink and a heady tropical night,' said Rose shaking her head. 'Oh, I sound like such a cynic, don't I? It comes with age. It's a bore becoming wise actually. It takes all the fun out of life.'

And when Libby got to know David better she could see why Tom was friendly with him. He was the typical product of a top public-school education; suave and articulate, witty and clever, but also emotionally stunted by the many years spent living in various boarding schools. He was equally at home standing on the bar after rugby matches at the Football Club quoting long extracts from 'The Wasteland' to a jeering but appreciative audience, or discussing politics for hours late at night in the Mandarin Grill.

Tom and Libby moved out to the balcony. It was huge; a cream awning stretched the length of it and the walls were lined with masses of soft cream chrysanthemums in terra-cotta pots. Giant palm trees in dragon pots set in each corner of the terrace trembled in the breeze. And the night was like all tropical nights; exotic, romantic, made for flirtations and too much drink and the hedonism that pervaded life in Hong Kong in the seventies.

'I feel so bad when I think of it now,' Libby said. 'I was so selfish. I never thought about you and Dad, or Charlotte going through such a bad time… And then later, after the kids and when Tom and I weren't getting on so well and he was always working, that's when it began. But I don't want to talk about the rest of it,' she said. 'Do you mind? It's all such a cliché.'

'You saved Charlotte,' Rose said. 'You persuaded her to come home. You don't need to apologise to me, of all people, about anything else.'

Libby sighed. 'I suppose that's another reason I went to Hong Kong. Because Charlotte and Ben were there. And then –

I can tell you this now Mum – I found that Charlotte needed looking after. You were right. They should never have married so young. It wasn't surprising that Ben got carried away by his life there. He was always going to get to the top and he was so clever and ambitious. Charlotte was never going to keep up with him. It was a typical Hong Kong story. She was always going to be left behind. And of course, the drinking didn't help.'

'You should have told me,' Rose said. 'But you were both probably trying to protect me. I get that. Our family is far too good at keeping secrets.'

They lived in a vast old flat in Happy Valley and unfortunately Charlotte decided almost as soon as they arrived in Hong Kong that she loathed the expat life with its dinner parties and maids in silly uniforms and hot, hot afternoons spent with mindless women lounging around club pools filled with shrieking children or in playgrounds that were bereft of grass and sizzled mercilessly in the summer sun.

Although she loved her children dearly Charlotte never really got to grips with being a mother of babies and toddlers. She lived in a constant muddle of rowdy children, chaotic living rooms and missed dental and doctors' appointments. She couldn't even entertain properly, according to Ben.

'He's become so bloody corporate,' she complained to Libby after a lunch they had held for a client. 'The apartment was untidy; the children were grizzly and played up at the table and he said the food was inedible.'

'You're not the most accomplished cook,' Libby reminded her. 'It's never been your thing.'

'That's true, but I have other attributes. Don't I?' Charlotte said hopefully.

'Of course you do. You either love cooking or you don't I reckon. No use trying to be something you are not.'

'He speaks to me as if I'm a naughty child. He's become so arrogant and pleased with himself. He never used to be like that.'

'Maybe it will get better as the children get older,' Libby consoled her. 'Everyone says that the hardest time in a marriage is when your children are young and you never get a good night's sleep.'

But things didn't get any better. Charlotte was a hoarder and her habit of storing things in unlikely places and never throwing anything out became more compulsive as time went by. Clothes were scattered all around her bedroom, hanging on coat hangers over the bedhead, jammed in clusters on hooks on the back of doors or thrown in piles on the top of the tallboy and the chest at the end of the bed. Secretly, Libby had some sympathy for Ben because it must be frustrating living with Charlotte given that, like Libby, he was by nature orderly. She knew from experience that Charlotte was much easier to love when you didn't have to actually live with her. Ben complained that her untidiness was catching and it was true that Charlotte's maid gradually gave up constantly tidying up after her and even the children's rooms were messy and the kitchen bench was never clear.

And now she was pregnant again.

'Ben is furious,' she told Libby one day as they half-heartedly pushed the children back and forth on the swings on a blustery wintry afternoon in the park they went to up on the Peak. Below them, the vast reservoir on the south side of the island and the South China Sea with Lamma etched beyond it were shrouded in low cloud.

'He doesn't seem to like anything I do nowadays,' she said. 'And this is the final straw. It is all *my* fault of course. He acts as though it was an immaculate conception.'

'It takes two,' said Libby, but she lay awake that night worrying about Charlotte and thinking that it was ironic that it was Charlotte's careless approach to life that had always got her into trouble, because it was precisely this aspect of her nature that Libby had always envied. She was witty and warm and funny, and particularly so when she had been drinking. Her long lunches were legendary and stretched long into sultry afternoons in her untidy apartment filled with comfy sofas and Indian carpets she bought because she felt sorry for the crippled man who came to her door selling them on Monday nights, and Korean chests that she bought from a friend who was married to a Cathay Pacific pilot who brought a few in every time he flew to Seoul. As the afternoon shadows lengthened and the empty wine bottles the maid tidied away cluttered up the kitchen bench, a hard core of drinkers would be left, all of them seemingly reluctant to go home.

Now, to Libby, the memory of those days was etched in her memory like a watercolour captured on canvas. A depleted table, fading light illuminated by large blue and white Chinese style lamps, women in light summer dresses still seated around the table with wine glasses in their hands, and children sprawled on exotic hand knotted carpets, the little ones half asleep and cranky; ready for their dinner.

'They were fantastic days, weren't they,' Charlotte said a couple of years later, on one of the many occasions when Libby had to put her to bed because she was hopelessly drunk in the unhappy way that was now always the aftermath of the short-lived euphoria she enjoyed after her first couple of drinks. 'Oh, *why* did we have to grow up?' Then she suddenly smiled radiantly as Libby pulled off her shoes for her and said, 'Sorry. I'm such a pain, aren't I? You're an absolute angel the way you always look after me.'

After she had tucked her in Libby slipped down the hall and out the front door quietly, passing the living room on her way, where she could hear Ben instructing the maid to bath and feed the children '*now.*'

'Charlotte isn't resilient enough to survive in a place like Hong Kong,' Libby said to Tom that night. 'She should live in a country town in New Zealand and muck around in gumboots all day. When she gets drunk and sad like that I always think of Keats and: "The sad heart of Ruth, when, sick for home, she stood in tears amid the alien corn".'

But Tom was sick of hearing the excuses Libby made for Charlotte's drinking and said harshly; 'Oh for God's sake. Don't romanticise her behaviour and relate it to one of your poetry lessons. She's just spoilt. She needs to pull herself together.'

'Mum would understand in a heartbeat,' said Libby. 'Even if you don't. She loves Keats.'

'What's the matter?' Rose said anxiously when Libby phoned her later. She was alarmed, as all mothers are, by late night calls.

'Nothing,' said Libby. 'Sorry. I forgot the time difference. I just wanted to hear your voice.' She decided not to tell her that Charlotte's life was rapidly spiralling out of control.

Libby and Tom named their first daughter Abbie. Rose told her having children would be the most profound experience of her life. 'Passion and love are fleeting,' she said, as she sat gloating over her grand-daughter. 'You will learn that in time. Mind you,' she added, 'I still have a weakness for a handsome face. Don't get me wrong.'

'We know you do Mum,' said Libby. 'And men have a weakness for you too. Unfortunately, as history would have it.' But the sarcasm was lost on Rose as she wrapped and rewrapped the baby to her satisfaction.

'I'm going to swaddle her,' she said firmly. 'I think it's weird how you sleep them on their tummies nowadays.'

Later the nurse bustled in and told Libby it was hospital policy that their babies sleep without being swaddled but Libby couldn't help thinking how lovely Abbie had looked all wrapped up like a beautiful parcel.

While Libby was in the hospital, Sophie, the wife of one of Tom's chambers colleagues, came to visit.

'Can you believe it?' she said when Charlotte popped in to see her that evening with a bottle of champagne and two glasses concealed in her oversized shoulder bag . 'It's only supposed to be husbands after lunch but that didn't stop her. And I was feeling so ghastly and ugly. She appeared like a vision in the doorway in a pale, ridiculously well-tailored lavender dress and Jackie Kennedy sunglasses which she always keeps on, even indoors. I felt as though I was listening to her through a fog. Abbie was crying on and off all night and I still didn't have a clue about breastfeeding. All that talk about "latching on" and "let down." I just don't get it.'

Sophie had two maids, Libby told Charlotte, and complained about them incessantly.

'"It's absolutely essential that you get another one when you have your second child," she told me. "You'll go mad otherwise," she said, baying away in her posh English accent, like somebody out on a fox hunt. "One for each child." And "Oh God. I always take mine on holiday with me. They fly Cattle Class with the children while we sit up the front fortifying ourselves with champagne. It's brilliant. Holidays without the slaves would be murder. And you mustn't tie yourself to the home," she warned me. "That will be frowned upon here and Tom will soon start to look around for greener pastures if you are not up to scratch".'

'Greener pastures. Up to scratch!' giggled Charlotte. 'Is the woman for real?'

'"You must come for lunch soon," Sophie said as she left. She only glanced at the baby and looked astonished when asked if she'd like to hold her.'

But weeks later, when Libby decided she would climb the walls if she didn't get out, she finally accepted an invitation to lunch from Sophie. She lived in a modern high-rise in Old Peak Road, in a flat with lashings of marble everywhere. Inside it was all peach and white; not a toy in sight, and a table laid on the balcony as formally as in a restaurant. A plump Filipino maid whom Libby imagined would look stunningly beautiful on her day off, but for now kept her head down like a shy child and was dressed in a demure uniform, served tea in fine china cups while another – also in uniform – took Sophie's two little girls dressed in Liberty print dresses downstairs to the carpark to play.

'This town is full of people like that,' Charlotte told Libby when she recounted the story of the afternoon to her. 'Those women will swallow you up and before you know it you'll be going to long boozy lunches – like me – and leaving your kids at home with the maid. Don't get sucked into it. You are better than that. And *please* don't end up like Ben and me. We have been corrupted by life here. Remember that weekend he took me to Macau for my birthday? On the way over on the hydrofoil I sat and looked out the window at that horrible brown soupy water, stirred up by the Pearl estuary, and I thought, what on earth am I doing here? I don't like this life or this part of the world and I don't think I even like Ben anymore. Our hotel was lovely, set in spacious grounds, surprisingly reminiscent of Europe, with cypress pine trees and clipped maze-like hedges. It should have been bliss. But when we lay by the pool in the morning, when I should have felt soothed by the soft sounds of the staff watering the plants and the chatter of the children in the pool – not mine so I should have been in heaven – I just felt weary and sad. Not a spark of joy in me. To be fair to Ben, he was trying, but everything was about his bloody company by then. I felt as though we were worlds apart because he loved Hong Kong so much and I didn't. I just wanted to go home. I wanted a back lawn and clean clear rivers and cold nights – and

Mum. "Postnatal depression" the doctor told me when I eventually went to him, but it was too late by then. Ben was having an affair with that cow from HR – I know it's still going on – and I had started drinking and I didn't feel alive again until you turned up here. Thank God for that.'

'You need help with your drinking,' Libby said. 'This place isn't for you. If you went home for a while, I think that might help.'

'What's this? An intervention?' Charlotte said. But she was as docile as a lamb the day Libby helped her to pack up and fly out with the family while Ben was away on a business trip and Rose looked after the kids while she went to 'dry out' and so that was that.

***

Charlotte spent a couple of months at the Hanmer Rest home. 'Rest' is a euphemism for relentless self-examination, she wrote to Libby, but in my case, it seems to be working. I'm getting there slowly and at least I don't have that ghastly feeling in my stomach any more. It was as though a rat had made its home there and spent its days gnawing away inside me.

It was late autumn, and sparse golden leaves hung like exhausted Christmas decorations on the avenue of trees that led into the town. The mornings were icy but when the sun came out the mountain air was clear and pure and it felt good to be alive. Charlotte walked along this avenue every afternoon after she had been to her group therapy session and written short notes to her three children. She kicked up the fallen leaves as she walked and the weight in her heart was lightened by the familiar sounds the leaves made. It was not only the treatment here that helped Charlotte; the healing also came from this return to a familiar place. Every whisper of the biting southerly breezes, the crunch of the gravel beneath her feet, the intense quiet of the pitch black nights, led Charlotte closer to becoming the funny, hopeful person she once was. The bossy, fearless sister Libby grew up with.

Sam was not surprised that Charlotte's rehab was so successful. 'She was always a fighter,' he said proudly. 'She was impossible to discipline as a child. Once she had her mind set on doing something there was no stopping her. She was determined to a fault. She gets it from me. Along with the alcoholism,' he added.

'I'm glad you can talk about it so flippantly,' said Rose. 'But you are right. You are both huge characters. That doesn't make you easy to live with though!'

But she smiled at him as she spoke so her words had no sting. Rose had become so serene as she grew older that Libby was quite envious. If getting older meant becoming so accepting maybe there was hope for her yet.

5

Two weeks after the funeral, after Tilda had gone away on a business trip and Edward and Charlotte had returned to work, Libby woke up one morning to bright sunshine and decided to go over to Akaroa. She was secretly relieved that nobody was free to go with her; if she was to clear up the house she would prefer to do it on her own.

The day was sunny and only a few feathered clouds swept across the sky, driven by a stiff breeze. Soon out in the countryside, she passed through the Kaituna Valley, then past Lake Ellesmere. A flock of mallard ducks, perfect dark v shapes in the sky, was flying towards the horizon and black swans, in twos, floated on the water, stretching their elegant necks towards one another and nodding as though in conversation. A group of Canada geese with white bibs and enquiring faces grazed in the reeds at the edge of the water.

There wasn't much traffic on the road and it was an easy drive past the marshy lowlands of Birdlings Flat to the quaint township of Little River. She stopped for a coffee and ate scones with cream and home-made strawberry jam that reminded her of childhood summers and wooden spoons and pots of boiling syrup spilling over on the stove top. A young couple were slouched in wicker chairs on the terrace outside the window; the

63

girl barefoot, with a tiny pursed-up mouth like a baby's, the Maori boy with the wide chiselled features of a chieftain. As they lifted their heads lazily to watch the smoke curling up from their cigarettes, Libby thought how perfect they looked. Like people in a play.

When she reached the top of the winding road leading to The Hilltop she felt her spirits lift as they always did when she arrived at the summit. She parked in the car park, the gravel crunching beneath her feet as she walked over to the viewing point to look at Banks Peninsula. It spread out before her, the fingers of the land jutting into the still water below, and the township of Akaroa a jumble of toy houses tumbling down the hillside opposite. The hillsides below were bald and dry, studded with tussock and grazing sheep, but the valleys were a soft green, filled with Macrocarpa trees. By the time she passed through the small settlements of Duvauchelles, Robinson's Bay and Takamatua, the tide was right out and the mud flats were dotted with dinghies and small family fishing boats, cast on their sides on the mud flats like basking seals.

The temperature was dropping as she drove into Akaroa and she wondered whether she should have booked into a motel for the night: the house would take some time to warm up. She drove slowly along the main street until she reached the side road where 'Belle Maison' stood.

She was surprised to see that a 'For Auction' sign was planted on the roadside at the foot of the pathway that led up to the house. What on earth was that about? The sign described it as: "An Akaroa institution, 4 beds, 2 baths, in original condition with all the beautiful features of its era. Ripe for Renovation." She looked up at the house from the road. It was as familiar to her as an old friend. On the ground floor there was a front porch with trellised columns and bay windows on either side of the front door. The top floor was gabled with sash windows on the two bedrooms and above, two carved wooden finials on the twin corrugated iron roofs.

When she drove further along into the village, she stopped the car outside the real estate office and got out to look in the window. What on earth was going on? The advertisement for Belle Maison was smack bang in the middle of the display window. Most of the other houses advertised were smart, contemporary holiday homes or functional baches. There was a photo of the front of the house, taken from its best angle, and another of the overgrown garden.

'Is there anything I can help you with?' A young woman with short bleached hair stood in the doorway; she was just about to light a cigarette.

'I'm Sam Prescott's daughter,' Libby said. 'I'm wondering who told you to put our house up for auction. I've come to sort everything out and clear up the house but we haven't decided to put it on the market.'

The girl looked flustered. 'I'm Sarah Foster. I'm actually marketing the house. I'm sorry. I didn't realise. Your sister Tilda phoned me and said she is the executor. Sometimes we get a random buyer who just drives past, so I thought it was worth putting up the sign and giving people plenty of notice. It's such a desirable property after all.'

She warmed to her theme. 'And the beauty of it is that because it was in your family for so long it hasn't been ruined by tasteless renovations like so many of the French cottages around here. If the new owner opens it up a little, puts in bigger windows, a skylight here and there it will be a real gem. At some stage it would be a good idea to find out from the Heritage Committee what you can and cannot do so that we can give that information to potential buyers. I loved your parents; they were the sweetest couple. They used to drive over to check it out quite often you know and they always popped in to say hullo.'

'*Really?* They never mentioned it.'

'They told me they liked revisiting all their old haunts. And it's best to sell in the spring,' she added hopefully. 'Even if it's a rotten day in Christchurch you'll often find it's a fine day here. And I'm not just saying that with my real estate agent hat on.'

'What about the southerlies?' Libby said. 'I remember they used to howl up the harbour.'

'Oh people exaggerate them,' said Sarah, looking at her reflection admiringly in the window and pushing her hair back. 'Anyway, they tend to slide past the township and hit the noses of the spurs in the harbour. You've always been sheltered up there.' She looked at Libby thoughtfully. 'Sounds to me as though you don't *want* to sell it!'

'It's not that,' said Libby. 'I would just like to have been consulted.'

'What the hell!' she said when she phoned Tilda later. 'Who are you to make decisions like that without telling us?'

'You're such a drama queen,' said Tilda dismissively. 'What did you think would happen? You're overseas. None of us here want the responsibility of another house. Our kids are older now; they're not interested in going over there. It's the logical thing to do.'

'I can see why she thought we'd all want to sell it,' Charlotte said when Libby phoned her. 'We're all too busy. You are right. She should have told us, but you know what; she's probably done us all a favour.'

'And why's that?' said Libby.

'Old houses are a drag to maintain. And every time you want to do something over there you have to consult the Heritage Society and then apply for permission from council. Do you really need that? And say *you* wanted to buy it – which I'm sure you don't as you don't even live here – we'd have to get it valued and you'd have to buy us out. Is that really a practical idea with you and Tom and all your problems?'

'I suppose not,' Libby grudgingly agreed. But as she unpacked her bag she was seething. The *cheek* of it!

Before she went to bed, she put her suitcase up in the attic room at the top of the house, where she and Edward slept as children, then went outside to look around. At the bottom of the gravel drive up to the back of the house, the garage, badly in need of paint, was covered by the thickened and gnarled vines of the wisteria climbing over it and up onto the guttering on the corrugated iron roof. She would need to get a gardener in, though it would be therapeutic to pick up a pair of secateurs and start chopping. Maybe now she could learn how to do all these basic things that people here took for granted. She only knew how to care for plants that lived in pots on balconies.

One Christmas Tom had given her a book on growing roses but reading it had been rather like reading a foreign language.

When she wandered back around the house she saw that the garden was full of enormous cobwebs, and she flinched as one spun between two bushes stuck to her face as she passed. She wiped it off with her hand. Here a narrow-paved path, now choked by wild grasses, led to the back door.

In the early days, before her father started drinking, he had built a wooden enclosure for a compost heap against the fence, so that her mother could easily toss vegetable and fruit peelings into it when she opened the kitchen door. In time, convolvulus grew over it and it blended into the landscape. This was one of the few practical things he had ever done. He was not a practical man, but he loved gardening. Eventually, however, he neglected even his beloved roses, and would be more likely to spend the morning nursing a hangover and listening to opera than working in the back garden. When their mother complained that he would be better picking the last apricots than lying about doing nothing, he would turn the music up and get himself another drink.

All this changed though after Sam stopped drinking. Libby's lasting memory now was of him and Rose sitting on the back lawn at Akaroa, on one of her last weekends there. She was making a cup of tea and watched her parents outside as she waited for the kettle to boil. Through the open window she could hear a background hum, like bees buzzing, of Saturday lawns being mowed and the calling of the commentator as Sam sat listening to the cricket while Rose read. Later, when the light began to sink behind the hills across the bay, and the fishing boats returned up the harbour, trailing wakes of silver, Sam got Rose's shawl from the bedroom, arranged it over her shoulders and then made her a strong gin and tonic, with two slices of lemon and a brandy dry with no ice for Libby. He didn't touch a drop himself by then. Not until after Rose died, and by then with the moderation of an old man who lacks the energy to do anything to excess.

She noticed as she went back in the front door that the lock was rusted. The agents should have changed it; it gave such a bad first impression. She had read somewhere recently that people decided whether to buy or not buy a house within a minute of coming through the front door. In that case she had better get it done herself.

Suddenly she asked herself what on earth she was doing here, in this house, in this small village, on a chilly spring evening. She must be mad. She missed her children. She missed Tom. She wanted to tell him what an outsider she felt back here. He was the only one who would understand. But he was the one person she couldn't confide in. Not anymore.

In the morning she unpacked the rest of her things and then sat on the window seat in the living room, looking out over the lawn to the sea beyond. The family had spent all their summer holidays here, right through Libby's childhood, until her first year at high school. What had happened that year? The official line from their parents was that life had become too busy, that as they became teenagers the children wanted to spend their weekends in town with their friends, Libby needed to study, Akaroa had become too crowded on public holidays. But something awful must have happened that summer, because afterwards her parents had even talked about selling Belle Maison. It was a particularly dry, hot summer and her parents had even more weekend parties than usual. But Libby could count on one hand the number of times they went there again in the next few years. It was also the last holiday that Max, Sam's best friend, was to spend with them before he returned to London after doing a locum in a hospital in Christchurch. Her father had begun to drink more than usual and some mornings the children would find him lying fast asleep on the faded divan in the sun room, as they ran through to get their togs off the clothes line for an early morning swim. When they came back he would be humming in the kitchen as he made a cup of tea, but his good mood wouldn't last and he would be grumpy again by lunch time.

The house went to rack and ruin that summer too. Rose had always been house proud, but now dinner dishes were left until the morning, the wooden furniture was unpolished, dusty Christmas cards lay in piles on the mantelpiece and the children were allowed to lie on the sofas in their wet togs, and trail sand through the house. Vases, once filled weekly with roses or hydrangeas from the garden, lay empty. More often than not, that year, Sam took to spending the weekdays in town.

'If babies choose to arrive during the holidays it's not *my* fault,' he said when Rose complained about being left with the children all week. 'You act as though I've personally organised my patients' deliveries just to spite you. Do you think I enjoy dragging myself out of bed at all hours to drive over that ruddy hill in the middle of the night? But it's my profession. It's what I do.'

But at least there was Max to keep them company. He seemed to have plenty of time on his hands. Often, in the afternoons, he would drive the family over the hill to Okains Bay, where they would spend the afternoon lazing in the lagoon or picnicking on the grassy verge above it. Vast sand hills, like the desert dunes they saw in their geography textbooks, stretched along the bay and when a blustery north-easterly blew the children would find sheltered places in the deep valleys between them and stretch out on their tummies, running the warm sand between their fingers or taking turns lying still like Egyptian mummies while the others buried them right up to their necks.

And that summer of '63 was the first time Libby saw anyone skinny-dipping. The children had wandered off to the far end of the beach to play on the huge piles of seaweed washed ashore by a recent storm, leaving Max and her mother reading their books after lunch. When they returned they found the two of them floating on their backs in the lagoon and something about the tone of their laughter, their mother's childish giggling and Max's low rumbling chuckle, made them stop and look at one another in surprise. Then Libby suddenly saw that they were naked. Their two white bare bottoms flashed as they dived in and out of the waves. The white blouse and blue slacks their mother had been wearing, and Max's trousers and checked shirt, lay neatly folded on the sand. Their orderliness was deeply shocking.

'Let's take their clothes,' Charlotte said. She sounded angry.

Edward ran down onto the sand, scooped up all their clothes and then called out, his voice as high as a girl's because it was breaking and tended to be at its most vulnerable when he was upset.

'What the hell do you think you are doing?'

Their mother stood up, her breasts startlingly white in the bright sunlight, and called back to him in her musical voice, 'Don't sound so angry darling. It's fun. *So* liberating. Come and join us.'

'Like heck we will!' said Charlotte to Libby. 'Let's go.' She stuck her chin up defiantly in the way she had when she had when she wanted to make a dramatic exit, but Libby thought she just looked a bit stupid as her togs were stuck up her bottom and her feet sank into the fine sand with each step so that she looked as though she was trudging up a mountain, not making a point. 'Come on!' she called to Libby as she got to the top of the first sand hill and saw that Libby wasn't following. Libby began to trudge after her, but then turned back and called out to her mother.

'We'll only give your clothes back if you promise to buy us fish and chips and an ice-cream for dinner.' She hated family arguments.

Their mother started wading into shore, but Libby noticed that she made no effort to cover herself up. 'What spoilsports you are!' she called.

Libby and Edward read quietly in bed that night.

'Don't tell Dad,' Edward said in a muffled voice as he turned the light off. And Libby didn't even bother to protest, as she usually did, that he hadn't bothered to wait until she had finished her chapter. 'It's our secret.'

Tom had taken to ringing her every few days.

'I don't know why you're so obsessed about your parents' lives,' he said when she told him she had been thinking about the years when the Akaroa house was locked up, they seldom went for holidays there and her parents were always bickering with one another.

'They're both gone now,' he said. 'Leave their secrets alone. Isn't it enough to know how happy they were together at the end?'

'No, it's *not* enough,' she said. 'I want to understand *why*. I only ever heard half the story from Mum. I never heard Dad's side. They never told us the whole truth.'

He laughed. 'All truth is subjective anyway. All lives are essentially about love, loss, betrayal, redemption.' He reeled the words off like a shopping list. 'All interesting ones anyway.'

'That's life in a nutshell is it?' said Libby. '"The World according to Tom." God, I hope you're not trying to justify your own bad behaviour by resorting to a sort of Pop philosophy.'

'Don't get on your high horse. You're so hard on me. I'm allowed to have an opinion.'

'Not anymore,' Libby said firmly. 'You've lost your right to have an opinion where I'm concerned.'

He laughed again. 'That's a hollow laugh in case you are wondering,' he said. 'Point taken.'

'Anyway, why do you keep calling?' she asked him crossly. 'You've made your bed. Now lie in it!'

He laughed. 'I haven't made my bed for thirty years. You know that.'

'That's how spoilt you get living in Hong Kong. It would be different if you lived here; I can tell you.'

'I just want to keep in touch. It's my past too you know. I loved your father and I like your family. Most of them, anyway.'

'Well I've told you already. They don't like *you* very much at the moment.'

'Look I just want you to know you can still talk to me about anything. I know you often get frustrated with all that family stuff. It can be stifling. If you need someone to talk things through with, I'm always here.'

'Talk is cheap,' said Libby. 'You try sorting out a holiday home that's full of years of accumulated family junk. Somehow everything has found its way here; all Mum and Dad's photos, and old letters and documents. The shabby furniture is easy. I can dump it. But what of the other stuff? I can't just toss all everything out. It's part of our family history.'

'You always said you wanted to write when you finished teaching. You could use all those old memories you're sorting through to write a novel. Weave a story around the letters and photos.'

'What would you know about creating a work of fiction? You make it all sound so simple.'

'I do it every day in court. I use the statements I have from my client and others to create stories that will convince the jury of my client's innocence. Or at least create a doubt in their minds. Mind you,' he added hastily. 'Of course, it's not fiction.'

'I sometimes wonder,' said Libby. 'You're a typical defence counsel. You always believe your client is innocent. Regardless. Anyway, you're impossible. Everything always comes back to you and the courtroom.'

She made herself a cup of tea and took it out to the balcony. The weather had changed since she'd sat here earlier in the morning. Then low white clouds had hung above the jetty like puffs of smoke and the bay was perfectly calm. A small runabout was chugging over from Robinson's Bay and she could hear the crystal voices of the children who hung over the stern calling to one another. Now angry black clouds were gathering at the head of the harbour and a smattering of rain began to fall on the roof. She shivered and zipped up her fleece. What right did Tom have to keep calling her anyway? And why should she take his advice. They were *her* memories to dwell on, not his.

But later, as she prepared dinner, Libby thought about what he had said about writing a novel. Hong Kong, in the seventies, was like a frontier town. China was over the border, communist and alien, but Hong Kong was a colonial haven with expats working for the Hong Kong and Shanghai Bank, the army, the police or, as Tom was, as Crown counsel for the Hong Kong government.

For a couple of days, she toyed with the idea. The protagonist in her novel would be a Crown counsel who goes off the rails. He would be a charismatic character who is unprepared but articulate in court, who loves gambling on the horses, is a sucker for pretty women and who is corrupted by the power he wields when he decides whether to prosecute cases or not. At first, it is just one or two cases, and he is handsomely paid by his friend – a solicitor with many influential clients – but later, as his tastes become more excessive, it becomes a way of life. He begins to spend his weekends in expensive hotel bars in Macau and meets up with a Russian beauty. She is a 'dancer,' controlled by her 'sponsor' a hardened criminal, a member of the Russian mafia which has infiltrated the Portuguese territory. He considers her his possession and does not take kindly to Libby's protagonist, Magnus, treating her as a girlfriend and not paying for every minute of her time. The plot would be an amalgam of stories about some of the characters she and Tom knew in Hong Kong over the years.

She sat conscientiously at her computer every day that week, recording her memories in a stream of consciousness that she hoped she could later distance herself from and shape into fiction. When she read back over it on the Friday night however, she decided it was a load of rubbish. She might as well focus on cleaning the house and learning to become a gardener instead. Even toned down, the true stories from the past would seem implausible.

6

Libby sat despondently on the top step leading to the first-floor landing. She simply didn't know where to start. The house had been used only occasionally over the past few years and the furniture, once contemporary, now looked battered and old fashioned, the knick-knacks were dated and the curtains had been so bleached by the sun that it was hard to tell whether they were cream or white. Over time the boxes and old suitcases left in the hallway cupboards had been covered in a thick layer of dust.

She wiped the top of one box to read what the label scrawled on it read – and promptly decided she needed to go down to the local store to buy some gloves. Once there she purchased a box of soft white cotton ones; they reminded her of the ones Rose used to pull on as they drove to and from the city.

'When you are older you must wear gloves when you drive girls,' she would tell them sternly, glaring over her shoulder at them as they bickered in the back seat. 'The sun will ruin your beautiful hands otherwise.' Like much of the information Rose had imparted, it only made sense to Libby now she was an adult. Then, they had raised their eyebrows at one another and Charlotte would nudge her and whisper, 'As if!' Now Libby looked ruefully at the age spots that had already spread all over her hands like a map of all the years she had spent unprotected from the sun.

When she got to the village it took her ages to shop for just a few basic supplies. In the corner shop she waited while the shop assistant, a young girl with a nose stud and greasy hair, conducted a loud conversation on her mobile phone. When she eventually found time to serve Libby, she kept up such an animated monologue on the weather, the upcoming spring festival, the new hairdresser about to open over the street that Libby escaped as soon as another customer came through the door, and went into the café next door for a coffee. But it was the same story there. She tapped her foot as she waited for the proprietor to finish wiping down the tables outside, place salt and pepper shakers on them, call greetings to various passers-by and then stand, legs akimbo, stand gazing up into the sky as he presumably decided what the weather was going to do. He seemed unable to chat and go about his business at the same time Instead of making her cappuccino, he leant on the bar, talking, while she willed him to get on with it. She felt pathetically grateful when a tourist bus spilled a whole bus load of Chinese tourists outside the café and he finally hurried to serve her.

After lunch she put on an old jumper to ease the cold. She had become a sorter, not a hoarder as the years went by, so she decided to sort the stuff into three piles as she went through it; rubbish (throw out and take to the dump) stuff she thought the family might want, and stuff to keep – old photographs, some letters etc.

By three o'clock she was exhausted but pleased with herself. She had put all the rubbish beside the garage and would get rid of it when she found out where the local dump was.

That left all the cartons in the box room; she would unpack two a day. The first carton she opened contained a small leather suitcase, the stitching coming undone in places and the lock broken; but it was in remarkably good shape considering how old it must have been. It looked like something from the 1920's or 30's. Inside there was an untidy assortment of loose photographs, some sepia but mostly black and white. She picked up one on the top; one of Sam and a few friends, standing on a beach with sand hills in the background. They were all dressed in the bathing costumes of the era; black woollen one-pieces with thin shoulder straps, and they had their arms around one another's shoulders. Sam had a wide smile on his face and was shading his eyes from the sun with one hand. Libby thought about the last time she had seen him, his old man's mouth as frayed as weathered rope. There was another framed photo of him posed for a studio photo; he was wearing a wide tie and a striped shirt and his signature was in the bottom right hand corner of the photo. Libby pulled up her jumper, wiped the dust off the frame and put the photograph on the mantelpiece. It was good Fung Shui to have photos around. She would make the house come alive again and she would make sure the ghosts she created from the past were happy ones. Tom had been right about one thing. It was much better to remember the good times, even if a little poetic license was needed here and there along the way.

She made herself a cup of tea and carried the case outside to the back lawn. A wooden bench sat over by the hedge, under the apricot tree. She sat there while she sorted through the photos, laying aside most to put back in the case. She kept aside one of her mother. Rose was dressed up, as though she was off to a wedding, or maybe the races. Her black hair was sleek, curled under in the style of the times and she wore a large hat with a huge feather on one side of it which swept down over the side of her face. She smiled demurely, her chin down, as though she was flirting with the camera. Her suit and blouse were immaculately tailored and over her shoulder hung a fox head fur. Her parents had both come from privileged homes but much of the ease of those years when they were young must have gone after their lives were disrupted by the Depression and then the war. The days of conspicuous inherited wealth vanished along with it.

***

Some habits from those early years lasted with Rose though; she still took meticulous care in her dress. Even when the children were young she would retreat to her bedroom at 4 o'clock every afternoon without fail. There she would change her clothes for something more presentable and freshen up her makeup. This involved applying Revlon powder, swept extravagantly over her face and blotted with a tissue, and then – puckering her lips in a pout – applying a rose-pink matt lipstick. After she had dabbed Chanel No. 5 on her wrists and neck, she was ready for their father's return. Before he arrived home, however, she would move through the house, a tray balanced on her arm like a waitress, collecting dirty cups and plates and taking them into the kitchen, removing any of the clothes that had been dropped during the day on the backs of sofas or kitchen chairs and straightening the cushions on the sofas. Finally, she would get out two cut glass crystal glasses, slice some lemon pieces and arrange them on a plate in preparation for the gins and tonic she and Sam always had at night.

If her parents were going out, her mother would take ages dressing, throwing things on the bed as she changed her mind about what to wear and then finally, when she was satisfied, she would down sit at her dressing table, dressed only in her petticoat, carefully apply her favourite Revlon bright red lip stick and finally take out her hair rollers and fluff up her hair. Suddenly she would be transformed into someone other than their everyday mother. Now she became a dazzling beauty with her bold lipstick, jangling bracelets and glamorous frocks with full gathered skirts that rustled in a delightful way as she bent to kiss them all goodnight and bustled out the door.

Libby wiped the photo, put it on the mantelpiece beside Sam's, and then, with a sigh of satisfaction, got back to work.

The next morning, Tilda arrived.

Libby had opened the front door to let some sunlight into the hallway and was kneeling on the floor in the living room sorting through a carton of books. Tilda shrugged off her coat and flung it over the back of the sofa.

'I hope that means you're here to work!' said Libby.

'And hello to you too,' Tilda replied, raising her eyebrows.

Behind her back Edward always referred to Tilda as the cuckoo in the nest and it was true that she was different from the other siblings. She had been blessed with Rose's effortless beauty; her face was as plump as a little girl's and she had the perfect features of a child's doll. At her best she was witty and amusing, at her worst manipulative and selfish. She enjoyed bearing grudges and managed to take offence so easily that you were never sure what you had said or done wrong.

'Yes thanks, I'd love a cup of tea,' she said when she saw that Libby had one beside her. 'It is bloody miles over that hill,' she said enunciating the 'it' and the 'is' is to embellish the statement. 'And the bad *drivers* you have to contend with! Actually, it's the slow old biddies who are the worst. Take me out and shoot me – preferably before sunrise – if I ever drive like that.'

Tilda worked hard at being different. Today she was wearing a coat made of faux fur in a leopard-skin pattern; the texture was so artificial it reminded Libby of candy floss.

'I could swear that sighed as you threw it on the sofa,' she said. 'Are you sure it isn't alive?'

Tilda shook her head. Her long auburn hair, extravagantly dyed, sliced through the air like a knife.

'It's new,' she said. 'Don't you like it?'

'I'm just teasing. And you look marvellous, as usual.'

Tilda picked up the coat from the sofa, put it on again, and said; 'I bought this because I could *see* myself in it with my long red boots and a black beret.' She looked at her reflection in the mirror over the mantelpiece, pushed one shoulder out and lifted her chin. 'What do you think?'

'It must be nice to like what you see when you look in a mirror.'

'I *am* rather "effective" looking, I always think.'

'Defective, you mean,' Libby couldn't resist saying under her breath as she turned to go into the kitchen to make the tea. But she was smiling when Tilda sharply asked, 'What did you say?'

'Nothing,' she said. 'By the way, I've been looking for the brass tray mum always promised me I could have; the one she got in India. It appears to have vanished. Have you seen it?'

The large brass tray was one of the exotic purchases Rose had brought back with her on the boat from Bombay, after she visited an aunt who was living there. For some years it served as a coffee table, supported by a trio of folding wooden legs, but in time the legs were put away in the cupboard under the stairs and Rose found a practical use for the tray, which was too large to display anywhere and fitted nicely between the refrigerator and the wall in the kitchen when it wasn't being used. Each day she carried it out to the washing line piled high with underpants and school blouses and Sam's shirts and gradually its glossy surface grew so tarnished that you could hardly make out the exotic passing parade on it: the maharajahs and the elephants, the umbrellas, and the Sanskrit writing.

Tilda didn't look up; she was scrabbling for something in her handbag.

'I presume you've seen it hanging on my wall at home,' she said. 'Why don't you just come straight out and say so.'

'Funny that she gave it to you. She always said I could have it. You all knew that, surely.'

'Well, she didn't actually *give* it to me. It was just hanging around after she died and I thought I'd polish it up. It's beautiful now. I get so many comments about it.'

'Don't worry. It's nothing in the scheme of things I suppose. I don't really care.'

'Well you obviously *do* care or you wouldn't have raised it,' said Tilda, pulling out her cigarettes.

'No. Really… Oh, please don't smoke inside.'

Tilda sighed, raised her eyebrows, put her cigarettes in her pocket and went through to the kitchen. She opened the fridge, and said over her shoulder, 'Gosh, if it matters that much to you, you can have it. It's just a brass tray. You have so many exotic things in Hong Kong.'

'That's not the point really though is it! You know I always loved it.'

'Nothing to eat here,' said Tilda, picking up her coat again. 'I'm starving, and I need a cigarette, so you get on with this and I'll pop down to the village and get us some lunch.'

'I still can't believe you just took it upon yourself to put the house on the market,' said Libby. 'Don't you think we should have all talked about it?'

'We *did* talk about it. It's just that you were on a plane at the time. As usual.'

'You really resent that, don't you?' said Libby. 'That you never lived overseas.'

'Not at all. And let's not get into all that. By all means, stay here, clear up, lay some ghosts; and then let's all move on.'

'Move on! Surely it's not that simple. You didn't think about asking the rest of us if we'd like to keep the house on as a joint enterprise, or even that one of us might want to buy it for ourselves.'

'Get real. You're separated now. There's no way you'll live here. Charlotte's on her own. Sort of. We don't want it. Our kids find it boring over here now that they are older. And Edward. Well; who would know what Edward wants. I don't think he knows himself.'

'Even so,' said Libby stubbornly. 'You should have given us the option. You've always just gone ahead when you think you're right, like a bull at a gate.'

'Oh and since when have you cared about life back here? If you want to buy the bloody house, you are welcome. Get a valuation done, make us all an offer.'

'Well I might just do that.'

'Well my advice to you is to think very hard about it before you go ahead. There's no secondary market for old houses over here anymore. People prefer modern holiday houses now.'

After Tilda had left to walk down to the village Libby went outside and sat in the garden. The apricot tree still had some late fruit hanging on it. She pulled a couple of apricots off but they were riddled with worms and she tossed them over the fence into the field beyond. She lay down on her back on the grass, closed her eyes and breathed in the smells around her; the fresh grass, the ripened apricots, the rosemary hedge. The sun filtered through the leaves of the tree onto her eyelids. Out of nowhere, a huge wave of sadness overwhelmed her. It was accompanied by the feeling she sometimes had when she woke in the early hours of the morning; as though some awful calamity was about to overtake her. She had never taken kindly to change. Maybe coming over here on her own was too much to ask of herself. She was already tired of being alone. She had always hated being away from her family. She had always hated the way other families did things differently. Homesickness was an affliction she had never conquered. She still blushed when she remembered some of the holidays away from home that had ended prematurely.

***

Her first real holiday away from the family had been at Waikuku, a beach not far from Christchurch. Their neighbours, the Murrays, who lived in a sprawling two storey mansion further down the road, had asked her to stay at their family bach for a few days. Although she was nearly eleven, she had somehow managed to avoid staying away from home until now. She would develop a high fever the night before she was due to go on a netball trip or a funny tummy before she was to stay with Auntie Nancy, her mother's scary sister. This time however, Rose and Sam had decided it was time they took a stand. When it became clear that the mysterious illness Libby had been struck down with the night before, with its wide range of puzzling symptoms, was not going to keep her safely at home in her own bed, she was indignant. She lay on her back on the lawn, rubbing her stomach, where the pain was getting worse by the moment. She needed to devise a cunning plan. As she looked up at the sky, past the roof of the shed, the corrugated iron sparkling in the morning sun, it came to her! After Sam had mowed the lawns he always tipped several loads full of newly cut grass into the compost heap he had built between the shed and the fence. She and Edward liked jumping from the roof onto the soft piles of fresh clippings. Today however, the compost heap was filled only with hard old vegetables and stiff dry corn plants that had been pulled out of the garden the week before. If anyone jumped from the roof today they might hurt themselves. With luck they might even break an ankle.

So Libby clambered up the wooden fence, pulled herself up on the roof and was just about to jump when Rose came out the back door to pick some silver beet for dinner. She looked up at Libby, shading her eyes from the sun.

'Don't do anything silly,' she said firmly. 'You are going to have a lovely time.'

'But I don't even *like* Sonia,' Libby said crossly. Sonia Murray, who was the same age as Libby, was boring. Libby only played with her if Edward was having one of his mean days; those days when he went off with his friends and told her to buzz off. 'Even you say she gets on your nerves with her grizzly voice,' she said.

But it was useless. She was talking to herself. Rose had already picked the silver beet and gone inside.

They drove out to Waikuku the next afternoon; it was a cold Sunday, with a light drizzle rolling in sympathy down the car windows. Libby hoped the journey would go on forever. With any luck her father might even get lost. He was always trying to find short cuts when they went anywhere. They stopped for Rose to buy apples and beans at a roadside stall to take to the Murrays before they turned off the main highway and down a side road that wound through marshy farm land to the coast. The township, when they came to it, was more like a cluster of houses than a community. There were a couple of rows of square wooden cottages with tin roofs and scrubby front gardens and even the village green they passed in the centre of the town was no more than a sandy wasteland. There was a children's playground in the middle of it; a slide, some swings and a roundabout. A man, his jacket collar pulled up against the weather, listlessly pushed a young girl back and forth on the swing and several children were fighting to climb up the slide. Libby wound her window down, and heard their laughter as they pulled one another back as soon as one of them got towards the top of the silvery slope. The row of fir trees that had been planted at the side of the green as a wind shelter leaned in unison away from the sea.

'Look at that!' said her mother, pointing at them. 'This place must be so exposed.'

'I feel a little bit sick,' Libby said.

'Nonsense. You'll be fine,' said her mother, but glanced anxiously at Sam. 'You won't be far from home you know.'

'We're only a car drive away,' Sam added.

'No. It's not that,' said Libby, trying to inject a note of weakness into her voice and coughing feebly. 'It's not that I'm worried about being away from *home*. It's just that I think I'm really ill now. I started to feel pretty sick again last night but I just didn't tell you.'

'You're probably just car sick,' said Rose briskly. 'It's the silly routes your father always insists on taking when we go anywhere further than the corner shop; cutting through the back streets, driving down back country roads that wander up hill and down dale, when all he needs to do is go from A to B directly like everybody else does.'

Libby wished that Sam would drive up hill and down dale forever, but all was now lost as they were drawing up outside the house, identified not by a number, but by the red painted corrugated iron roof on the garage at the end of a short shingled drive.

'Here we are,' Sam announced unnecessarily.

'You'll have a super time,' said Rose. She leaned over from the front seat and pushed Libby's hair back from her face. 'We all have to learn to stay away from home sometime,' she said gently.

'I *know* that,' said Libby, but she didn't look at her mother and pushed her hand away.

'It's not much of a house, is it?' Rose said doubtfully. 'But at least it's stopped raining.'

Before anyone could answer her, the front door was flung open and Mrs. Murray emerged. She stopped to light up a cigarette and leaned on the wooden verandah railing, waiting for them. She was wearing tight scarlet shorts. Rose only wore shorts like that to garden in.

'I don't like her,' Libby said. 'She looks cheap.' Perhaps the tight shorts would be enough to make her mother and father climb back into the car (for they were now getting out with stupid smiles on their faces) and take her straight back into town.

'Don't be silly,' said Rose, leaning in the window and opening her door from the inside. 'She's a very nice person. And I don't like you using that word. You sound like a snob.'

'We'd better get on the road sooner rather than later,' said her father quietly as they walked her to the front door. 'Don't stay for a cup of tea, will you? It will only make it worse.'

The late-night call from Mrs. Murray came just as Sam was settling down in bed to read his book.

'I couldn't let her suffer all night,' she told him, as he stood barefoot in the cold hallway shrugging on the woollen jumper Rose handed him. 'I know from bitter experience that the one thing that cures homesickness is a couple of terms in boarding school, but I wouldn't recommend *that!*'

'You'll grow out of it,' Sam said as he drove Libby home, uphill and down dale, along pitch black country roads and through the sleeping city. 'There's no point in forcing these things.'

'I hate having to fit in with the way other people do things, do you?' Libby said, looking at him for reassurance.

'I hate it too,' he replied.

'I am going to live with you and Mum for*ever*,' Libby told him sternly as he tucked her into bed.

'That's fine by me,' he said, and she heard him whistling as he walked down the hallway.

7

Libby got up from the lawn and wandered around the outside of the house. The house was set up off the main road, directly opposite the War Memorial: it was so close that she could see the Anzac Day wreaths, withered now like papery imitations, arranged on the wide steps leading up to the cenotaph. The names listed on the monument, the de Villiers, the Browns and the Williams, were mostly from old farming families from the peninsula. How far they must have felt from home, as they fought and died in Flanders, or at Gallipoli or in the sands of the Desert War.

Sam had earned the Distinguished Service Medal he kept in the top drawer of his tallboy when he was a medical officer in the desert. He never talked about it, but Rose told the children he had defied the German command after the Allies had suffered a brutal defeat at Tobruk and he went onto the battlefield, tending to the wounded and dying. Libby thought guiltily how her generation had taken so little interest in the past and asked so few questions about the war. Sam never spoke about it.

It was Daisy who had found a photo of him in an old box of photos one year when they were staying there, and put it on the mantelpiece in the living room. 'What on earth for I don't know,' Sam grumbled when he saw it there. But Daisy said that it was a half-hearted grumble and he stood for a long time looking at it. In it he stood with a group of other young medical officers, their uniforms fitting them as easily as dinner jackets.

The little summerhouse overlooking the memorial, where Sam used to sit and read the morning paper on fine days, was as unkempt as ever, but nestled complacently amongst the shrubs and was hidden from the road by the hedge which ran around the front of the property.

Libby stood beside the hedge and looked back at the house. How fine it was; perfectly proportioned and unassuming but with just a hint of grandeur that distinguished it from the other houses in the village. Then she walked out to the front, leaned on the gate and looked back at the house, wondering what prospective buyers would think of it. The bay windows, shaded now by faded striped canopies, gave the house a pleasingly friendly air, as though its eyelids were drooping and it was half sleeping, enjoying the afternoon sunshine. The next owner should replace all the small lattice windows with big windows though; that way light could pour into the house and bring it into the 21st century.

In the late afternoon, just before Tilda set off back to Christchurch, they walked down to the small jetty at the far end of the bay, and then along past the tennis courts and cricket ground. The pavilion beside the cricket pitch was being renovated; it was covered with scaffolding, and a couple of the painters who were sprawled on the grass having a smoke whistled at them in a half-hearted manner as they approached.

Tilda laughed. 'We still look ok from a distance then. Watch their whistles trail off in disappointment as we get closer.'

'Some things never change in this part of the woods, do they,' said Libby. 'I thought wolf whistles were not considered "harmless" nowadays. I do love being back here though, don't you?' she added. 'It's like old times.'

'You're romanticizing it,' said Tilda. 'You've been away too long. It's actually excruciatingly boring here; I can never wait to get back to town. Oh, look how well tended the tennis courts are now. There is actually grass on them! Remember what they were like in our day?'

***

When her parents had friends from Christchurch over in the summer, and after a few drinks, a spontaneous game of tennis was often organised. At that time of year when there was not much rain, the batting areas on the cricket pitch were bald of grass and the tennis courts were baked like hard clay. It was an unspoken rule that the men must take the young ones with them if they planned to be away all afternoon. Fortified by fizzy drinks, the children would settle down in the shade of the pavilion, but would soon grow bored. The older ones generally headed off to the jetty nearby, or started up their own game of bar-the-door, leaving the younger ones to fend for themselves. Consequently, Libby was always left behind. And the men's tennis games always stretched long into the afternoon, dragged out by contested line calls and sets that seemed to go on forever. Only Edward, who was an accomplished player, was occasionally allowed to join in.

Libby smiled to herself as she remembered a day when Charlotte had been told to 'buzz off' by the others and had slouched back, sulking, to the oval.

'It's not fair,' she said. She had been trying to join the older children who were now jumping from the end of the jetty into the water. The challenge was to swim around the end of the jetty – past the pylons covered with sharpened barnacles that sliced at you like knives if the current washed you onto them – and then scramble up the ladder on the other side. It was really a working ladder, used to inspect the piles holding up the jetty, but the children, over time, had become adept at pulling themselves up the rusted rungs to the top. The timing had to be just right. If the waves were too strong they threw you against the ladder; if you tried to climb up between surges the lower rungs had more treacherous barnacles growing all over them.

'It's not fair,' she said again, throwing herself down beside Libby. 'I hate them. They're so mean.'

'Shall we make daisy chains?' said Libby. She was happy, lying on her back on the grass. She had been day dreaming. In all her day dreams that summer she was wearing the patent leather red shoes – her first ever slip-ons – that her mother had bought her for her birthday at a church "Bring and Buy". Today she was imagining herself playing tennis in them, at some fabulous tournament, with the crowds roaring and her parents watching in awe as she flew back and forth across the court, her second-hand red shoes flashing in the sunlight.

'No! That's boring. I don't want to play with you anyway,' said Charlotte. 'I think I'll run away,' she said. 'Then they'll all get into trouble with Mum.'

Libby sat up quickly. 'Oh, don't do that,' she said. 'Then Mum and Dad will just have a fight. Anyway, where would you go? It's getting cold and you'll get hungry.'

'I'll just hide for a while. Don't you *dare* tell them!'

She stomped off, heading for the back of the pavilion, but just then the sun began to slide behind the hills across the harbour.

Libby shivered and pulled on her cardigan. 'We'll be going soon anyway,' she called out to Charlotte's retreating back. 'And shouldn't you put your jumper on?'

Charlotte turned back. 'I'll bet they wouldn't even notice I was gone,' she said, but she came back, snatched her jumper from Libby and sat with her back to her, chewing on a piece of grass.

But Libby had forgotten the after-match drinks. The men slowly drifted away from the tennis courts and gathered at the foot of the small stand at the end of the cricket pitch. Sam passed around bottles of beer, and they stood in a circle, chatting. Lights began to go on in the houses in the surrounding streets, the sky darkened over the hills and the others began to wander back from the jetty, huddled in towels and quickly scrambling into their clothes. Libby caught snatches of the men's conversation.

Three of the four men were doctors, and Sam and Max were obstetricians, so any holidays they had were planned around delivery dates.

'I know a chap who refuses to do house calls nowadays,' said Max.

'How can he call himself a doctor?' Sam asked.

'It must be tough on your marriage living the way you guys do,' said Bruce. He was the only businessman in the group. His family owned a biscuit factory. The children thought it the most enchanting occupation ever and one they would like to aspire to – along with being a fireman or a policeman – when they were older. Imagine what it must be like to have an endless supply of biscuits and chocolates! They loved it when he visited at Christmas because he always brought the same gift; a huge tin of biscuits from his factory. The tin itself was thrilling enough; a bright red shiny container the size of a bucket with raised patterns of biscuits all over it. It was filled with broken biscuits not fit for the commercial market and this made it even more appealing as they could sift through for the biscuit parts they particularly liked. Initially, they would play stones/scissors to decide who got first choice. By the time their parents got to choose, all that would be left would be the crisp layered biscuits filled with a coconut cream filling. The children hated those.

Bruce handed Max another beer and said, 'I hear you have decided to move back to London earlier than planned. That came out of the blue...'

Libby shivered suddenly. She pulled her cardigan around her and rubbed her arms to keep warm. She hoped the others wouldn't mention this to Rose when they got home and she asked, as she often did, what the men had been gossiping about.

Not that it mattered as it turned out, because Nancy must have got wind of it. They were sitting outside in the front garden the following evening. Max had driven back to town but the rest of them would leave the following morning. It was a mild evening and the adults were sprawled in the wicker chairs on the lawn, nursing their gins and whiskies. Rose was leaning against one of the pillars, smoking a cigarette and idly picking off some of the dead lavender heads. Sam was inside, pouring more drinks.

Nancy was laughing at something Bruce had said and then she leaned back in her seat and called over her shoulder to Rose, almost as an afterthought, 'You know that Max is going back to London soon?'

There was a sudden silence. Libby thought that it was like the game called Statues that Sam used to play with them sometimes when they were younger, when, whatever they were doing, they had to freeze when he clapped his hands.

'Surely, you've heard?' said Nancy, when Rose didn't reply. 'After all; you and Max are *such* good friends.'

Rose turned around and narrowed her eyes in that way she had where she kept her head down, but looked up at you and called you by your full name so you knew you were in trouble, and then she turned away and began to pick at the lavender again.

Libby said, 'Nobody's talking.'

'Don't be stupid,' Charlotte said.

'I thought you of all people would know,' Nancy repeated.

Their mother looked up at her and shook her head.

'You just love this don't you,' she said. 'And to tell me in front of the children.'

'What do you mean?' said Nancy innocently. She turned back to the others and shrugged her shoulders. 'You're the one who has made your own bed. Now you have to decide whether to lie in it or not.'

'You've always had a nasty streak,' said their mother. 'I don't know where it comes from.' She walked over to the wall at the side of the garden. It marked the point where the valley began and the hill sloped down, through the wild apple trees to the valley floor. There the stream ran as clear as glass, over the stony creek bed and into the harbour. There was a brief flicker as she lit another cigarette and in the darkness, there was only a silhouette as she leaned on the wall, turning her back on them all.

Just then Sam came out carrying more drinks on a tray.

'Who died?' he said cheerfully.

Later, Rose came in the French doors to the living room, where Libby, Charlotte and Edward were playing cards. She closed the door behind her.

'You really should be in bed,' she said. 'Can I play?'

Libby got off the sofa and sat down on the floor.

'Of course. We're playing five hundred so it's better to have four.'

Later Libby lay awake for a long time. The light of the full moon crept around the edges of the curtain and she studied the patterns it made on the ceiling and walls, half-closing her eyes to conjure up animals or people's profiles. When her mother looked in on them later she said, 'Still awake?'

'I've got a tummy ache,'

'I have too,' said her mother. 'I'll snuggle up with you for a while. That will make it better.'

8

One afternoon, before Rose went away, they were sitting in the garden at Akaroa. It was a sultry still day and huge black clouds had been rolling down over the hills all morning

'There's a storm on the way,' said Sam. 'I'll go down and get some drinks in.'

'Why?' said Rose, putting both hands to her head dramatically as she did when she was annoyed by something. 'Why is *drink* the first thing you panic about being without? If there was an earthquake, or a war or a great flood, you'd be worrying about whether the drinks cabinet was full. Normal people would think about getting in bread and butter.'

'Who wants to be ruddy *normal?*' Sam said. He got up and folded up his deck chair, banging it down clumsily as he threw it on the porch as he went inside. Several paint tins – he had been painting the back door screen off and on for months – fell from the balcony onto the ground.

'And watch those paint tins,' called Rose. 'Mind you,' she continued, 'why bother! The paint has probably dried out by now. When did you begin that job? Was it a year ago? Two? And get some bloody bread when you're down there.'

'You're talking to yourself Mum,' said Libby. 'He can't hear you.'

'He drives me mad,' Rose said.

'Does it really matter if he gets a few drinks in?' said Charlotte.

'Yes, it does,' said Rose. 'He drinks too much.'

'At least he's fun,' Charlotte mumbled as she got up from the lawn.'

'What was that?' shouted Rose. 'What did you say?'

She suddenly leapt up from her chair and grabbed Charlotte by the shoulder of her cardigan. Charlotte pulled away, but their mother held on. There was a sickening sound like a paper bag ripping as the sleeve tore along the seam.

'Now look what you've done,' said Charlotte coldly. 'You're crazy.'

'Oh, sorry,' Rose said, her voice trembling.

'Don't touch me. You're such a nag! No wonder he drinks!'

'Why do you always take his side?' Rose said angrily. 'It's not *fair*.'

'Don't, Charlotte,' Libby said. 'Leave her alone. *I'll* go down and get some bread for you Mum.'

'That's alright darling,' said Rose. 'You're always the peacemaker.' Then she added, suddenly cheerful as she looked up at the sky. 'He's right. It feels like rain so maybe he'll get caught in a downpour while he's out.'

Auntie Nancy, who had been watching the scene with a tight smile, said, 'That's not a very nice thing to say Rose,' and began packing up the tea cups and putting them on the tray.

Just as they got inside there was a huge crack of thunder and in a flash the sky darkened as rain began to fall. Lightning flashed outside the window and the hills opposite soared into view as though someone had switched a light on, and then just as suddenly disappeared into the darkness.

As Libby and Charlotte were setting out the Scrabble on the coffee table, the front door opened and closed very quietly.

'Dad,' Libby called out. 'Do you want a game of Scrabble?'

'Later,' Sam said as he came into the room. Then, with an exaggerated swinging off his arms and putting his head down as if he was about to march off to war, he said, 'I'd better make my peace first.'

They heard him say hopefully as he went into the kitchen, 'I bought you some chocolate.'

'Thanks,' Rose said, slicing the word off like a knife.

'What's wrong with you? Sulking?'

The fridge door opened and closed with a soft clunk.

'Say something. Don't be childish.'

'You always have to ruin everything, don't you?' she said.

'Me!' said Sam. He sounded genuinely astonished. 'You're the one who ruins everything with that sour face of yours, the exaggerated sighs every time I have a drink or sit down listening to music, or – God forbid – make any effort to enjoy myself.'

'So you have to have a drink to enjoy yourself do you?'

'No. It's just sociable. Better than putting a damper on the whole holiday for everyone by rushing around tidying up all the time like you do.'

'So if I didn't do it, who would?'

'Is that a rhetorical question?'

'Don't be smart. It may come as a surprise to you that things don't just jump up and put themselves away, and clean themselves. Toilet rolls don't just mysteriously appear on holders, towels on towel racks, flowers don't cut themselves from bushes and arrange themselves in vases.'

'Really. Well you learn something every day. I always thought they did.'

'Don't be sarcastic.'

'And who works hard to bring in the money so you can spend all day arranging flowers in your nice holiday home?'

'Oh, don't start that!'

'Oh, shut up,' Charlotte yelled suddenly and pushing all her Scrabble pieces onto the floor she ran out of the room. Her bedroom door slammed behind her.

'What a happy family we are,' said Libby to an empty room as she picked up the pieces.

The next morning, keen to start out on the long road to redemption, Sam placed a cup of tea on Rose's bedside table.

'Nothing but the best for you madam,' he said. 'A perfect brew served in your best china.'

'"Madam" doesn't cut any ice with me,' Rose said, before turning over dismissively and snuggling down into the bedclothes again. But when he had left the room she turned over again, winked at Libby who was tucked in beside her, and sighed appreciatively as she took her first sip.

Sam put his head around the door a couple of minutes later. 'Would you like to go out to lunch?' he said hopefully.

'I'll think about it,' said Rose.

That day Sam worked extra hard to get back into Rose's good books, as the next day the Frasers, their parents' friends, were coming to stay. They arrived just after breakfast, much to Rose's chagrin.

'Talk about desperate,' she called over her shoulder to Sam when she saw them coming through the gate as she washed up the breakfast dishes. 'I thought you said they were coming at lunchtime?'

Felix, Libby's godfather, put a bottle of Johnny Walker on the sideboard as he came in, before advancing on Libby with short bouncy steps that always reminded her of a ballet dancer's.

'My *favourite* girl,' he said as he hugged her for a little longer than she thought was strictly necessary. 'You get more beautiful every day,' he added, taking her face in his hands and pulling her so close that she could see the map of red lines running all the way down the sides of his nose and across his cheeks. 'You are like a ripe peach.'

Doris, his wife, a tiny blonde who Sam described behind her back as a 'retired bombshell', said sharply, 'Leave her alone Felix. Girls that age hate being pawed over.'

'I wasn't pawing her,' he said indignantly. 'You like being hugged by your Uncle Felix, don't you Libby?'

'I don't mind,' she replied quietly but as soon as she could escape she hurried straight off to the back lawn to join Edward who was kicking a ball at the back fence.

'I don't know how she can stand the way he carries on,' she said. 'I'm never going to marry someone like that.'

'You won't have to,' said Edward. 'You'll be lucky if anyone asks you.'

Libby ignored him, and flopped down on the lawn. 'And even at this hour he stinks of whisky. It's gross.'

'At least the Frasers always bring the good weather with them,' Libby heard Sam say to Rose that night as they sat having drinks outside.

'You sound so smug,' said Rose. 'As if you have been vindicated for asking them over.'

It was true though, thought Libby. The moon was enormous; a luminous buttery balloon hanging in a deep black sky. The hills beyond the harbour were folded over one another, the shadows rolling over them like blankets. It was impossible not to be happy.

But the next day it was the same old story. Sam wanted to put drinks in the fridge; Rose said there was no room because of all the food she had got in for 'his bloody friends.'

The bickering went on all morning.

'God you two are *ridiculous*,' said Charlotte eventually. 'You're always fighting for possession of something, even a stupid old fridge.'

'It's the *principle*,' said Rose. 'I spend days preparing the food and then he just takes stuff out willy-nilly and fills it up with his silly bottles.'

'Well where am I meant to put them? You can't have warm wine and beer.'

'Fill up some tubs with ice, fill up the bath, prepare beforehand; I don't really care what you do as long as you get that stuff out of my fridge.'

'What a ruddy fuss about nothing,' Sam said, but he removed all his drinks with much clinking and banging and then slammed the door as he went out.

'No doubt he'll fortify himself with a drink when he goes to get some ice,' Rose said.

'You can't resist getting at him, can you?' Libby said. 'It's better to just go along with him.'

'Why should I?' said Rose incredulously. 'Wait 'till you're older and trying to cook for everyone. Then you'll understand. You all spoil him! But unlike your father; I'm too busy to sulk.' Turning her back on Libby she started to put all her food back in the fridge.

And Sam *was* drunk when he and Felix came back. They avoided Rose and went straight into the living room, where Sam put on one of his favourite operas, *The Pearl Fishers*. They were both fast asleep, their heads flung back on their armchairs, and snoring like old men, when Rose went in later, irritated by the loud music. She turned the player down and went outside and Libby, watching anxiously through the sunroom window, saw that although she was usually gentle with her roses, today she was hacking at them like an enemy and pushing them roughly into her basket. Afterwards she sat for a moment in the sun with her head thrown back to it and her eyes closed and she was calmer when she came back inside. She was arranging the flowers in tall crystal vases by the time Sam stirred.

'Like a drink?' he asked her. He was relaxed after his little nap and he smiled gratefully at her when she replied, 'Yes please.'

Later that night, as they lay in bed, Libby whispered to Edward, 'Maybe Charlotte is right. She says Dad's drinking is destroying us all.'

'They're destroying one another,' said Edward. 'I don't want to talk about it. Go to sleep.'

'But one night after Mum came back,' Libby told Tom. 'I asked her why she hadn't left Dad when he drank like that. "I won't put up with that when I get married," I said firmly. "You will understand when you get older," Mum said. "You stick with people through good and bad. You'll see."

'I can still see her sitting at her dressing table, talking to me in the mirror and idly brushing her hair. She smiled at me so radiantly and said, "Dad was forgiving too you know."

'I was still so naive then. Still a child. Something told me not to ask her what she meant.'

Charlotte, as opinionated as ever, said that Libby can only move forward if she looks backwards and arranged for her to see Brian Thompson, 'the 'best counsellor in Akaroa.'

'That is hardly a glowing endorsement as there wouldn't exactly be much competition in a village this size,' scoffed Libby. But the sun was shining and as it was always easier to just go along with Charlotte when she had a project in mind, she agreed to go to three sessions and then decide whether it was worthwhile.

'So far it has all been a complete waste of time,' she told Charlotte crossly after her first visit. 'You and your bright ideas. I'd rather talk to *you*. At least you give me some advice, even if I decide not to take it. But he just sat there saying nothing. It was hopeless.'

And she hated the way Brian expected *her* to do all the talking. She had never been an eloquent story teller when it came to talking about her own life. And although that morning, she had related a rather self-deprecating anecdote about herself, to start the second session off on an entertaining note, he did not appear to be amused.

'One observation I have before we move on,' he said, rather pompously. 'Is that I think your efforts at humour only mask your pain. We need to confront your sadness, not gloss over it.'

'Oh, do we *really* have to go over all that?' said Libby. 'I was hoping you'd just give me some ideas; a bit like a life coach, whatever that is. I'm not really comfortable with deep analysis. Did I tell you that Hong Kong gets a hold of you?' she continued, in an effort to distract him. 'It's like an intense love affair. And even when you know it would be best to walk away you can't bear to leave it. And how realistic is that? China won't sit back and allow us our freedoms forever but we expats just keep on believing.'

'I can see you want to talk about Hong Kong again,' he said. Rather wearily, Libby thought. 'So perhaps the thought of leaving your life there behind is a stumbling block for you? Let's talk about that shall we.'

'And I hate the way he drapes a long lock of what's left of his hair from one side of his head to the other. It's ridiculous,' Libby told Charlotte as they debriefed later. 'What's wrong with being bald anyway? And I'm not happy about sharing my feelings with him. Why should I! He doesn't even know me. For all I know he might be totally indiscreet and spend every Friday night in the bar at the end of the wharf mocking me to all his mates. I've always found therapists some of the most indiscreet people I know. Only trumped by lawyers. He's got a long mean nose,' she added. 'And his eyes are too close together.'

'Oh *now* who is being ridiculous,' Charlotte said. 'I only hope you are being open with him. I know what you can be like. It's impossible trying to get to the bottom of anything with you. You just go round and round in circles and then change the subject. The trouble is,' she said, snapping her finger as though she had just had an epiphany. 'You have the soul of a bloody poet. You are the only person I know who thinks in metaphors and that's why you can never explain yourself clearly. In short,' she said, shaking her head. 'You can't see the wood for the trees.'

'That's unfair,' said Libby. 'It's just that nobody here, apart from you, ever understands. How can I explain to him, someone who's never lived there as you and I have, that Hong Kong is a city that made me lose sight of myself? That when I look back it's as though I became a completely different person. I mean, what say I told him that after you've lived there for a long time and you return to your home country you're like a lost sheep, just wandering around searching but never ever finding your flock again. Would he understand what I was trying to say?'

'Not a chance,' said Charlotte. 'Only expats would understand. Just keep it simple.'

'Well I *will* tell him that the people we first met there were remarkable,' said Libby defensively. 'Like characters from a Scott Fitzgerald novel. He is bound to find that interesting.'

'I doubt it.' said Charlotte. 'I think you'll lose him completely if you say something like that. It sounds so pretentious. Don't try to overcomplicate things. Speak in plain English.'

'Now don't hold back this time will you,' she said sharply, revving the engine in a scary way as Libby slowly extricated herself from the car when she dropped her off for the third session. 'You've always put a distance between yourself and other people when they get too close. Even the family; it's your *modus operandi*.'

'That's rubbish,' said Libby, but she twisted her hair around her finger and quickly changed the subject.

'You've got a cheek giving me lectures. Look at *you* when you were drinking,' she said sternly, leaning in at the passenger's window before Charlotte had the chance to put it up. 'Counselling did nothing for you. You had to go to that place in Hanmer Springs to dry out before you got better.'

'*Exactly*,' said Charlotte. 'For your information, we had tons of counselling there. I got sick to death of it, but it did help. Mind you,' she said thoughtfully, 'I'm not like you; I've always enjoyed talking about myself. Come to think of it, I am one of my favourite subjects. I'll pick you up in an hour. My hair's a mess; I'm off to the hairdresser.'

'Going to the hairdresser would do more for my mental health than going to a therapist,' said Libby wistfully. 'You know I love having my hair done. Can't I come too? You could wait for me.'

'No,' said Charlotte. Then she gave Libby the finger and called out the window as she sped off. 'I'll take you to my hairdresser when you make some progress.'

Libby shook her head as she watched her go but the gesture cheered her up immensely. Charlotte could always make her laugh.

'I did as you said,' she told Charlotte later. 'I tried to just tell him simple stories about my life there. But of course, he still didn't get it.'

She looked out the window of the café they were sitting in. It was part of a country-wide chain so they could have been anywhere; with the ubiquitous view overlooking the open carpark with only a few people going to and from their cars and beyond that the a new development of suburban bungalows stretching along the main road outside.

'I told him that if you live on one of the hillsides, on the island, and open your windows, the city actually hums like a huge machine. And it's a machine that never ever shuts down. And there are neon lights and signs and sky scrapers and noise everywhere and yet you can walk on hillside paths above the city through the bush and hardly see another person. And the people we met there in the early seventies were amazing. The expats were beautiful and spoilt and hedonistic. It was glorious.'

'Do you call that plain speaking?' scoffed Charlotte.

'Let me finish,' said Libby. 'I did add detail. I told him how difficult it was at first, because I loved my life in London. I confessed that I actually *followed* somebody I fancied to Hong Kong. I confessed that I'd used the excuse that you were living there, but really, I was looking for the big romance. I told him that I was just about to get a promotion at school, and that the romance didn't last and do you know what he said? "Women often decide to follow a man halfway around the world just as they are about to become successful. I wonder why that is?"'

'Oh, he sounds like someone out of the Ark,' said Charlotte.

'Yes, I think he was trying to be profound but I didn't respond. It was a rhetorical question after all and wasn't *he* the one who was meant to be providing *me* with answers? And then, because I could tell he was sick of hearing about my love affair with Hong Kong, I told him about some of the things I wouldn't be sad to leave behind. That cheered him up no end.'

9

'Your mother was a spoilt woman,' said Nancy. That's a joke, Libby thought. Nancy, the youngest of a large family, had always been the mollycoddled one. Especially by Rose. Now Nancy was crouched in the back seat of the car, with a blanket over her knees, her face as petulant as a teenager's. You could tell she was looking for trouble. In old age upsetting people had become her raison d'être. She had elevated it to an art form. Once a beauty, with strong aristocratic features and lush brown hair she wore swept back from her broad forehead, age and disappointment had soured her good looks.

Libby had driven all the way back from Akaroa to take her for an outing from the residential care home she lived in. When they got out of the car to have afternoon tea in the tearooms at the top of the Port Hills, Libby helped her out of the car and then watched her as she shuffled towards the entrance. She felt a sudden surge of anger. Why did she have to look so *old*! It was probably the drink. She now consumed a bottle of gin every two days or so, according to the tell-tale nurses who had the misfortune to look after her. And why was *she* still here, and not Rose? Charlotte was the only one in the family who Nancy had any time for. Edward said it was because Charlotte always visited Nancy bearing gifts and always the same one; the largest bottle you could possibly buy of Nancy's favourite, Gordon's gin. On her infrequent visits Libby usually took one too, but she had run out of time today and had grabbed some flowers wrapped in cellophane and ready to go from a bucket outside the petrol station opposite the retirement home.

'What good are *flowers* to me,' Nancy said as soon as she opened the door 'There's hardly even room for a vase in my bloody little prison.'

'I'll give them to one of the nurses then,' said Libby briskly, and before Nancy could object she marched her out to the car, plonking the flowers down on the receptionist's desk as they passed.

Nancy's vast bloomers showed as Libby helped her into the back seat and she caught a whiff of stale urine and mothballed clothes.

'What a lovely day,' she said cheerfully over her shoulder as they drove off.

'It's just like any other to me,' Nancy retorted like a series of bullet shots. She always spoke crisply and enunciated every word. 'They're all the same when you get to my age,' she continued. 'Every bloody day is the same. Bloody awful. Just you wait,' she added for good measure.

Not bloody likely, Libby thought to herself. She said quietly, 'I'll make sure I kick myself into touch before I get to your stage.'

'What's that?' said Nancy. 'What's *that*?' she repeated, leaning forward.

'Nothing,' Libby said. 'I just said I hope I'm as alert as you when I get to your age.'

'You don't hope that at all. You don't even like me. And don't forget I taught you that rhyming game madam. I'm not stupid, you know.'

'That's true,' Libby muttered. 'But you're also a pain in the bum.'

'What?'

'I said, here comes the sun.'

'It won't last,' Nancy said. Like most old people, she could hear perfectly well when she chose to. 'It never does. Four seasons in one day. Christchurch is not my cup of tea you know. Your mother always liked it for some reason. I never wanted to end up here. Give me Auckland any time.'

'You must miss Mum,' said Libby, although she knew she was asking for trouble. 'She was a wonderful older sister wasn't she?

'What!' Nancy snorted. 'That's what you think my girl. I could tell you a few stories.'

'I'm sure you could,' Libby said quietly. 'But I don't want to hear them.'

'What was that? Speak up. Enunciate!'

'I said go ahead. But I've heard them all before.'

'She was a silly woman really,' Nancy said, undaunted, and settling back with a contented smile on her face. Nothing pleased her more than pulling someone apart. 'So impractical, always dreaming about this and that, and lost in her books so she never heard a word anyone said. I'll never forget the day she fell asleep on the beach at Akaroa. You and Edward were just toddlers; you could have drowned!'

'Where were you?'

'Minding my own business. Reading my book in peace. You weren't my children!'

'I liked her absentmindedness. It meant we could do what we liked.'

'Too right you did. You were a wild bunch. I don't know how any of you survived.'

'Well, thank goodness there was none of that rubbish PC stuff in those days. We were free to take all the risks we wanted. That's what children are meant to do if you ask me.'

'PC stuff. What's that?' said Nancy.

'Political correctness.'

'Political correctness my arse!' Suddenly she farted, and Libby, startled, looked at her in the rear vision mirror.

'Nancy,' said Libby, shocked. 'Where did you pick up that language?'

Nancy ignored her. 'Your mother was so patronising to me you know.'

'That's not how I remember it.'

'Your father should never have forgiven her. She didn't deserve it.'

'Forgiven her for what?'

'For going away.'

'She came back,' said Libby. 'Maybe she had her reasons. Dad wasn't easy. He drank too much in those days.'

She didn't wait for Nancy's riposte, braking hard in the crisp gravel as they came into the car park, jumping out quickly and throwing open the car door to help her out.

When they were seated, Libby ordered a traditional afternoon tea. Nancy, silent for a change, squinted at the city stretched out below them. Beyond the plains, low clouds hovered like a mist at the foot of the mountains on the horizon.

'*And did those hills,*' Nancy suddenly sang, her voice surprisingly robust for someone her age, '*in ancient times…*'

Libby joined in. '*Walk upon England's mountains green.*'

'Music's one of the only things worth living for when you're old,' Nancy grumbled, and then continued.

'*And was the holy Lamb of God, in England's pleasant pastures seen.*'

The tea rooms were almost deserted on a Monday afternoon. A young Japanese couple in walking gear, glanced over in mild surprise, but the tall waitress with the wide Slavic face of an immigrant smiled encouragingly at them from the corner of the room where she leaned against a pillar, picking at her nails.

'It was the one thing I liked about church as a child,' said Nancy, when they had finished the first verse. 'The hymns.'

'Me too,' said Libby. 'What's your favourite?'

'Glorious Things of Thee are Spoken.'

'Let's have a sing song, 'Libby said. 'You choose, then I'll choose and we'll see if we remember all the words.'

'Don't be silly,' Nancy said. 'We'll just make spectacles of ourselves.'

But she could never resist showing off so they sang them all; all the hymns that went up year after year on the hymn board at the front of the dour Presbyterian church Libby had been dragged off to on alternate Sundays by Rose: 'Praise My Soul, the King of Heaven,' 'How Great thou Art,' 'Immortal, Invisible.' Nancy finished all the cakes, Libby got her another pot of tea, and the Japanese tourists left the tea rooms, bowing shyly as they passed their table. The sun even came out for a moment illuminating the cobwebs stretched between joints of the rafters in the neglected corners of the room.

'I'm surprised you remember all the words,' Nancy said. 'You children were always so badly behaved in church.'

As Libby helped her into the car Nancy said grudgingly, 'That wasn't too bad after all. And I'll be home in time for a gin before dinner,' she added. 'But I won't ask you to join me as there's only enough for one stiff drink left in the bottle. Shame Charlotte didn't come with you bearing practical gifts as usual.'

When they weren't at the beach, her mother and Max played Scrabble or cards in the afternoons. Neither liked to lose and the children could hear the rise and fall of their voices as they squabbled over words or, as he often did, argued about whether Max had cheated at cards. Libby had a school friend, Julia, staying that summer; she was the daughter of divorced parents, a condition that Libby found both shocking and exotic at the same time. She was English and had come to live in New

Zealand only a few years before; she was worldly and confident in a way that made Libby conscious of her own naïveté.

Rose always said Julia's mother reminded her of that awful Mrs. Simpson, but when Libby asked 'Who's Mrs. Simpson when she's at home?' Rose said, 'Never you mind', and went back to her book.

Then, just when it was time for Julia to go home to Christchurch, her mother rang her to say she had business to attend to and Julia must stay in Akaroa for a few more days.

'While she is she is lording it up somewhere, I'm left with an extra child to entertain,' Rose complained to Sam when he called that night. 'She didn't even have the manners to ask me whether it suited. Just told Julia to let me know she'd be staying on. I'd feel sorry for her if she wasn't such a little madam. She's far too sophisticated for Libby.'

Although Libby professed to be happy about the arrangement, she was secretly dismayed. For the past week she had endured whole afternoons propped at one end of her bed looking wistfully out the window, (where Edward always seemed to be bowling or hitting a cricket ball to the boy next door or lying on his back on the lawn reading,) while Julia, painstakingly enunciating every word in that posh voice of hers, read her poetry to her. At first Libby found the recurring theme, the amorous yearnings of a young girl, quite interesting, but it soon became repetitive, and Libby longed to join Edward and his friend outside when she heard the clunk, clunk of the ball and their raucous laughter, beckoning her out into the late afternoon heat.

Worse still, the previous afternoon, half way through an exceedingly long poem that Julia called an Ode, and just as Libby heard the gate creak and looked out to see Edward head off out with a tennis racket in his hand, Julia suddenly leaned languidly over and put her hand down Libby's top.

She slid her hand into Libby's bra and started fondling her breasts. Libby had been thinking about her breasts a great deal lately. She longed to ask someone whether what was happening to her was normal; they were full of lumps the size of half crowns, but Charlotte, the one person in the world she would dare to ask, was staying with a friend. They also seemed to be getting larger by the day and boys were beginning to stare at them when they talked to her.

Now, she looked down at Julia's hand, and then glanced desperately at the door. Should she spring to her feet and run, or would that be childish? What if her mother came into the room and saw what was going on, or worse still, Edward! She could feel her nipples prickle as Julia touched them and part of her wanted to lean into Julia's hand and rub itself against it. She shifted back on the bed and pressed herself right up against the wall.

'This is boring,' she said. 'Let's go to the wharf.'

Julia looked at her coldly and then rolled over onto her stomach, and said dismissively, '*You* go. I can't be bothered.'

But the next day Julia phoned her mother in the morning, and left on the bus for Christchurch in the afternoon. It was another beautiful day, not a cloud in the sky, and Libby waved her off on the bus, and then whistled as she walked home with the late afternoon lying across her shoulders like a warm scarf.

'Back to your old self I see,' said her mother wryly as she and Edward crept out early the next morning to go fishing off the wharf. 'And for goodness sake, you two, put on some shoes!'

Libby was so ashamed of the incident that she kept it to herself, until she told Tom, years later. When he laughed it off she felt exhilarated, as though she had been absolved of a huge burden of guilt.

'Jean-Paul Sartre said that Hell is other people,' she said. 'He was probably thinking of people like Julia when he said that. I still can't stand having people to stay.'

'I don't think he had you in mind when he wrote that,' said Tom. 'Let's face it. You are just damned unsociable.'

Later, as Libby sat outside in the garden, smoking the solitary cigarette she allowed herself at the end of the day, she remembered another night – just before the end – when she had repeated the same phrase to Tom. They were having Sunday dinner at one of the clubs they belonged to in Hong Kong. It was one of the evenings when the pollution wasn't too bad, and they could see clearly, right across the Bank of China Building, the HSBC headquarters and the IFC Centre, over the harbour to Kowloon and the nine hills beyond. Tom was unusually quiet; she had been telling him about the problems their friend was having at work. 'Sartre said "Hell is other people",' she said. 'The more I see of life the more I agree with him.'

'I've always wondered what he actually meant by that,' Tom said. He shifted irritably in his seat, his mouth set in a tight line. 'He was such a miserable bastard. Why would you be impressed by anything he said?'

'Don't sound so angry. I'm just making conversation. He probably just preferred his own company to other people's mindless chatter.'

'He was a pretentious intellectual conscientious objector! He was never happy...'

'That might well be. Who said the purpose of life is to be happy? Only idiots think that.'

'Well maybe I'm just an idiot then. Life seems pretty meaningless if you have a philosophy like yours.'

'What are you talking about? At least I think about what life is all about. You're so busy working you don't give yourself *time* to think.'

'You've got too much time to think if you ask me. You analyse things too much. You need to start living your own life and stop living other peoples'.'

'What do you mean?

'Well take the girls for instance. You're far too close to them, always ringing them and worrying about them. Let them get on with their own lives. And what about *me*?'

'What *about* you? Don't tell me you feel neglected?'

'I think all men feel neglected after they have been married for a while. When did you last ask me about what case I am doing, or do something spontaneously thoughtful for me?'

'Oh God. Like what? You sound like a baby. You know I love hearing about your cases. And I've always been fascinated by your work; how many times have I brought my English classes to watch high court cases as part of English projects? But I work too you know and I haven't noticed you asking me anything about that! Oh it's so pathetic,' said Libby. 'Why do I feel as though I am suddenly in the middle of a mine field? Are we talking about something more than what bloody Sartre thought? It was just a harmless remark.'

But he was silent and didn't look at her. He was watching two teenagers arguing a point on the tennis court below.

'It's sad,' Libby said. 'We have become like all those couples we used to watch in restaurants when we were young. Remember? We felt sorry for them because they were at the same table but as far apart as planets.'

10

The last summer they spent at Belle Maison, before Rose left, was ruined for the children by the incessant arguments between their parents. Even after they returned to town, and Sam went back to work, the bickering continued.

All through her childhood Libby had been used to hearing the same reassuring sounds last thing at night; the gush of her father's bath running, the slurp and gurgle of the bath water draining and afterwards his bare feet padding down the hallway. Then, if she was still awake, she often fell off to sleep to the soft sounds of her parents chatting. But that summer everything changed and more often than not she lay chewing on her lip listening to her parents' raised voices, as sudden and shocking as the small earthquakes that occasionally rattled her bedroom windows at night.

A week or so before they returned from holiday, Rose and Sam told the children they had decided to let out the house.

'I'm fed up with running around after other people,' Rose said, seeing the children's shocked faces. 'Every weekend it's the same. Your father's friends turn up, they start drinking and they expect to be fed. They bring their children with them and then let them run wild. It's one meal after another. It's no holiday for *me*.'

'She never complained before,' Charlotte grumbled to Sam later, when she found him reading outside in the garden.

'It's your mother's decision, not mine,' he said, not even glancing up from his newspaper. 'Why don't you ask *her* why she's suddenly had enough?'

'Is it because Max has gone?' Libby said. She was getting her togs off the line and had her back to him as she spoke.

'What is *wrong* with you lot!' Sam said angrily. 'It's impossible to get any ruddy peace around here!' He snapped his newspaper shut and disappeared inside.

Charlotte caught up with Libby as she went out the gate to go down to the beach.

'What a stupid thing to say,' she said. 'Now you've made him mad.'

'I don't care,' said Libby, slamming the gate shut behind her. 'Sometimes I hate them both.'

When she was woken early the next day by a rooster crowing relentlessly from somewhere on the hillside behind the house, Libby lay thinking about all the lies and deceit that went along with being an adult. The children were told that Rose had gone on a long holiday when she went away, but everyone except the children must have known that she had gone away with Max. Perhaps Tilda had always known too; that would explain why she left home as soon as she possibly could, to go nursing, and why, that year, she kept her distance from the family.

She drew the curtains and looked out. It was a miserable day, with rain falling in horizontal gusts. The prevailing wind tossed foaming grey waves across the harbour. A solitary walker trudged his way along the beach, hugging his jacket around him in the cold. The sight of him only reminded her of her own loneliness.

She had never really thought about how lonely some people's lives must be until she stopped working. Even when the girls left home she hadn't been lonely. In fact being alone seemed like a desirable state after all those years of looking after people.

And then one day last year, when she had been to the gym very early, she passed her Filipino helper as she drove up the steep drive leading to their apartment block. She had driven past her before she realised that it was Carmen, who had been with the family for thirty years, because from behind she looked like one of the old broken shouldered Chinese women in the markets who had spent their lives carrying heavy burdens. Libby was shocked. When did Carmen get old? When she first came to work for them in the late seventies she was a sturdy young woman with long glossy black hair and smooth features, like a baby's. Everything about her was soft, especially her voice. When she called to her friend in the next block as they hung out the clothes on the roof each morning, Libby thought how beautiful their voices were. Soft and melodious, they sounded like birds singing out to one another.

The next morning, after Tom had gone off to Chambers, Libby lay in bed wondering whether Carmen was lonely now the girls had gone and she no longer had a big family to look after. Recently she and Tom had moved into a smaller apartment, so Carmen now lived out, in a small boarding house in one of the high-rise blocks on noisy Des Voeux Road. When Libby had helped to move an old television there for her she was upset to see that the space Carmen shared with three other helpers had no living area.

'You must have to spend all your time in your bedroom,' she said.

'Oh, that's all right ma'am,' said Carmen, in her lilting voice. 'Now I can watch anything I want to on TV. They even have a Filipino channel. The other girls don't have TVs so they think I am the lucky one.'

'But it's the size of a box room,' said Libby in dismay. 'You've made it look so nice though,' she added quickly. The room, although immaculate, was crowded with many of the presents and hand-me-downs she had given Carmen over the years. Cardboard boxes, no doubt filled with more cast-offs to take back on her next trip home, were piled neatly up one wall, almost reaching the ceiling. Several of them had been pushed together to make a table and covered with a floral yellow and blue table cloth Libby had bought in a French market years ago and then discarded. An old framed poster from Libby's teaching days hung on the wall facing the door. The words, 'I am half sick of shadows, said The Lady of Shallot' were in bold print along the bottom.

The print was of John William Waterhouse's painting, with the lady depicted in this interpretation as a wistful, tragic heroine. The tapestry, in glorious gold, she has spent her life creating in her tower near Camelot is draped over the prow and drags in the water behind her. When Libby told her the story Carmen listened spell-bound and stood very close to the picture, like a child looking at illustrations in a picture book, as Libby pointed out that the crucifix and rosary next to the candles suggested her spirituality and explained that the Lady of Shallot was not permitted to join the world and lead a real life. She was effectively a prisoner.

But now Carmen too was gone and all the bric-a-brac of her life with them, the posters, the photos, the old cushion covers and clothes, had gone with her. She sent Libby photos of the small house she had been able to build in Cuyapo, her village in the NE Philippines, with the gratuity she had received from them for all her years of service, and there was The Lady of Shallot; hanging in pride of place on the living room wall.

It made her guilty to think that she had been too busy when the girls were young, to wonder what it must be like for women like Carmen to move away from their country and families to look after somebody else's children. After the girls went off to university, Libby often took her with her when she went out to Stanley market for the morning and afterwards they would have coffee and Carmen would talk – shyly at first – about her home in the countryside, the avocados her brothers were growing and her plans to have her children living with her when she retired and could build a house of her own.

She missed Carmen; the flat was so quiet without her. Sometimes she thought she preferred Carmen's company to that of some of her own friends. The thought of not seeing her again was too much to bear. She climbed back into bed. Maybe she should just stay there all morning.

11

The Sunday night before Sam died Libby and Tom, as they always did pre-Oscar, went to see one of the nominations. Afterwards they climbed up a flight of steps to a French restaurant tucked away in a cul-de-sac set above Queens Road East. It was on the bottom floor of a low-rise colonial building and overlooked a small terrace set with a few wrought iron tables and chairs. An old banyan tree, its aerial prop roots spreading over the parched earth below, provided some welcome shade on hot afternoons for those prepared to brave the searing heat.

'If that isn't a potential Oscar winner, what is?' said Libby. 'Don't you think?'

But Tom spoke quietly, as though they were having a completely different conversation.

'Maybe we've just been married for too long. We talk about our property, and other people and politics, but then there's no passion left. We're like a couple of old mates.'

Libby, who now was studying the menu, looked at him, startled.

'What a hurtful thing to say. Where on earth did that suddenly come from? I think this is a great time of our lives. The girls have gone, we have the same interests.... Come *on*!'

she said. 'The thrill of being young and in love has to be replaced by something more substantial as you grow older. That's just the way life is. I like the way we are so kind to one another now. I felt bad about myself when we were young and passionate and always fighting. Now I simply cannot begin to imagine how I'll get by without you.'

But he still didn't look at her. He was watching an old woman outside, pushing a cart loaded with debris from a building site nearby. She was as tiny and fragile as a child, but her face was a mass of wrinkles and her back was curved like a question mark.

'Look at her,' he said, as though Libby hadn't spoken. 'Bowed and broken from her long life of hard physical work.'

Libby said, 'There's someone else isn't there?' Later, she wondered how she suddenly knew, and then just as quickly wondered why she hadn't known all along.

Now he turned to look at her and she felt a sickening wave of panic as she saw that he had tears in his eyes.

'It's Amy, isn't it?' she said. It was as though someone had just kicked her hard in her stomach, torn out her heart and stamped on it. Her feet were numb; she couldn't feel her fingers. Amy was the bright young barrister who had been his junior on several big cases. She was an Oxbridge graduate with all the confidence that goes along with coming from a wealthy Chinese family, an English public-school education and a myriad of connections in the city.

'I'm so sorry,' he said. 'I wouldn't hurt you for the world.'

She was incandescent with anger.

'What a ridiculous thing to say! I wouldn't hurt you for the world. It means nothing, *nothing*. Of course, you've bloody hurt me. And *look* at me when I speak to you! You must be mad!'

'I am *not* mad,' he said calmly, shaking his head as if talking to an unreasonable child.

'And think ahead for God's sake. What will you have left when the sex is stale? You'll be a pathetic old man whose children despise him. And you know how ambitious those young barristers are. Any QC in a storm. You're not the first one you know...'

'That's just gossip. Don't believe everything you hear.'

'It's not gossip. Speak to anyone in your chambers. And she's only in her thirties. Next thing she'll want to have a family.'

He looked disconcerted. 'I don't want any more children,' he said; then added wistfully. 'I thought we could still be friends.'

'*Friends,*' said Libby. '*Friends!* You've got to be joking. I don't want to be your friend. You've been watching too many movies. My friends are people who are loyal to me.'

He tried another tack. 'You show no interest in my work anymore.'

Libby shook her head incredulously. 'Don't try that old line. You know bloody well that I find your work interesting. You know what?' she said, leaning over the table and stressing every word as though he was hard of hearing. 'I don't need to hear any more of this. I'm going home.'

'What? Before you've eaten,' he said. 'You said you were starving.'

She shook her head. 'I can't believe you just said that. You're from another planet. It's almost laughable. Sometimes I think you're on the spectrum.'

'I thought we could come to some sort of understanding. *You* did this to me once remember!'

'But I didn't *leave* you, did I? And we were young and it was a difficult stage of life; we had little children, no sleep, not enough money, too many parties. You were never home, totally absorbed in your career. We've worked so hard to get over all that. I can't believe you are throwing it all away.'

'I've been unhappy. You must have seen that. It's not easy for *me* either you know.'

'Oh of course you've got to tell yourself *now* that you were unhappy. We all do that when we try to justify falling in love with someone else.'

'What?' Tom said sarcastically, 'You're some sort of mind reader, are you?'

'Yes, I am where you are concerned actually. That's how well I know you after all these years. I can tell by the set of your mouth whether you are happy, sad, and grumpy, tired, stressed, bored... Anyway, you know what! I'm too old to put up a fight. I'm going to leave you to it. You can make your own bed now. Literally.'

'What do you mean? You can't just walk away just like that!'

He put his head in his hands like a man in deep shock and for a fleeting second she almost felt sorry for him. Then, looking more hopeful. 'You've got the girls to consider.'

'Did you consider them when you started fucking her?'

'Don't use that language,' he said, looking around nervously at the other diners.

'Yes,' she went on, ignoring him. 'I'll go home to see Dad. 'And you know what?' she finished triumphantly. '*You* can tell the girls. *You* can deal with all their problems for a while. It's time you did that anyway.'

She leaned over the table. 'I feel as though they are bleeding all the life out of me with their problems at the moment. Abbie doesn't know what she wants to do with her life; Cleo is so busy with her career she doesn't have time for anything else and Daisy's so bloody moody she thinks about nobody but herself and her social life.'

She picked up her handbag, very deliberately, from the seat beside her. 'Come to think of it, I've had enough of you *all*, actually.'

'Well, there you are,' said Tom. And, and then, like the proverbial bull in the china shop, he went on. 'Well that's one good thing that could come out of this, isn't it?' He warmed to his theme. 'Maybe now you can think about yourself, do what you want to do for the first time in your life. It will be good for you.'

Libby stood up, pushed her chair back and looked down at him. 'Gosh, I hadn't realised how grey you've become. Good luck with the child bride.'

'Fuckwit,' she added, and walked out, taking a bread roll from the basket as she went. She would eat it on the way home.

12

'Let's talk about Tom,' said Charlotte. 'If we're to work this out one way or another you've probably got to think back on the good times as well as the bad. At the moment, you're so angry with him that he doesn't sound like the Tom we all know. And love.'

'Oh, I get sick of you all thinking he's so fantastic,' Libby snapped. 'Let's face it. The very things that draw you to someone in the beginning – in Tom's case his charm and sense of humour – can be the very qualities people seem to lose when you live with them every day don't you think? Particularly charm. We all know it can be turned off and on. And when your children are little, and you are both working, and the most fun you have is when you go out with friends, all that charm gets turned on for other people. Charming people don't waste it at home.'

'But surely that came later,' said Charlotte. 'What about the early years when Tom turned his charm on for *you*?'

'Oh yes,' said Libby. 'They were brilliant.' She twisted her hair around her finger as she did when she was thinking.

'It's hard on a marriage when your children leave home though,' she said. 'You sort of have to start all over again. Kids act as a buffer. And also; something fundamentally changes when you have children doesn't it. I'm sure you found that too?'

'Yes,' Charlotte said. 'But we are not talking about me.'

'There is nothing like becoming a mother, is there?' Libby went on. 'Nothing prepares you for it. When Abbie was born it was the best, the very best moment of my life. I love my girls like a tigress. I want to live their lives for them, keep them safe. If anyone harmed them I would kill them. Without even thinking twice about it. If I had to die for them I would. There you have it,' she said as she turned away from the window. 'There you have motherly love in a nutshell. It is all encompassing and always forgiving. And if I'm being totally honest with you, I don't think Tom loves the girls with the same passion as I do and maybe that has always been a problem for us.'

'Men and women love their children differently,' said Charlotte. 'I think you're being unfair. What about Mum and *her* mothering! You are always so nice about her. Didn't you feel abandoned when she left us? Angry? I know I did. And scornful when she came back and expected us all to forgive her. Just like that. Mum was always so entitled. So beautiful and so entitled.'

'I was so happy when she came back I would have forgiven her anything.'

'Sadly, that's what children do isn't it. Mine were the same. They don't care how selfish their parents are. They just want them to be together and ….'

'Mum wasn't really selfish,' Libby interrupted. 'I think she was just so beautiful that there was bound to be a drama somewhere along the way. And when she came back – well – she became the perfect mother again.'

'My point exactly. There you go making excuses for her. And nobody is the perfect mother. Sometimes I think you live in La-la land.'

'Well that's how I like to remember her,' said Libby defensively. 'But don't worry. There are some things I'll never forget. Certainly not the day Mum left.'

13

It was an autumn morning in Christchurch, and an icy wind had kept them all inside that morning. Rose was packing her clothes into two suitcases, in an uncharacteristically disorganised way. Their two old Labradors followed her from room to room, constantly getting under her feet, until finally they lay down by her suitcase and put their heads on their paws, looking up at her with milky eyes.

'They look as though they are crying,' Libby said, as her mother threw some underwear into one of the cases.

'Don't be ridiculous,' Rose said. 'Dogs don't cry.' But she patted both dogs on the head and pulled their ears gently before she left the room. It wasn't unusual for their mother to go away by herself; in fact, once a year at least, she visited her mother in the North Island. But this time it felt different. It was so sudden for one thing.

'The house can't breathe this morning,' said Libby.

The windows and doors remained tightly closed, the curtains in the living room weren't drawn back as they always were by the time the children got up, and there were still empty glasses on the coffee table, an overflowing ash-tray and Sam's book lying open on the arms of the sofa.

The children had fallen asleep the night before to the sound of raised voices and slammed doors, and when they had driven home from Akaroa, after a long weekend where the rain had been so heavy that they couldn't even go for a walk, and Rose crashed and banged about the house organising it for letting, Sam drove without speaking, taking the corners on the winding hillside so fast that the car kept skidding on the gravel and the small stones peppering the side of the car sounded like hail stones in a storm. One by one the children fell silent in the back seat, until Edward could bear it no longer and called out, 'Slow down Dad.'

Their mother, who had been gazing out the window as intently as a tourist seeing the countryside for the first time, turned to Sam, touched his arm gently, and said, 'For goodness sake! You'll kill us all.'

Sam took her hand and placed it firmly back on her lap. The children could see the bleak look on his face in the car mirror before he said matter-of-factly; 'I don't care.'

But then he smiled at Libby's reflection and said, 'I don't mean it Chooks.' 'Chooks' was his most affectionate name for her.

When they got home, Sam went straight into the drawing room. When Libby looked in to say goodnight he was sitting in his arm chair, drinking whisky. He had taken the bottle from the silver tray it always sat on, on the side board, and was sitting with his feet on the coffee table, the bottle resting in front of him.

That night, for a change, Edward let Libby climb into bed with him and listen to 'Journey into Space' on the radio. He turned it up very loud, but even then they could still hear the shouting.

The next morning, Rose packed her bags.

'Where are you going Mum?' said Libby. She and the dogs were following her around the house as she packed.

'I'm going back home to England, just for a short time.'

'Why do you call England home?'

'Oh, we just do – my generation I mean. My parents always did so I suppose we do too.'

'I'll never call it home,' said Libby. 'Why would I?'

Rose sat down at her dressing table and carefully applied some lipstick.

'There. Now I feel better,' she said. 'Come here, I'll put some on you. Just a little touch.'

'Who are you going to see,' Libby said.

'Don't talk. Purse up your mouth; like this. Just an old friend. There. How lovely you look.'

She stood behind Libby, with her hands on her shoulders and they looked at one another in the mirror.

'What a beautiful woman you will be.'

'Who?'

'Someone you don't know. I knew her at school.'

'What's her name?'

'Mabel.'

'How come we've never met her?'

'She's been over there for a long time.'

'Who's going to look after us?'

'You'll be fine. Ruby will come in to clean and make the evening meal every day and Nancy is going to help out.'

After her mother had left for the airport in a taxi, Libby sat on the window seat in her bedroom, until Sam came home. Over the low dry stone wall covered with ice-plants and through the big walnut tree that stood by the front gate you could see the road outside. Sometimes she would sit in the crook of the lowest branches and wait for him if she was bored but now she was waiting for Rose as well. She played a scene over and over in her mind of Rose, about to board the plane, and then turning back at the last moment, realising that she couldn't bear to leave the family and make such a long trip, to another country, on her own. And Rose would never be able to leave her dogs for long either. Not now she had seen them crying. Sometimes Sam complained that she cared about Monty and Basil more than she did the children. And him. If she closed her eyes and thought hard enough and imagined Rose turning around and coming home again, it might come true. But by the time the street lights were going on, and Sam's car turned into the driveway, she knew Rose wouldn't be coming back.

Libby took up the same position on the window seat, in the bay window, every Sunday afternoon after that and only when Sam called her to dinner would she budge. For Sunday was the day of the week that she knew her mother would come home. Sundays were sad days and boring and endless. Sunday was the day of the week when the family felt the loss of Rose the most. It was unthinkable that she wouldn't remember what Sundays were like and not return soon.

'You can't will her back you know,' Sam said gently to her one Sunday, when he decided he was going to take the children out for a drive. 'Sitting here all afternoon won't bring her back. Wishing won't make it true.'

'Yes, it will,' said Libby. 'You go. I'll be fine here.'

Even now Libby cannot endure goodbyes. Her sisters never come to the airport to say goodbye to her, and she doesn't drive her daughters out to Chek Lap Kok airport in Hong Kong after they visit. She tells them the Airport Express is a far more efficient way to get there.

'Of course, you know she just abandoned you. Without a second thought,' Nancy told Libby one night, years later. She was staying with Libby and Tom in Hong Kong on her way to London and had had one too many gins after a long night dining at the Hong Kong Club.

'She went off, just like that, to be with Max. Then, typically, because that's what he was like; he probably decided he couldn't be bothered with all the drama. Rose, so miserable without you children – although it didn't stop her leaving you in the first place. I bet he couldn't wait to get rid of her.'

'That wasn't what she told *me*,' said Libby. 'She told me *she* left him. She missed us all too much.'

'Well she *would* say that, wouldn't she? Rose never let the truth get in the way of a good story. The truth is that she came home, her tail between her legs. And so sanctimonious once she had come back. Like a reformed alcoholic! She ruined *my* life too you know, by coming back,' she called over her shoulder as she made her way down the hallway towards her bedroom, slamming the door emphatically behind her.

'What on earth was that about?' Libby said to Tom as she got into bed.

'She's just a sour old bitch,' he said. 'Take no notice of her.'

'I suppose she resented those months she spent helping out when Mum was away. Not that we wanted her there.'

'Turn out the light, and forget it,' said Tom. 'She loves stirring things up. Always has.'

But Libby, her stomach churning and her head still blurry with drink, lay awake for ages thinking about it. Nancy was always there. Always ruining their fun. And always angry.

She had even ruined their annual Pine Cone Collecting trip one year. An annual outing that should have brought back warm memories, not unpleasant ones.

14

In mid-autumn they always went on a family trip to the Waimakariri River to collect pine cones to store for the winter months ahead. One Sunday when Rose was away, they awoke to bright sunshine in a cloudless sky.

'This might be the last gasp in an Indian Summer,' said their father.

'What's an Indian Summer?' said Edward.

'One that goes on and on,' said Sam. 'Until you think it will never end.'

'Oh,' said Edward disappointed. The phrase sounded so exotic.

Nancy was cheerful for a change, making a huge performance of packing a picnic lunch for them all and even starting to sing as they drove through the suburbs and out of the city. She had a beautiful voice and when she was in a good mood, usually after a few drinks, she would sometimes play the piano and sing to the children.

'People's singing voices say nothing about them,' Libby whispered to Edward, 'because inside she's mean and sarcastic.'

'What was that?' Edward said loudly. 'Did you say that Nancy…'

'Shut up!' She hit him but he shrugged her off and gave her the Chinese Torture, twisting her upper arm in a vice so painful that tears of pain and anger welled up in her eyes.

'That's *enough* you two!' said their father. 'I'll stop the car and put you out and you can walk home if that continues.'

'And you'll have no lunch,' added Nancy.

'Why can't she mind her own business,' Edward whispered to Libby. '*She* needs a dose of the Chinese Torture.' Libby giggled and rubbed her sore arm.

'*Summer Time, when the living is easy,*' Nancy and their father sang.

'*Fish are jumping and the river runs high.*'

'What a glorious sight the trees are at this time of year,' said Nancy. 'I never tire of this drive.'

'I know,' said their father. 'It's as though we are suddenly in a world made up of fields of gold. Everywhere you look.'

'Yuk,' whispered Libby. 'Why does Dad act so drippy when she is around?'

Now they were driving down the long avenue of poplar trees, along the gravel road leading to the river. The trees' branches stretched vertically up like raised arms reaching into the blue sky and were smothered with bright yellow leaves. They would always park the car in the gravel beside the river, Sam applying the brakes suddenly so there would be a satisfying crunching sound that Libby loved, and then they would wander into the small forest of pine trees with the carpet of old pine needles beneath them and the bone grey dried up pine cones, perfectly shaped like old skeletons that lay scattered on the ground. When they were thrown on the fire at home they crackled and popped and burned wildly, setting the paper crumpled up beneath them alight and creating enough combustion for the coal to be shovelled on top so that the fire would burn quietly for hours.

'The landscape out here is so perfect isn't it,' said Nancy. 'What a good idea of yours to come out here Sam.'

'I hate it when she's in a good mood,' said Edward, making a face at Nancy's back as she got out of the car. 'It's almost worse than when she's just her normal horrible self because she's so sickly sweet to Dad.'

Normie, Nancy's son from a brief disastrous marriage, was with them that day. He had been packed off to boarding school down South the year before, but it didn't seem to have toughened him up as Nancy had hoped it would. He hero-worshipped Edward, who took advantage and always managed to get them both into trouble when they went on outings with the family.

'You let them get away with murder,' Nancy would scold Rose, whenever this happened. 'Your children are so wild.'

After they had collected the pinecones and put them in old sugar sacks into the car Sam said they could play for a while so they raced down to the river bank while Nancy laid out the picnic and Sam lit up his pipe.

'It's freezing,' said Edward as he knelt down and put his hand into the river. The water there was always cold, because it flowed down from the Southern Alps before joining the sea near Woodend. Sam had taken them to the river mouth a few times to look at the delta but there were fierce currents where the waters collided with the sea and it wasn't safe for swimming.

Here though the water ran clean and clear and you could see the honed white and grey stones, like giant polished pebbles, on the river bed. Although the water was shallow at the edge, in the middle, or in hollows by the sandy bank, it was so deep that you couldn't see the bottom.

'There's been a lot of rain this year,' Sam called out to them as he helped himself to a sandwich. 'Be careful.'

The children started to play a game at the side of the river. They had found a flat sandy place, with a cliff of hard sand above it that crumbled and broke up when they jumped onto it and they could slide down the edge of it to the river bank below. They soon tired of this though and seeing that Nancy and Sam had fallen asleep on the rug, they wandered down to a larger sandy beach, where several large logs were lying, stranded there by flood waters the week before.

Edward pointed at the smallest log.

'Perfect for you Libby,' he said.

'It looks a bit slippery,' said Libby doubtfully. It was all slimy and still had horrid spiky branches on it.

'Don't be a wimp,' said Charlotte.

'We'll pull off some of the sharp bits,' Edward said gallantly.

He and Charlotte began to drag it down to the river. The branches cut deep patterns into the sand and it took all their strength to drag it over the stones at the water's edge and into the deeper water

'You get on it Libby,' said Charlotte. 'We'll follow you.'

'Why do I always have to go first,' Libby said quietly to Edward. 'Look at the river. It's so swift out there in the middle. What say the log rolls over?'

'It won't,' he said. 'Just hang on tight.'

Libby looked pleadingly at him – sometimes he could be counted on to come to her rescue – but this time he had turned away.

'You're the lucky one,' said Charlotte. '*We'll* have to look after Normie so we'll have to put him between us on that *huge* one.' She pointed out a massive log, so cleanly cut that it was obviously from a timber yard upstream somewhere.

Normie, who was dawdling behind them, looked anxiously over his shoulder, back up the river bank.

'I don't think Mum will think that's a good idea,' he said.

'Don't be a coward,' said Edward. 'Go on Libby. You show him how easy it is.'

Libby slowly took off her t-shirt and jumper and shorts. She had her togs on underneath. Edward and Charlotte held the log steady for her in the calm water, as she climbed on.

'Maybe you'd better wait 'till we get the other log down,' said Edward. He looked across at the white foam, boiling like a kettle, in the middle of the river, around a jagged outcrop of rocks.

'We'll have to stick together,' he said reassuringly.

Libby clung to her log, hoping the larger one would prove too heavy for the others to drag to the water's edge, but, despite Normie's half-hearted help, they were soon standing waist deep in water alongside her.

'Yippee,' called Charlotte, 'Bombs away!'

As they pushed the logs out the water became deeper and Libby was able to push off from the stony bottom and let the current carry her away. There was a channel of calmer water further out and she found herself floating in quite a sedate fashion, holding on near the end of the log so that it wasn't too hard and the rough bits on the trunk didn't scratch and tear at her as they had when she had been dragging it out in the shallow water. The others were having a more difficult time as they had to try to balance themselves on the log and it tumbled and rolled until they too got into the deeper water.

'We shouldn't go too far,' Normie called across to Libby.

'Just round the next corner,' Charlotte shouted. 'Then we'll ditch the logs and walk back and get some more.'

But this was easier said than done. Around the next corner, the landscape changed dramatically. Suddenly they found themselves in a vast plateau of tributaries set in a grey landscape of shingle. All of them were flowing into their section of the river. The current grew stronger and carried them further and further out into the middle of what was now a wide expanse of water. It was all Libby could do to keep her head above water as the river seethed and churned around her, tossing the log around like a stick. The cold took her breath away. Then she saw that the others had abandoned their log; all she could see of them now was their heads bobbing up and down. She thought she heard Charlotte call out, so she let go of the log and watched it buck and thrash down the river ahead of her. It was difficult to keep her head up, but she remembered her father telling her not to fight rips if you got into one at the beach, just to relax, swim across them and make slowly for the shore. She supposed it was the same in rivers. Just up ahead she could see another piece of sand, and a little inlet, where the water looked calmer. She lay on her back and started paddling with her hands as best she could, although the current kept pulling her this way and that. And then suddenly the water around her was still and quiet and she was in the little side water. She pulled herself onto the bank, so exhausted that she just lay there. The others, miraculously, had managed to get there ahead of her. For a moment they all stretched out on the sandy bank like indolent sunbathers. Then Libby began to shiver violently with the cold.

'You *bloody* idiots!'

They looked up to see Nancy on the top of the sand bank above them. She was silhouetted against the late afternoon sun, hands on hips and clearly *very* angry.

Charlotte rolled over and put her head in her hands. 'Oh cripes!' she said. 'Now we're in for it!'

'*You're* in for it, you mean,' said Edward smugly. '*You're* the ring leader.'

Before Charlotte could reply, Nancy came slithering down the bank, bringing showers of sand with her. Fury radiated off her like waves of light.

'You children are a just a bunch of headless chickens!' she yelled. 'You're *mad*! I don't mind you drowning yourselves – in fact go ahead – but don't drown *my* son as well!' She hauled Normie to his feet – he had been lying gasping like a beached fish on the sand.

'And *you're* as bad as them, you little chump,' she hissed as they disappeared over the top of the bank.

Charlotte shaded her eyes with her arm as she watched them go, and then rolled nonchalantly onto her tummy again. The sun went behind a cloud. There was a silence.

'Well that was fun,' Charlotte finally said, jumping to her feet. 'We'll do it again next time. But let's not take Normie. He's a *pain.*'

Their father gave them a terrible telling off when they had made their way – pushing through overgrown gorse bushes all along the river bank – back to the picnic spot. But he squeezed Charlotte's shoulder as they walked to the car and winked in the mirror at them as Nancy ranted and raved at them on the long trip home.

'Mum would have laughed,' said Libby as he tucked them in that night.

'She probably would have,' said Sam. 'But that doesn't make it right. You really *are* a pack of ruddy fools,' he said as he turned out the light but they could hear him chuckling to himself as he walked down the hallway.

'It's good to hear Dad laugh.' Edward's voice was muffled as he turned over in bed.

'But why do we have to take Nancy everywhere we go. She hates us.'

15

'And I can't believe it took me so long to see the truth,' Libby said to Charlotte. 'I bet you knew all along.'

'Not so,' said Charlotte, leaning down to stroke her threadbare old Labrador that lay snoring gently at her feet.

They had been for a walk along the beach and were now sitting outside a café overlooking the long wharf at Brighton, watching the waves roll in, one white foaming row after another.

'It all finally fell into place that afternoon when I drove out here to Brighton. How could I have been so stupid?'

'You're not stupid. It's not uncommon to refuse to see things that don't fit into our narrative; that will just be too much for us to bear. You had Mum's infidelity to live with and Dad's drinking. And you were just a kid. You've always looked at life through rose-coloured spectacles. Pardon the pun. I just thought it was best to leave out that part of the story be until you were older. And you always looked up to Dad so much so I didn't want to spoil that for you.'

'Are you saying I don't face up to things?' said Libby

'Not at all. What I am saying is that when we are children we sometimes have to block out some of our memories; the really bad ones, just so we can survive. Even as adults we do the same thing. Don't forget I did the equivalent of Psych 101 at

Hanmer,' she added, smiling. 'And remember how you said that although you were shocked when Tom told you about Amy, part of you had known for ages that there was something wrong.'

'Anyway, tell me about that day at Brighton. You *must* have known about Dad and Nancy way before then. I'm sure Tilda and Edward did. We just didn't talk about it.'

Poor Nancy. Rose would always come first where men were concerned. Rose had told Libby the truth that afternoon at the airport, but not the whole truth. She had spared her that. Because the truth is that Nancy must have been devastated when Rose came back. She must have realised that she was only a substitute for her sister, only second best. It probably happened after one of those weekend lunches Nancy helped prepare: the adults outside on the lawn and the children packed off to the waterfront fish n' chip shop to get their dinner and sit on the wharf, legs dangling over the side, while they ate their fish and sausages in batter so thick that you could break it off like pieces of Christmas cake icing. No doubt it was one of those radiant summer evenings when street lamps along the waterfront hung like pale balloons in the sky and the breeze came up across the water, bringing the sounds of hungry squawking seagulls with it.

Nancy was everywhere the summer after Rose left, preparing meals, filling the house with flowers, driving the kids mad with her bossiness and greeting Sam with a strong whisky when he returned home from work.

How she must have despaired when Rose decided to return home, just as the days grew shorter and she had begun to think she might be able to settle in for the winter.

***

At first the day Rose returned was like any other day. Libby awoke to a cold, rainy autumn morning and the familiar gnawing pain that she always had in her stomach now. It was a Sunday and she was playing cards with Edward. They looked up as someone turned the light on.

And there she was. Rose. She was back.

'It's so gloomy,' she said. 'You should have the light on. And if it's dark, it's easier for Edward to cheat.' She had an unsuitably light summer dress on, small pink and green flowers on a black background and a pink cardigan thrown over her shoulders. She was biting her lip in that way she had when she was trying not to cry. She had the sort of beauty that always struck you like an electric shock and when Libby saw her face, the glossy brown curls cut around it and her perfect laughing eyes, she thought she was seeing a ghost.

'You can't imagine how *wonderful* it is to see you,' Rose said.

Libby got up from the floor and went straight to her. Rose brushed her hair back from her face. 'You've grown,' she said. 'In such a short time.'

They both turned to Edward, but he was still sitting on the floor, looking down at his cards as though thinking about his next move. Their mother raised her eyebrows at Libby and hugged her again. Then she went over to Edward, knelt down, took his head in her hands and said, 'Hullo darling. You look so tall too. Stand up so I can see you.'

He stood up slowly, still looking down at his cards. She hugged him awkwardly, the cards clenched in his hands between them, then quickly stood back.

'I've bought you something,' she said.

'*Really*,' Edward said. 'You thought that would make up for it?'

Rose rummaged around in her bag and then held out her peace offering. It was a tin toy soldier, dressed in one of the famous English regimental uniforms.

'And we all know who helped you to choose that!' Edward said, and throwing his cards down on the carpet he rushed out the door, slamming it fiercely behind him.

'Why on earth did he say that?' Libby said. 'He's missed you *so* much Mum. You know what he's like. He just doesn't know how to show it.'

Rose smiled wanly, pushing her hair back in an agitated fashion. 'He'll be back.' She crossed to look out of the window and wiped away some of the condensation so that they could see the sodden lawn outside. 'What a difficult age his is.'

Libby looked at her incredulously. '*Difficult*! You *have* been away for ages Mum. And you went so suddenly. Of course he's angry.'

'Sorry. I didn't mean that. I just don't know how to handle this.' She looked at Libby with that little tilt of her head she had when she was perplexed about something. 'Can you help me?'

'Oh Mum, you're hopeless,' said Libby, exasperated. Not for the first time she thought how unfair it was that Rose's beauty meant she could get away with so much. But she hugged her and said, 'He'll eventually forgive you. He'll forgive you *anything*!'

'And boy did he make Mum pay,' Libby laughed.

'He had everything you need to get on in life, that boy; good looks, brains and incredible charm. He was – still is – so witty. Let's face it, we all adore him. You can't help it. But remember what a nightmare he was. For years. Dropping out of university, getting into drugs, drinking too much and wasting all that promise. *That's* how he got Mum back for going away and leaving him, I reckon.'

'And me. You're right. I wanted Mum back so much I would have forgiven her anything. But it taught me an important lesson. You can't trust anyone. We are all on our own at the end of the day. And we can't all be like Edward. Some of us in a family have to be peacemakers; never rock the boat. There's nothing bad about that, is there?'

'Of course not,' said Charlotte. 'But then I've never hero-worshipped him the way you do, so I've never tried to make excuses for him. And it didn't surprise me when he went off to London and became a financial trader. They're all wide boys at heart. And he made far too much money for his own good. Retiring back here at his age with that trophy wife of his. It's crazy.'

'Well we should be happy for him,' said Libby. 'And we should be happy that he has Susie to keep him grounded.'

'Susie!' scoffed Charlotte. 'She's a pain and has *no* sense of humour, but you are right. She keeps him grounded. Mum and Dad spoilt him and I always thought Mum recognised he had a fatal moral flaw. In and out of trouble all the time. We mothers try to cover up the weaknesses of our children, don't we? It's only natural.'

'Well I loved him just the way he was,' said Libby sulkily. 'And let's face it; *you* were no saint. I am never sure who the main ring leader was anyway. You or Edward. You both got us into trouble. Constantly.'

'That's not true,' said Charlotte indignantly. 'My ideas were always original. And I was *always* the leader. Edward just went off on his own and did whatever he felt like. And,' she added self-righteously, 'I never *stole* anything.'

'Oh, you can't really blame him for *that*. Remember that was the Christmas after Mum came back. I think it was just attention seeking on his part.'

***

It was unfortunate that Edward chose to ask Sam for his overdue pocket money on a morning where Sam appeared to have got out of bed on the wrong side. It was Christmas Eve.

'There'll be no more money for you this year my boy,' Sam said as he rejected the request without even raising his head from his newspaper. 'What with your poor school report and general bad behaviour. And don't think I haven't noticed that you disappear out the back to play cricket every time it's your turn to dry the dishes. Libby always ends up washing and drying. Money doesn't grow on trees you know. You have to work for your pocket money.'

'Don't worry about it. The beauty is in the giving, not the cost of the gift,' Rose said when Edward grumbled about it to her later, as the children lay glumly on the lawn watching her hanging out the clothes.

But she didn't seem to appreciate the gravity of the situation and spoke carelessly over her shoulder as if she was thinking about something else. It was a cloudless summer day and after she had finished she stood for a moment, raising her face to the sun. Then she glanced at them all and said brightly, 'You'll think of something,' and settling the brass tray she always used to carry the washing out on her hip, she went inside.

'Well that's just *great*!' said Charlotte. 'That means Libby and I can't ask for money either thanks to you Edward.' She looked up hopefully as Rose reappeared at the doorway.

'And none of your silly ideas Edward,' she said, and shut the door firmly behind her as she went inside again.

'What a bloody cheek,' said Edward. He picked up a clod up from the garden and hurled it at the wooden paling fence. '*What* silly ideas!'

Charlotte sat up and looked across at him scornfully. 'She *may* be talking about your stupid Christmas present to her last year.' She lay on her back again and gazed thoughtfully up at the sky. 'You idiot,' she added for good measure.

The Christmas present she referred to was one that Edward had given Rose the year before. Never one for saving his pocket money, that year he had embarked on the ambitious plan of stealing all his Christmas presents from Woolworths. His first few ventures into the world of shop lifting went off without a hitch. His siblings that year were to receive gifts that were far superior to the usual paltry offerings.

His gift for Rose was his *pièce de resistance*; a hideous china coffee pot in the shape of a black cat, the paw being the spout. He showed it to the girls who openly scoffed at it while later acknowledging to one another that Rose would be thrilled with it, as in her eyes, Edward could do no wrong.

Emboldened by his success, Edward set out the next day to choose something special for Sam, but a watchful shop assistant had become suspicious of the young man who had taken to loitering in different departments of the store over the last few days. It was unfortunate that Sam answered the phone when the manager of Woolworths phoned home. Edward had been caught red-handed with two packets of golf balls stuffed in his pockets and was awaiting collection by at least one of his parents in his office

Fortunately, the store manager was a kindly family man who said he would let Edward off with a warning, providing anything else he had stolen over the past week or so was returned. The girls' presents were sulkily returned to Sam, but Edward was adamant that Rose's had been paid for, and by now Sam just wanted the whole situation to go away.

'He's a ruddy fool,' he complained to Rose that night when she said that young people often went through a phase when they shoplifted. 'There's no excuse.'

'Oh, but he means well,' said Rose. 'They all do really. He and Charlotte just get a little bit carried away at times.'

'Don't remind me,' said Sam, brushing his teeth with unnecessary vigour. 'I could write a weighty tome about their philanthropic ventures. The Rover episode took the cake.'

Then, he chuckled as he climbed into bed beside her. 'But then what can we expect of them. Between the two of us, we have probably mucked them all up for life.'

'You were definitely the leader,' agreed Libby. 'I'll give you that. But you got us *all* into trouble. Constantly. What about the Rover episode?'

'Oh *that*,' Charlotte said dismissively. 'That's a good example that no good deed goes unpunished. We were just trying to be kind.'

*****

'I've got it!' said Charlotte. She had rolled onto her stomach and was reading the newspaper. 'Look at this.' It was an advertisement for "Beautiful black and white farm puppies, half-sheepdog". 'It says "To give away to good homes". This will be great for Aunty Nancy. She's always in a bad temper nowadays. She's been like that ever since Mum got back. You'd think she'd be happy that she doesn't have to look after Dad any more. This is just what she needs.'

Libby, the only one of the children to ever think of consequences, asked cautiously. 'Don't you think we should check it out with Mum first?'

'Mum!' said Edward incredulously. 'We've got on without her for ages. And she'll say no before we even get to explain what a good idea it is. A puppy for *free*. It's a *gift*.'

'Literally,' said Libby sarcastically. 'A free gift for us, but maybe not for Nancy.'

But Edward ignored her and anyway it was, as always, too late. The others had already sprung to their feet and were clambering onto their bikes and she found herself in her usual position – tagging along behind them – as they embarked on an epic trip across town to a suburb that was as unfamiliar to her as a foreign country. It was a blustery day and they battled against a head wind, but it was behind them when they cycled back later in high spirits. Their Christmas present for Nancy, 'which cost us nothing,' as Charlotte kept reminding them, lay on an old swimming towel stuffed in the basket at the front of Charlotte's bike. Rose was surprised, but not worried, that they had missed lunch. But she was horrified when Charlotte, with all the flair of a magician, produced the puppy from behind her back.

'You can't just give somebody a *puppy*,' she said. 'Nancy works, and odd hours at that! A puppy is like a baby. Who's going to look after it when she's not there?'

Momentarily, Charlotte and Edward looked taken back. The whole spirit of the enterprise hadn't allowed for small matters of a practical nature. Undeterred for long though, Charlotte could always be relied upon to come up with an answer.

Nancy's house has a generous, fenced back yard. There is a side door into the garage. They will build a warm home for the puppy there, (although, they agree later, there is no reason why the puppy shouldn't remain inside the house while Nancy is at work.) They, personally, will take turns cycling around to her place, (after all it is only around the corner) and taking the puppy for a walk every day. Perhaps, they agree as an afterthought, it might be good for Rose to take a turn too. It will get her out of the house. Rose rolled her eyes scornfully at this suggestion, but Edward, emboldened by his own storyline, goes on to describe the scene when Nancy is presented with Rover, (for they have already named him,) on Christmas morning when the family gathers after church to open their presents from under the tree. She will be deeply, deeply moved. She will, at last, have something to lavish her love on. They imagine that tears of joy may even roll down her face.

'And Nancy doesn't cry easily,' Charlotte reminded Rose. 'Not like you Mum.'

'Imagine away to your heart's delight!' scoffed Rose. 'Tears of *anger*.'

'She will be a changed woman,' Edward continued, undaunted. 'Every day when she comes home Rover will be waiting for her. He will curl up beside her when she has her first sherry of the evening. He will still be there when she downs her last gin.'

'Don't be cheeky,' said Rose. 'She's entitled to a few drinks now and then.'

'You must be mad,' said Sam when Rose told him later that, seduced by Edward's homily, she has capitulated. 'You can tell he's part sheep dog. He'll be as wild as hell and should be on a farm, not cooped up like a chook in Nancy's back yard.'

However, there was nothing to be done at this late hour on Christmas Eve, so the next morning, when the family arrived back at the house after church, Sam poured Nancy a couple of generous cream sherries. He followed this, with extravagant bonhomie, with several staggeringly strong gins so that by the time Nancy was presented with her present from the children she was in a state of advanced alcoholic euphoria.

'She would have welcomed a lion cub with open arms,' Sam boasted to Rose in bed that night.

'Just wait. She's always grumpy the next day after all that drink,' said Rose dismissively. 'And I'm the one who'll get it in the neck.'

She was right. Christmas Day, with Nancy softened up by drink, was the high point in this saga. For Rover would not remain a docile puppy for long. The sheepdog in his genes meant that he should have been trained to herd sheep, and decades of inbreeding meant that there was a wild strain in him that made him resistant to any form of behaviour modification.

'I told you it would end in disaster,' said Sam unsympathetically to Rose, when she complained that Nancy was cross with her. 'Like most of Charlotte and Edward's mad ideas.'

And unfortunately, not only did Rover prove resistant to training; he also became increasingly territorial and possessive of Nancy. For some reason, he took a particular dislike to the local postman, Mr. Wright, a cheerful man who normally enjoyed his retirement job, cycling around the suburbs in a leisurely fashion delivering the mail. After Rover had attacked him for the second time, lying in wait behind the thicket hedge, before inflicting several sharp nips on his skinny aged legs, he plucked up the courage to speak to Nancy about it.

'I'm not an unreasonable man,' he said tentatively, for he had been the victim of Nancy's sharp tongue on more than one occasion. 'And I *like* animals. I even have a cat!' he added triumphantly. 'It's just that it's making me anxious every time I lean over to put the mail in your letter box. It's as though he lies in wait for me. After all, I'm not a young man,' he said glumly, hoping to appeal to her better nature.

'A *cat!*' replied Nancy with barely concealed contempt. 'Cats are only for sissies. Might I suggest a change of plan to you that may just sort out your problem with Rover?'

Mr. Wright, hoping for the best, nodded politely, but his hopes were quickly dashed.

'Do you really have to whistle that loudly as you cycle along?' said Nancy. 'To be frank with you,' she continued, warming to her theme. 'Dogs have infinitely superior hearing to us and even *I* find that tiresome shrill sound annoying when I'm sitting in my sunroom minding my own business. And after all,' she said, before shutting the door resolutely in his startled face. 'He *is* a sheep dog by breeding. It probably confuses him.'

But sadly, after a third, more serious attack, and an official complaint from the Post Master General followed up by a visit by the local constabulary, Nancy reluctantly decided that Rover had to go.

'You let your children do the most ridiculous things,' she said to Rose when she phoned to tell her about it. 'I'd actually become quite fond of him, so now they've made my life worse, not better.'

'He's just territorial.' Rose said. "He wants to protect you. It's rather sweet really.'

'Territorial's fine and good,' snapped Nancy. 'Next thing they'll be taking me to court! And that's so bloody typical of my life,' she grumbled. 'I always get the consolation prize and now even that is taken away from me. Everything I start to love is snatched off me.'

'What do you mean by that?' said Rose. 'Sometimes you talk in riddles.'

'As if you didn't know,' Nancy snapped before she put down the phone. 'Or care.'

Fortunately, one of Sam's regular house calls, a charitable one, was to a convent of nuns who lived high up on the port hills. He persuaded the Mother Superior that Rover, with his protective nature, would make a good guard dog for them. But Rover, like Greyfriars Bobby, was a one-man dog. He found his way back to Brown's Road three times, chewing through the rope the nuns tied him up with after his second escape, and travelling over fifteen miles back home to Nancy. She found him at the back door, exhausted and hungry, but pathetically pleased to see her, after she returned from night duty at the nearby hospital where she worked as a sister in Emergency. The nuns had had enough. Besides, they told Nancy, Rover had begun to growl threateningly at the Monsignor when he cycled up the drive to say Mass each morning. Perhaps the scrunch of his bicycle tires in the gravel reminded Rover of the postman who had annoyed him so much in the past.

'What's that crazy dog doing here?' Sam said when found Rover stretched out on the living room sofa when he returned from a night call later that week. 'He looks as though he owns the place.'

'Oh Nancy was threatening to *send him to the country*,' Rose explained, handing him a generous glass of whisky. 'But I couldn't have that. He'll just have to settle in with us for a while. He loves the children.'

So settle in he did and it wasn't until years later, when Libby herself was a mother that she realised that being 'sent to the country' was a euphemism that adults used when explaining the sudden disappearance of family pets to their children.

'It's funny how I keep remembering the past,' Libby said when Tom called that night. 'It must be being back in the house. Why do you keep phoning me anyway?'

'I wanted to talk to you,' he said. 'And you know, I'm still concerned about you and want to know that you are ok.'

'Well don't bother,' Libby replied. 'It's not your job anymore.'

'I've been in the hospital all day,' he said finally. 'They think there might be a problem with my heart. I might have to have a couple of valves replaced, or stents put in.'

Not Tom, the natural athlete, surely! Although it was true he had gained a little weight over the years, with his thick brown hair barely flecked with grey and his lanky build, he still looked surprisingly boyish. And he had to tell her this just as she was beginning to feel a little better. It was just another splinter driven into her heart. It was full of them now. She knew him so well. He would be sitting on the other end of the phone, willing her to reassure him, like a scared little boy wanting to be told that everything would be alright. He would be twisting a piece of his hair in his fingers, as he always did when he was worried about something.

'Doctors love telling you the very worst about any condition. Lots of people have stents put in.'

'I know. It's still quite a major operation though. No wonder I've been feeling so tired.'

'You'll be fine. You're so fit. And young. Well… relatively.' She hesitated before saying anything else to console him. How cruel hurt and anger made one.

'I hope you are right,' he said. His voice was lighter. She had made him smile at least.

'I'm always right. That's what annoys you about me. How is Amy taking it?'

'That's the first time you've used her name.'

'I'm being nice. It won't last.'

'She's frightened, of course. She's younger, so she's not accustomed to her friends getting older – or dying.'

'You are *not* going to die,' said Libby firmly. 'And it's pathetic to use the word "friend"!'

'I deserved that,' said Tom. 'But you know what I mean. We're at that age where we start to think about it. We go to lots of funerals. Death is suddenly all around us.'

Compassion for him swept over her like a brush stroke. Later as she lay in bed, wide awake in the early hours, she conjured up images of the past, snatches of their life together.

She watches from the doorway as Tom gently pats dry scraped knees at bath time, they laugh in the car on the way home from a parents' evening when the drama teacher tells them that their daughter Cleo is, 'quite frankly, a *pain* in class.'

'A pain in the *arse* more like it,' Tom says as they leave the school hall.

'I just wanted to hear your voice,' he said.

Ordinarily, there was so much more she would have tried to say. How she loved him, how they'd get through it together, what a strong brave man he was and how much they all needed him. How she'd put him on a special diet and they would live life at a slower pace. How he must now give up all that wine he drank every night and not feel he had to finish off the bottle. She would be bossy and consoling and motherly all at once. But someone else had taken her place now, so she simply said, 'I'd better get to bed.'

'I'm quite frightened.'

'I know.'

'How's Charlotte?' he said. 'In trouble as usual?'

'She's fine,' said Libby. 'As mad as ever. The dreaded ex is still being elusive; and difficult about money! But she seems contented on her own.'

'I've always had some sympathy for Ben,' said Tom. 'Is she still building that yacht in her backyard? She'd be hard going for anyone to live with.'

'That's not fair. She's got so many good qualities. She's kind and funny. And authentic.'

'But you said yourself that she was probably difficult to live with. All that drinking and disorder. Men hate that.'

'Oh *really*. Anyway, I can say those things because she's my sister. You can't. Especially now.'

'You're right, 'said Tom. 'But was she always like that?'

'Always,' said Libby. '*Always* getting us into trouble. Dad never forgave her for chopping down the quince tree you know. He used to go on about it all the time. Mind you, Charlotte actually did Dad a favour because Mum stood up for him whenever Charlotte complained she'd been unfairly treated. Maybe that was the beginning of the rapprochement.'

'It *was* one of Charlotte's better efforts,' said Tom. 'I've always liked that story. In fact I love all those stories you tell about your madcap family.'

16

It was a baking hot summer's day. Bored, Edward, Charlotte and Libby lay on the back lawn. Their parents, who didn't often get out on their own, were at a family wedding. The three children chewed on pieces of fresh grass.

Their father's last words before he started the car had been, 'And don't get up to any mischief.' They looked at one another with genuine astonishment as the car vanished around the side of the house.

'Who does he think we are?' Edward said. 'I'm deeply wounded.'

Libby looked at him adoringly. She loved it when he spoke like that.

'He means *you*, not us,' said Charlotte. Edward rolled over and kicked her. He was still in trouble because of the shoplifting incident the previous Christmas.

Wedding plans were in full progress for Tilda's wedding later in the summer and the three younger children had felt sorely neglected over the last couple of months. Even a private preview of their annual circus, performed on the lawn outside the back shed last weekend, had been poorly attended, their mother making the feeble excuse that she had to get on with her sewing and their father disappearing off to the TAB just as it was about to start. So, it had been a motley group that attended; the Reynolds' boys from over the fence who were roped in at the last minute as audience *and* circus staff, the old couple from over the road whose grandchildren were in from the country for the day and Mrs. Dobson, the highly strung widow from next door, who was simultaneously captivated and appalled by the Prescott children and their goings-on.

On this particular occasion they had planned a number of acts, described in the programme as both skilful *and* dangerous, some of which would be performed on an old iron pipe they found behind the shed. The ends fitted snugly into the junction of the lowest branches of the walnut tree and the quince tree in the back garden and when placed between the trees it served as a sort of tightrope. The bar was lowered or raised a few branches by the two youngest Reynolds' boys, depending on whether the act was a trapeze walk, (Charlotte, with a broom as her balancing pole) a series of daring acrobatics on the high bar, (Edward) or the spectacular finale. Libby was surprised to be chosen for this. Normally Charlotte or Edward would vie for this role as it would be considered the showpiece of the great event. She received her instructions from Edward, and in particular, his final comment, with a degree of scepticism.

'It'll be easy,' he said. She was to get on her bike at the front gate and pedal furiously as she approached the back garden down the side of the house. The speed she would reach from this long approach would ensure that the momentum she had by the time she reached the bar, set at waist height, would help to propel her over it in a perfect somersault. Landing triumphantly on her feet on the other side she could raise her hands above her head, bowing left and right as she did so, just like the Russian gymnast, Larisa Latynina, who was, as Edward reminded her, her heroine. When she timidly pointed out that she hadn't had a chance to practice yet he looked at her scornfully. 'Don't be such a *nerd,*' he said. 'We're performers. Remember?'

It was unfortunate, they all agreed later, that there had been no time for a full rehearsal because owing in no small part to the laws of physics, which nobody had bothered to consult, Libby took a nasty tumble during the grand finale, whereby the bike, continued on its trajectory under the bar and collided in perfect symmetry with her forehead as she attempted to complete her somersault. The injury sustained was sufficiently serious to render a ban by their parents on any circuses in the foreseeable future and a cancellation of any privilege for the next two weeks.

'You nearly gave poor Mrs. Dobson a heart attack,' Rose scolded Libby as they waited to have her head stitched at the doctor's. 'For some reason she's very fond of you children.'

So here they were, stuck at home all afternoon, rather than catching the bus into town and seeing a film at the cinema, as Rose had promised they might when she broke the news that most of the younger cousins and *they* in particular, were *not* invited to the wedding.

To add insult to injury, Sam wound down the window of the car just as he reached the end of the drive and called out. 'And don't lie around sulking all day.'

'We could help with the preparations for the wedding,' Charlotte finally announced. She had been lying on her back, but now she rolled onto her stomach and smiled. Her two front teeth were missing as Edward had struck her in the mouth with his bat while they were playing cricket the week before. The lisp she would have until a bridge was made gave her voice less authority than usual so Libby pretended she hadn't heard her.

Undaunted, Charlotte continued. 'They'll need the back lawn to put up the marquee. But do you notice something?'

'No,' said Libby, relenting. 'What?'

Edward affected indifference. He had no time for other people's ideas, especially Charlotte's.

'There's not enough room for a marquee with the quince tree there,' Charlotte said. 'It will have to go!' She pointed accusingly at the tree as though she expected an argument from it. Each year Sam made an occasion of picking the fruit off the tree so that Rose could make quince jam. The jam was horrible, almost as bad as the tomatoes and silver beet that he always said they would acquire a taste for one day.

According to the children, the only thing the tree was good for was quince fights. In late summer the rotting fruits could be scooped up from the ground and thrown over the fence at the Reynolds boys, or, when they were bored on a Sunday afternoon, lobbed over the front wall at passing cars.

Libby looked up at the tree from her perspective of lying below it on the grass. It was a large tree that their father had pruned to an umbrella shape so that the children could lie under it out of the summer sun. On this fine afternoon its leaves glistened brilliantly, as though somebody had polished them.

'Dad likes that tree,' she said warily. 'If it's *there*, it's there for a reason. Dad must have thought about where the marquee would go.'

'He probably hasn't had *time* to think about it,' Charlotte said. 'Anyway, Mum says he's hopelessly impractical. Imagine his surprise if they come back and we've moved it for him. It will save him hours of work.'

'It's not like a chest of drawers. You can't just *move it*!' Libby said stubbornly. 'Maybe the marquee will fit nicely beside it.'

'Oh, don't be *silly*!' Charlotte said. 'Not with the walnut tree there and all.' She sprang to her feet and strode up and down the lawn. She reminded Libby of Sam when he had paced out a cricket pitch for them the year before.

'Look! The marquee would be at *least* this big. I've seen them. They're *huge*.'

'You're mad,' said Edward. 'He'll hit the roof.' He jumped to his feet and sauntered off into the house.

'Spoil sport!' Charlotte called to his retreating back. Then she turned to Libby. 'Come on,' she said. 'Let's get started.'

Reluctantly Libby followed her into the shed. Hanging on the far wall along with a few other garden tools was a large saw.

'Do you think that's *big* enough?' Libby said doubtfully. 'And it's pretty old and rusty.'

Charlotte ignored her; she had the ability to act as though she was hard of hearing when it suited her, and taking the saw off the wall she headed back outside. Libby followed her and found her shading her eyes from the glaring sun as she looked at the tree. There was something so theatrical in her pose that Libby's heart sank.

Charlotte turned to her, and tapping the saw in her hand as if measuring the weight, she said, 'I can't wait to see Dad's face; can you?'

Libby screwed up her face at the thought, but she knew when she was beaten. 'I still think you should have asked him first,' she replied.

Chopping down the quince tree – a glorious specimen of *Cydonia Oblonga*, a member of the Rose family, as their father constantly reminded them after the event – proved to be a far harder task than Charlotte had anticipated. The outer bark was tough and kept peeling off when she tried to saw through it. Beneath it, the fresh white bark looked as hard as iron. The saw teeth kept sliding off as Charlotte pushed the saw clumsily back and forth across it.

'You look all red and blotchy like you do when you've been playing basketball,' Libby said unkindly, after she had watched her for a while. 'Shall I have a go?'

'No need,' said Charlotte. She threw the saw down on the grass and wiped her face with her arm. 'All we have to do now is *push* it,' she announced confidently, as though chopping down trees was something she did every day. 'Come on.'

They both pushed and pulled at the trunk and finally it splintered away from the base of the tree, although large pieces of the bark were still attached to it. There was a loud noise like a rifle shot as one of the lattice windows in the shed broke when a branch tumbled onto it.

Charlotte screwed up her face and then said cheerfully, 'they probably won't notice it if we don't say anything.'

Now the tree lay sprawled awkwardly across the lawn, a tangle of branches bearing buttery yellow fruit. And now the back yard looked decidedly bare – reduced to an expanse of dry summer grass – with the walnut tree on the boundary of the veggie garden to their left; and the clothes line, the hen house and the wooden paling fence at the back no longer screened by the quince tree and its foliage. Worse still, the remaining stump of the felled tree oozed a horrible white substance, like pus from a wound, and Charlotte was now covered in it. It had attached itself like glue to her hands, her clothes and her hair that she had continually brushed back from her face as she worked. Libby looked despondently down at the glossy red slip-on shoes their mother had bought her at the church Bring and Buy the weekend before. Now they too were ruined and when she moved her feet they made a sucking noise as though she had been wading in mud. She surveyed Charlotte's handiwork with growing trepidation. The whole back yard looked diminished by the loss of the tree. Even Charlotte must be able to see that something vital had been lost.

Suddenly there was a scrabbling sound on the fence on their boundary with the Reynolds' property next door and Ralph Reynolds' head appeared above the wooden palings. He hauled himself up, looked into the backyard, scratched his straw-like hair, and shook his head.

'Your father will kill you,' he said eventually, in his toneless voice.

Charlotte glared at him scornfully. 'Get lost,' she said. 'You're just jealous,' and she leant down and in one refined movement scooped up a hard clod of earth from the garden and chucked it at him. It struck the fence with a solid thump and then burst open. Ralph's head abruptly disappeared, and then just as quickly popped up again.

'Just you wait 'till your father gets home,' he said. His head disappeared again, but his voice rose prophetically from behind the fence, 'You're dead!'

'Oh that's right. Run away!' yelled Charlotte, incensed, and stooped down to pick up more ammunition. 'Hay head!'

'Perhaps if we tidy up the stump,' Libby suggested quickly. Charlotte's temper was easily aroused and she would relish nothing more than a full-scale war. 'Then I'll put one of Mum's table-cloths over it. That will look good.'

She left Charlotte scraping and sawing at the stump, while she went in to the house and searched through the linen cupboard until she found a hand embroidered table-cloth their mother had brought back from a trip overseas.

'Do you think it matters that it's a bit sticky?' said Charlotte. They had carefully draped the cloth over the stump but the gooey sap kept seeping through the material.

'The tree looks as though it's crying,' Libby said.

'*Righto*,' said Charlotte, as though she hadn't spoken. 'Let's get on with it.'

But as Ralph had predicted, Sam did *not* appreciate what they had done. It was just that the *timing* was bad, Charlotte said later in her own defence. She blamed Ralph and his stupid Punch and Judy show for this. His provocation had ruined the whole thing. Her *original* plan had been that the first thing Sam would see when he and Rose arrived home was the tree artfully arranged on the front lawn with baskets of the golden fruit all around it. But the whole operation took longer than anticipated as the tree was heavy and hard to manoeuver in the baking late afternoon sun. As it was, Sam and Rose came up the drive just as they reached their destination but before they had time to set the stage. Their father's anger at the sight of his beloved quince tree being dragged onto the front lawn like a 'slaughtered animal', leaving in its wake a trail of broken rose bushes, was heightened by the fact that he had had a few drinks and was looking forward to a late afternoon snooze.

'What a fuss about nothing,' Charlotte grumbled, as she and Libby, confined to their room for the rest of the day, lay despondently on their beds. She was still rubbing her hands together as Sam had used the wooden spoon on her. 'He *picks* on me,' she said. 'You always get away with everything,' and turning her back on Libby she picked up a book and said over her shoulder, 'That's the last time I try to help out.'

Libby thought glumly to herself that knowing Charlotte, there was little chance that she would remember this promise for too long.

Rose popped her head in later and came and sat on the end of Charlotte's bed. 'I know you thought you were helping,' she said, a half smile on her face. 'But you know how much Dad cherishes his garden.'

'He was so *mean,*' said Charlotte, turning her face to the wall dismissively.

'He's just upset. It's always better to try to understand why people are angry,' said Rose, squeezing her shoulder. 'It's easier to forgive them when you do.'

Charlotte said cryptically over her shoulder. 'I haven't noticed that anyone is particularly big on forgiveness in this household.'

'You're right,' said Rose briskly. 'But it's never too late to start.'

'What did you mean by that,' asked Libby, when Rose had gone.

'Oh sometimes you're so thick,' said Charlotte, as she picked up her book. She was rubbing her sore hands together gingerly. 'Always the baby, always being spared the truth. And the wooden spoon. It's not fair. Mind you,' she added. 'That's the first time Mum's really stood up for Dad. So maybe I should be the hero, not the villain.'

17

Libby got up before daylight on Christmas Day. It would be her first one without Tom for over 30 years. It had rained intermittently during the night and now everything was drenched; the lawn, the trees, the sagging old deck chairs she'd been too tired to fold up the night before after the neighbours, (he a retired university lecturer, she a 'career housewife' as she proudly described herself) popped over for a drink. Sally had pursed her tight little mouth, whether in sympathy or disapproval Libby couldn't be sure, when she'd explained why she was alone on Christmas Eve: three daughters overseas – two with Tom in Hong Kong and one in Europe skiing.

She set out up the hill just as the sun was rising, hoping that a walk might lift her spirits before the family arrived. What on earth was she dreaming of staying here for Christmas? Last night as she lay in bed tossing and turning in the early hours she felt the same overwhelming waves of homesickness rolling over her, that she'd felt when her parents left her with the Murrays, all those years ago. Homesickness was a word that so aptly described the condition itself. She had forgotten that it was actually a physical affliction. What a baby she was though; she must pull herself together. Every time she thought of the day ahead and wondered how she would get through it, her eyes filled with tears. She must be mad. And now Charlotte had decided to go away early this year she would be stuck with Tilda and her family. For the whole day.

'*Alone again, naturally*,' she sang wistfully as she scrambled over the stile leading to the path which led up the valley. But only a few sheep raised their heads lazily at the sound, before returning to their grazing. Suddenly her mobile rang; it was the harsh 'bark' ringtone she had recently allocated to Tom.

'Good morning,' he said cheerfully. 'You are up and about early. I tried the house.'

Secretly, it lifted her spirits to hear his familiar barrister's voice, cultivated by all that time spent presenting arguments in court and now with age, confident and as mellow as an old wine.

'I hate it that you are always so cheerful,' she said. 'In these circumstances. Why can't you sound a little sheepish? If you'll pardon the pun as I am on the hillside surrounded by lots of those. Looking stupid as sheep do. And what are you doing still up? It must be about one in the morning there?'

'I'm not used to wrapping presents without you. The girls are out partying and I've been trying to do all the things you usually do the night before.'

Libby sighed loudly. 'Oh, why do they never learn that it's a bad idea to go out on Christmas Eve? Now they'll be all hung over and grumpy tomorrow. Is your girlfriend there with you?'

'Are you joking?' Imagine the reception she'd get here. Anyway, she'll spend the day with her parents.'

'Like the filial little daughter, she is!'

'Now, now!' he said, but not unkindly. 'I'll bet you are gloating.'

'I am *not* gloating. I would have been absolutely amazed if you'd been insensitive enough to ask her to be there anyway, with those two forthright daughters of ours around. But despite what you think, I don't want you to be unhappy.'

'Yes, you do.'

'Hmm. Well. For a little while maybe,' Libby said pretending to think about it. 'But not forever.'

'It's going to be terrible having Christmas Day without you. I can tell the girls are dreading it.'

'Same here. I feel so stupid. I don't actually think I can get through the day.' Suddenly she found herself crying again, in great gasping sobs like a child's.

Tom said, 'Please don't cry. I hate it. We'll call you at lunchtime.'

'I feel so lonely here. I've been away too long. We are all so different now. And nothing seems so bad from a distance.'

'I thought you said you wanted to enjoy some solitude?'

'Not on my own though.'

He laughed. 'Isn't that the whole point?'

'Oh you know what I mean! Can you come over to see me?' She hated herself for saying it. 'No, on second thoughts, don't. That would be ridiculous.'

He said far too quickly: 'I'm in the middle of a case anyway. I can't get away. Not in the next couple of weeks. After that I could come over for a few days, but only if you agree not to spend the whole time telling me off. It would probably be a good idea for us to talk things through without all the anger anyway. Do you think we've moved on?'

'Moved on! What a cliché. Even after all these years you have the ability to astound me.'

'Why don't you just try to enjoy the day,' he said, changing the subject. 'You'll feel better when you've spoken to the girls. By the way, I've even put their presents in pillow cases, the way you used to do.'

'Easier said than done,' snapped Libby. 'Just enjoy the day! You say that so glibly. And I just hate the way it will be so totally different from any Christmas Days we've had before.

Mind you, not all our Christmas Days were perfect. Only retrospect and time make memories so idealized.'

'It's sad that the girls are older, isn't it?' said Tom. 'I used to love those early Christmases we had here.'

'Don't talk about it. I'll start crying again,' said Libby. 'Tell the girls to call me later. But not if they are still drunk. And warn them I'll know by their croaky voices!'

She put the phone back in her pocket, and continued to sob loudly as she walked along the path, through the paddocks, and up the hill. But by the time she walked back down the road she was only making the sort of hiccupping sound that children do after a hefty bout of crying, and when she flung open the garden gate she was dry eyed and thinking about Christmas lunch and what she needed to do. She even hummed to herself as she got out the plates for lunch.

They arrived late of course. Tilda had never been on time for anything in her life. She swept in, her mouth pursing her lips like a petulant little girl, and pecked Libby's cheek in an absent minded way.

'Stupid idea coming all the way over here.' She headed straight for the kitchen, carrying a tray covered with a tea towel which she dumped on the bench. 'There. The Christmas pudding as promised. And I did try to make a pavlova but it didn't work. I think you are meant to leave the eggs out overnight but I forgot. The traffic was *dire*,' she continued in a cross voice. 'Where on earth would everyone be going on Christmas day?'

Hugo smiled wryly at Libby as he hugged her. 'Charming isn't she,' he said. 'Don't worry. She's just in one of her foul moods. Christmas has that effect on her.'

'I know how she feels,' Libby said. 'But it wouldn't hurt her to put on a good face occasionally. It seems strange to me celebrating Christmas Day in the summer,' she said as he put some bottles of wine he'd brought with them into the fridge. 'Not that it feels much like summer today.'

Her heart sank as she noticed through the window that a blustery wind was now sweeping up the harbour and white capped waves were surging in from the heads and slapping onto the beach below.

'When are we going to open the presents?' Joe, Tilda's sullen 16-year-old, was whining to no one in particular as she went into the living room. He spoke in a droning monosyllabic voice that set Libby's teeth on edge. She could never understand a word he said.

'Enunciate for God's sake,' she longed to yell at him. But she simply said, 'Pardon?'

'We've had to come all the way over that hill and Christmas day will be half over before we open them.'

'Let's forget the champagne then. Why don't I get tea or coffee or drinks for whoever wants it, and then we can start,' Libby suggested.

'Good idea,' said Tilda. 'Let's get it over with.'

'Not the most gracious comment my darling,' said Hugo, winking at Libby.

'Well what do you expect? I'm bloody exhausted. You do nothing for Christmas. *Nothing.* And let's face it; it would have been so much easier to stay at home.'

Libby felt tears well up in her eyes again. Tilda glared across the room at Hugo who was shaking his head at her.

'What's that "fuck you" face for?' she snapped at him. 'Don't be a hypocrite and get all virtuous on *me!* Who was it who complained all the way over here?'

'That's right,' Hugo said. 'Share that Christmas spirit around a little by telling tales and making Libby feel even worse than she does already.'

'Good one Mum,' said Joe sarcastically. 'Come on Libby, let's pop the champagne and get this show on the road. Forget the cups of tea.'

Libby smiled at him gratefully. Maybe there was hope for him after all.

But all this was so different from what she had planned. *Her* girls would be in Hong Kong today, opening their presents first thing, grumbling as they got ready for church, drinking too much at one of the Open Houses they always attended on Christmas day morning…. She suddenly wished she was a million miles away from here. She hated it. She wanted *her* children with *her*. Not her sister's. She wanted Tom with her, not Hugo.

'Don't be so mean,' Claudia said. An overweight teenager with the soft features of her mother but a much warmer heart, she had been sitting silently on the sofa. Now she came and pulled Libby down beside her and put her arm around her. 'Libby's done a brilliant job and we're going to have a fabulous day.' She looked up at her mother. 'Imagine how she must feel without her family here today Mum. Give her a break!'

'Thanks Claudia,' Libby said. She couldn't resist adding. 'Don't worry Tilda. You can have Christmas day at home with your family next year.'

'I need a drink. *Now*,' Tilda responded. 'Sorry, it's just been one of those weeks.'

'Well don't take it out on other people next time,' said Hugo.

Everything went wrong after that of course. It always did when she cooked a special meal. It didn't matter how well prepared she was or to what lengths she'd gone to. She just couldn't seem to coordinate the whole assembly of a meal or time it so that everything was ready to be served simultaneously. And it was like trying to master mathematics or the economy. She simply couldn't be bothered putting the effort in.

'It is all in the organisation,' Tilda said when she came into the kitchen to supervise. 'You have to plan these meals like a military operation. There *are* no shortcuts.'

'What a bore it all is,' Libby said grumpily. 'I've never understood what the fuss is all about. Really, I'd rather read a good book.'

'And the kids don't like parmesan cheese, said Tilda when she saw that Libby had shredded it on top of the cauliflower. 'They have rather unrefined taste buds I'm afraid, but there you go. You should have asked me to get you some cheddar at Barry's Bay on our way. Oh well. No use crying over spilt milk I suppose.'

'Oh, I should have thought of that,' said Libby apologetically. 'Cheddar is in our DNA. Remember how Dad loved stopping at the cheese factory on our way over here.'

Every time they went to Akaroa, Sam would insist on stopping to pick up huge blocks of cheddar cheese, like soft yellow bricks, at the Barry's Bay Cheese factory, an elegant white building sprawled at the bottom of the long winding road descending from the summit. By then at least one of the children would be complaining of feeling car sick after enduring the series of hairpin bends that Sam took at speed, so they were always happy to stop and taste the different varieties of cheddar arrange on toothpicks and offered to them by the owner, Mr. Boyce. A surprisingly debonair man for this neck of the woods, he was always dressed in moleskin trousers and a cream viyella shirt and the children were fascinated by his long moustache, gleaming with wax, that he constantly twirled between his fingers. 'As though he is rubbing butter into flour,' Rose complained. 'It's so unhygienic because next thing he's slicing up the blocks of cheese we buy and wrapping them in that oily thick paper.'

'Didn't you bring cream and brandy butter?' Libby said, trying not to sound critical but looking in quiet despair at the small Christmas pudding sitting in solitary splendour on a tray on the kitchen bench.

'Oh I just assumed you'd have those,' Tilda replied, far too quickly. And then dismissively waved her hand as if the matter was settled. 'And it doesn't matter about the pavlova because you said you'd do a fruit salad. It was all getting just too hard.'

Now Libby could hear a heated discussion starting in the living room.

'This Maori issue is completely out of hand,' Hugo was saying loudly as she came into the room. 'Have you read the latest?' he asked Libby, waving the morning press at her as she came into the room. 'They now want to call Akaroa "Whakaroa". What next?'

'Well what do you object to exactly?' said Claudia. 'It *is* a Maori name you know Dad, although someone from your generation couldn't be expected to know that of course. Or care.'

'What a cheek!' snapped Tilda. 'And don't speak to your father in that sarcastic tone. Your generation is *so* arrogant. For your information – when we were young we had loads of Maori friends and never thought anything of it. It's like inverted racism the way you all carry on about it all the time.'

'But that's the whole point. You treated them like the Pakeha and had no interest in their history or culture.'

'Well personally I find all this self-examination so artificial,' Tilda continued. 'It's all so over the top. What about *our* history. Suddenly that stands for nothing and we have to spend all our time apologising for our past. I'm never even sure what we are meant to have done wrong.'

'You're talking absolute bullshit Mum!' said Joe. He was sprawled indolently on a large floor cushion, right in the way of everyone entering the living room. 'That's such an ignorant thing to say. You were all so prejudiced.'

'That's a pretty sweeping generalisation isn't it?' said Libby as she stepped over him and refilled Hugo's glass. 'Nowadays your lecturers at university fill you full of historical revisionism which you accept hook, line and sinker, without even questioning the interpretation of historical events. Many, many countries were colonised – always have been – and the legacy of British colonisation is not all bad. Of course our generation's view of the world needs to be re-examined, but you have to remember that social media has had a huge influence on your generation. You've practically forgotten how to think for yourselves. You are so heavily influenced by Facebook, Twitter and all these jolly celebrities blogging endlessly about political issues of which they have no real understanding. I don't think any of you read newspapers anymore and anyway, there's no deep analysis of issues in the papers here.'

'Do you really think you are in a position to be critical?' Joe interrupted, springing up and going over to the sideboard to get himself another beer. 'You haven't lived here for years and years.'

'But sometimes distance isn't a bad thing is it? Don't you think we need to start looking forward, not backwards? What about the rights of the large Chinese and Indian communities living here now. Aren't we all meant to be equal in a democracy?'

'So you are basically saying we are xenophobic, are you?' said Tilda. 'Not like you, with your sophisticated global outlook!'

'Mum that's not fair,' said Claudia. 'Libby has a point. She's just saying that New Zealand needs to stand outside itself occasionally and look at itself and its problems to get a better perspective.'

'But she's so patronizing,' Tilda snapped. 'Let me remind you, Libby, that we live in a free liberal society here. We don't exploit people the way you do in Hong Kong, with your privileged expatriate way of life and your maids, or should I say slaves.'

'Don't be ridiculous. And we call them helpers for your information. Not maids. That is exactly what I am talking about. That smug, complacent, judgmental attitude. All of Asia and loads of European countries still have home help.'

'What sort of excuse is that?' said Tilda. 'And look at you. Even after you had retired and the girls left home you still had help.'

'That's because we cared for our helper and decided to keep her on until *she* wanted to leave us and retire. Look, it's not even worth talking about.'

'The kids are probably right,' said Hugo. 'It's good to see their generation forcing us to re-examine the past.'

'Oh shut up all of you,' said Claudia. 'Libby, I think the turkey's ready.'

'Why can't I learn to keep my mouth shut?' Libby said when she spoke to Abbie on Skype after they had all left.

'Yes, you could work on that,' said Abbie. 'Sometimes you tend to sound like an extreme right winger and yet you're the kindest, most compassionate person I know.' She shook her head. 'But I think you are a lost cause so I'd just carry on the way you are if I were you. You're too old to be converted. Sadly.'

18

Edward came over in the early evening for a dinner of leftovers.

'I'm sorry Susie couldn't come. She was exhausted after making lunch, so she and kids decided to stay on at her sister's.'

'Don't worry about it,' said Libby. 'We'll just eat in the sunroom then.'

But when she told Cleo about it that night she said, 'Nice. Not.'

Daisy called out in the background, 'That's bloody rude Mum. Susie would know that you'd have set the table and catered for them all. What a loser!'

'Christmas Day is always a disaster,' Edward said when she told him about the lunch.

'Always has been. Somebody always falls out with somebody, or somebody always behaves badly. Remember that one we had when I offended Nancy after church and she wouldn't come to lunch? Mind you,' he added, 'Although Mum was upset we had a much better time without her.'

'Oh God. I'd forgotten about that one. Don't remind me,' said Libby. 'We were horrendous teenagers, weren't we? Mind you, that stupid minister was also to blame.'

***

'And don't think you two are getting out of going to church, Sam said sternly. 'You're going. Hangovers or no hangovers. You didn't turn up to the midnight service last night, although you know how much it means to your mother, so you can ruddy well come to my church this morning to keep her happy, although personally I couldn't care less if you stayed at home. You both reek of cigarettes and alcohol.'

Libby winced and looked over his shoulder at her reflection in the hallway mirror. Her face was blurred, like a badly taken photograph and her eyes had the faraway look they always had after a big night out. *And* she felt like throwing up.

'Do we *have* to go?' said Edward. 'I'm not sure I can last.' But he spoke with little conviction. His face was as pallid as clay and he said his head was hurting so much he could barely speak, so that Sam, who had turned away, appeared not to hear him.

Libby shook her head at him. She knew there would be no negotiation on a day like this.

'Did I behave badly last night?' she asked Edward pleadingly, hoping he would take pity on her.

'Yes you did,' he said, visibly cheering up at the thought of somebody else suffering hangover remorse. 'You slid down the bannisters in the house party we gate-crashed *and* you spent all night hanging around some guy you fancied even though he was far more interested in that really pretty girl with long black hair. The one who was the complete opposite of you,' he added gratuitously.

'Oh thanks,' said Libby sarcastically. 'That's all I need. I can't have been *that* bad because I didn't lose my shoes or anything.'

'You were bad. Very bad,' said Edward shaking his head like a disappointed teacher. 'I'd ring up and apologise to the mother and father if I was you.'

'Are you kidding?' said Libby. She never knew with Edward, but he had said enough to make her headache worse and not for the first time she told herself that she would never drink again.

Fittingly, it was a glum summer's day; the sun grudgingly emerging from the low clouds at intervals and a blustery wind lashed at the trees outside the window.

Unfortunately, the service that day was conducted, not by Sam's favourite minister the Reverend Wilson who generally wandered off into the philosophical in his sermons, but by 'Master Bates,' as Sam called him, who had recently suffered some sort of mental breakdown so that now his gloomy world view was inflicted on his congregation every week. Today, much to Sam's chagrin – for he always insisted on timing the sermon – he spoke for more than the 15 minutes that was traditionally allotted to this part of the service. As if this wasn't bad enough, his theme was about the futility of war. He chose as his starting point, the unofficial ceasefires along the Western Front around Christmas 1914.

'We should not continue to glorify either of the Great Wars,' he said in a trembling voice. Libby wondered whether he was hung over, like her and Edward; but perhaps he was just deeply moved by the sound of his own voice. 'In fact,' he continued, 'We New Zealanders had no business fighting in either War. There must have been other ways, such as diplomacy and mediation, for the politicians to put the world to rights.'

He wound up the sermon by reading Wilfred Owens's *The Parable of the Young Men and the Old* and Libby found herself listening intently, for the first time during the service, the words boring like nails into her throbbing head. It was a sonnet she would remember always and teach years later, as part of a unit on WWI poets. At first reading her students are puzzled by it as many of them come from different religious and cultural backgrounds, so they have never heard the story of Abram and his son, but when she explains the parable, and the theme of the poem, they are spellbound, as teenagers are when the riddle of poetry analysis begins to fall into place.

The Parable of the Old Man and the Young

So Abram rose, and clave the wood, and went,
And took the fire with him, and a knife.
And as they sojourned both of them together,
Isaac the first-born spake and said, My Father,
Behold the preparations, fire and iron,
But where the lamb for this burnt offering?
Then Abram bound the youth with belts and straps,
And builded parapets and trenches there,
And stretched forth the knife to slay his son.
When lo! an angel called him out of heaven,
Saying, Lay not thy hand upon the lad,
Neither do anything to him. Behold,
A ram, caught in the thicket by its horns;
Offer the Ram of Pride instead of him.
But the old man would not so, but slew his son,
And half the seed of Europe, one by one

'The man's a complete fool,' Sam muttered to Rose as the collection was taken afterwards. 'He's meant to be giving a Christmas Sermon not a WWI Poetry Reading.'

'He had to go and ruin the last carol too,' he grumbled as they shuffled out of the pew. The Reverend had reminded them, just as they were about to sing the last hymn, that Silent Night was sung by both the Germans and the English in their own tongues on that Christmas Day so long ago.

'As if we didn't know that!' Nancy said scornfully. 'He's so young he's got no idea what the last war was like for us. Christmas Day is not the time to open up painful old wounds.'

When it came to their turn to speak to the Reverend Bates as he lay in wait at the top of the church steps Sam strode straight past him, but Rose stopped to wish him a Merry Christmas.

'Don't breathe on him,' she cautioned Edward.

'I hope you haven't invited the bugger in for a drink,' Sam said, as they met up afterwards on the pavement outside.

'*Shhh*,' said Rose. 'Of course, I had to, but he probably won't come after seeing you storming out with a face like thunder.'

Edward, who Libby suspected was still a little drunk, began to talk in an overly animated way about the sermon, waving his arms around in a manic way and enunciating as though talking to a group of deaf people.

'I'll bet he was thinking about Vietnam,' he said. 'We shouldn't be there.'

Nancy stamped her foot on the pavement and the others flinched as the small bowler cloche hat that was sitting precariously on the side of her head, wobbled in an alarming fashion.

'How *dare* he!' she said. 'To belittle all those young men by going on about how no freedoms are worth fighting for. That stupid, *stupid* man. How did he think *we* would feel? Our generation gave up so much.'

'It was a sermon about peace if you think about it,' said Edward, always the bull at the gate. 'All that jingoism is madness. And we have to stop glorifying all those "sacrifices for the sake of freedom." Too much patriotism is dangerous.'

'Oh *stop* it Edward,' said Rose. 'He's stirring you up Nancy.'

'Stirring me up! What a spoilt brat you are Edward! How would you like it if you got up every morning, opened the paper, and saw that several of your young friends had been killed?'

'My point exactly,' said Edward triumphantly. 'That was the whole thrust of the sermon; that war is simply not worth the loss of young lives.'

'*Shut up Edward*!' said Libby. 'Just *shut up* and get into the car.'

'Spoken with the glorious arrogance of youth,' said Sam. 'Just ignore him Nancy.'

'Yes, let's just stop arguing and get on,' said Rose. 'There's so much to be done.'

'Oh that's so typical,' snapped Nancy, turning on Rose ferociously. 'That's all you can think about. Your precious dinner and your precious family. If you think I'm going to spend Christmas Day with a couple of hung-over brats who have the audacity to mock everything we all fought for you've got another think coming. Especially if that idiotic man is coming too,' she added, looking over her shoulder at the Reverend Bates, who finding most of his older parishioners appeared to be shunning him, was lurching towards them with a hopeful smile on his face.

'I think he's a secret drinker,' she pronounced. 'And not one who'd be fun to spend time with.'

And with that she darted off over the road and started to walk down the avenue of trees leading to the main road home.

'Oh look what you've done now Edward,' said Rose in dismay. 'You've ruined Christmas Day. Sam; go after her!'

'Like heck I will,' said Sam. 'She's been spoiling for a fight all morning. And as for you two! What appalling behaviour. You haven't done a thing to help your mother, you come in at all hours, you're still drunk, you stink of cigarette smoke and your voices are so hoarse that none of us want to hear a word you say. Just shut up and keep out of my sight. And don't bother standing up for Edward, Libby. You always make excuses for him or try to get him out of trouble. I bet he's the one who encouraged you to stay out late last night. When are you going to learn that he's not perfect? In fact, he's just a ruddy bad influence.'

'Never,' whispered Libby as she turned away. It wasn't negotiable. To her and Rose, Edward would always be perfect in their eyes. Nothing would change that.

And although she and Edward, chastened, podded the peas for Rose when they got home from church, and Libby, unbidden, put out the Roses chocolates in the traditional bowl on the table while Edward brought extra chairs through for the table, the day was still ruined. And Libby escaped to the back toilet as soon as Tilda arrived with her ghastly, noisy children, where she vomited her heart out before making her way, ashen and nauseous, to the table for Christmas lunch.

'I never understood how Dad could forgive Mum for abandoning us, did you?' Edward said as he got into his car to drive back to Christchurch.

'Gosh,' said Libby, taken back. 'That came out of the blue. We've never even talked about it.'

'But then we don't talk about things in our family do we,' said Edward briskly. 'And I haven't got time now. I've got to get back. It's just that remembering that day makes you wonder whether we all went off the rails for a while, after Mum returned. Everything we do has consequences. You begin to see that when you are a parent yourself.'

Libby put her hand on the window as he went to wind it up and said, 'I didn't understand then, but I'm beginning to now. Sometimes forgiveness is the only way out.'

19

'Did I tell you that Amy has moved out?' said Tom. 'She can't handle the thought of living with someone who isn't in rude good health. It makes her feel old, even though they say my heart will be ok now I've had the stents put in. She said she needs some time to think.'

'You're joking! Well what does that tell you about her?'

'It's actually a relief to be on my own for a while.'

She didn't respond.

'Don't worry about me, will you,' he said, after a hopeful pause went unrewarded. 'I'm fine. It helps to talk to you, and at least it means the girls will be nice to me again.'

'Not *that* nice,' said Libby. 'You're fooling yourself if you think they'll get over it just like that. And don't expect *me* to suddenly be your confidante again,' she added for good measure. 'I'm good at bearing grudges.'

'I know that! I don't expect you to. I could come down to see you now of course? And we could talk.'

Libby continued on as if she hadn't heard him. 'No, you had your chance after Christmas, when I was at my lowest ebb, and you didn't come. Work always comes first with you. That's probably why Amy's getting sick of you. Young women require relentless adoration. And you *do* know how you'll end up the way you are going don't you? You'll be one of those sad old expats who stagger through Central to The Hong Kong Club every morning. All limping along like a team of Hopalong Cassidy's, nursing their aging hip and knee replacements. Then after spending an hour or so wistfully reading *The Spectator* and *The Times* in the library and dreaming of better days, you'll slip downstairs to the Chairman's Bar where you'll meet up with some other old codgers for lunch, all of you unable to bear the irrelevance of retirement and unwilling to relocate to a place where you don't have aging maids who've been with you forever to pander to you. *And* by then Amy will be long gone and happily ensconced with a younger replica of what you once were.'

'You really do have the most extraordinary imagination,' said Tom. She could tell he was smiling. 'Writing should definitely be your second career. I wish you could be a little kinder to me,' he added plaintively. 'Would that hurt you?'

'You know, I don't actually enjoy being unkind,' Libby said. 'You've made me like this. If I am honest though, there must have been something wrong with our marriage anyway, because if this had happened when we were younger, I probably would have murdered you.' She sighed. 'It's funny. We've always got on fine when we speak on the phone.'

'Well that's a start,' said Tom.

'Don't you think you should give him another chance?' Charlotte suggested, when Libby told her Tom wanted to come down to see her for a couple of weeks. To *talk*.

'It's not that much fun being alone at our age you know.'

'It's not *that* bad,' said Libby, who was standing on a chair looking for a vase in the kitchen cupboard above the fridge. 'You don't have to worry about regular meals, you don't have to go out with boring couples you don't like, no pestering for sex when you're reading a good book.'

'Hmm… Actually you're making it sound quite attractive,' said Charlotte. 'But what about those long Sundays when you have nobody to watch TV with or chat to, and going to weddings on your own, and finding a compatible friend who doesn't drive you mad to go on holiday with. *And*,' she added triumphantly. 'Imagine having to date again at our age. How gruesome would *that* be?'

Libby shuddered. 'No way! I just wouldn't bother.'

Charlotte had arrived unannounced that morning just as Libby came in from the garden with an arm full of roses. There was more bad weather on the way so she had rescued some of the blooms that had survived the rain gusts that had blown through the previous night.

'Oh let *me* do that,' said Charlotte, climbing down from the kitchen stool as Libby jammed the flowers into the Waterford vase she had just washed. 'What a mess you're making of them.'

'I like an unstructured arrangement,' said Libby defensively. 'It suits the country house look.'

'No,' said Charlotte. 'It's just shapeless. Even unstructured has a structure; and you need to trim the stems, like this.'

Libby leaned on the bench and watched her. 'I suppose I *should* take his previous, on the whole, devoted behaviour into consideration.' She followed Charlotte into the living room. 'Should I?'

'It wouldn't hurt,' said Charlotte, placing the vase of flowers on the mantelpiece and standing back to admire her handiwork. 'And time's an amazing healer, as Mum used to say. And have *you* always been such a saint?' she said, raising her eyebrows. 'No, don't tell me. I don't want to know. And can't you remember the early days? You were mad on one another. It was like the romance of the century.'

Libby laughed. 'Gosh you do exaggerate. It's true though. We were so happy at first.'

'Can I give you some sisterly advice? Do you think you could try and distance yourself from him for a while? Stop discussing your relationship with him every time he calls you. Men hate discussing relationships. And don't mention Amy. Don't even show any interest in her. Pretend you are incredibly busy and have lots of new friends and interests. In other words, get a life. Remember that he's confused and angry too at the moment. Probably with you as you are getting in the way of his grand passion. And passion has a use-by date. I think the research shows it's a couple of years at most. After that Tom will be thinking more rationally. Small things about Amy will begin to irritate him. Mark my words.'

'That sounds so calculating. I'd be playing a part. Like a role play.'

'Yes,' said Charlotte triumphantly. 'Just like that. Pretend to be one of your drama students. It's worth a shot isn't it? And look at me! I've always been unable to commit to anything. It was fine to play about when I was younger because you always think there might be something better around the corner, but there aren't so many corners to turn as you get older. And on that note, it's probably the right time to tell you, while we're sort of on the subject, that I have a new man.'

'What?' said Libby. 'Why haven't you told me about it? That's brilliant. I've been so busy talking about myself – going on and bloody on – and we never talk about you. I know you've been lonely.'

'Yep,' said Charlotte. 'I've finally found someone who's funny, loving, kind, thoughtful and never boring.'

'OMG,' said Libby. 'All those worthy qualities. It's unheard of. Let's preserve and bottle him immediately.'

'Oh I don't think so,' said Charlotte. 'It's not a younger man, as you'd expect with me. He's too old to preserve and bottle I reckon. He's literally the guy next door. But he's perfect for me. And he's practical. He can hang paintings and unblock the drains. What more could you want? I've always said that in another life I'd marry a builder not a banker.'

'What are you like,' said Libby. 'Honestly!'

That night Abbie arrived to stay for a week and after she had gone to bed Libby and Charlotte stayed up, finishing off the bottle of wine they'd opened. When Libby went to into the kitchen she glanced at her reflection as she passed the hallway mirror.

'You know I actually look reasonably attractive when I've had a few drinks,' she told Charlotte when she came back with another bottle. 'But I know I'll look pretty average again in the morning.'

Charlotte laughed. 'Don't be silly. You're gorgeous. Perfect. And there you go, putting yourself down again. Where does that come from?'

'It's true,' said Libby. 'Naturally beautiful people like you wake up looking beautiful. People like me only look attractive after a couple of wines.' She laughed. 'Maybe I just need to drink more.'

'I'm not naturally beautiful, said Charlotte scornfully. 'You're as bad as Mum, always telling us we looked like super models. Then she always added we were clever as well.' Like Libby, she never dealt well with compliments.

'Tell me about your man,' said Libby. 'I am *so* happy for you, but you dropped that on me as though it is of no consequence. As though you're telling me you've just bought a new dress or found a new dentist. Are you being so blasé because you are scared of being hurt?'

'Maybe,' said Charlotte, waving her hand dismissively. 'Maybe. I'll look silly if it doesn't work out. Look at this. Doesn't it take you back?' A documentary about Cilla Black was on the TV and she was singing '*You Don't Have to Say You Love Me*' and Libby joined her as Charlotte handed her an imaginary microphone and danced out onto the terrace.

'It's good to know we're not gaga yet. We still know all the words. After all these years,' Charlotte boasted.

A full and perfect white moon – like one in a child's picture book – floated outside, luminous in the pitch black sky.

'The music in our day was so much better than the rubbish they listen to today, don't you think?'

'What are you two like,' Abbie suddenly called out before Libby could answer.

The loud music had woken her up and she had been standing in the dark kitchen listening to their conversation. Now she came out onto the terrace rubbing her eyes and looking grumpy.

'There's nothing sadder than people your age listening to old songs and living in the past.'

'You'll be the same, young lady,' Charlotte said. 'The past isn't always a foreign country. Sometimes at our age you just need to go back there for a few minutes.'

'The trouble is,' added Libby. 'At your age you don't think of us as real people; with a life and an interesting past. I was the same with my parents. Now I regret taking them for granted and not asking them more questions about when *they* were young. *We* were anxious and vulnerable too you know. So were our parents. Probably more so because of the war.'

'Definitely. It's just that your generation is so narcissistic,' added Charlotte emphatically. 'Nobody ever asked us how we were "feeling" every five minutes.'

'That's a little harsh. You didn't have the pressures we have nowadays,' said Abbie. 'No social media. No Instagram. Every time I look at it there is some loser posting photos in an exotic location; photos of their hotel room, every meal they eat, and the cool friends they holiday with. How do you think that makes us feel? Inadequate. And is that intentional?'

'I'm just saying,' said Libby. 'One day you'll wish – like I do – that you'd been a kinder daughter.'

'Don't worry Mum,' said Abbie. 'I won't leave it too late to be good to you. I know I think about myself a lot at the moment. That's what you do at my age. It's obligatory. And by the way, you are perfect in my eyes. *Sometimes*. You too Charlotte. You're my role models. I bet you met your lover online Charlotte and that is why you are being coy. But good on you. Now, can you turn the music off? And get to bed,' she added sternly as she returned to her room clutching a warm glass of milk. But she was smiling as she said, 'Sleep tight.'

'What a wimpy generation they are,' said Charlotte. 'No stamina. But how sweet was that. Sometimes I think Abbie is the mother and we're the children. She's far too wise for someone her age.'

'Is that why you won't tell me about him?' Libby asked her, shrugging her shoulders incredulously. 'Because you met online? As if *I* would be judgmental.'

'No. As if. You know how useless I am with all that technical stuff. I can only just manage Facebook, let alone a dating site! It's just that I don't want to talk about it yet. I'm like you in that way. The gods will punish me if I'm too happy.'

'What is it with us?' laughed Libby, shaking her head. 'I reckon it's age. We always feel as though we're living on the edge of some calamity. I'm sure that's why I'm so obsessed with order now. I'm only content if everything is in its place. Because family life isn't like that. There is always someone to worry about and disaster just waiting to strike. So the wolves must be kept at bay and preferably behind and beyond the paling fences.'

'You are too deep for me,' said Charlotte, yawning. 'What on earth are you talking about? Off to bed with you madam.'

'Where did it all go? The joy of our youth?' Libby asked Charlotte the next morning as they sat in the kitchen nursing sore heads and looking disconsolately at the dishes still waiting to be washed.

'I never leave the dishes overnight,' said Charlotte, frowning. 'And I think the joy was all an illusion; an illusion fuelled by drink and youthful hormones.'

'No. It was more than that,' Libby said. 'There were moments when I was young when I was simply and utterly happy.'

'But it was usually when you were in love. Life kicks in at a certain stage and you just lose all that exuberance for living.'

'You two do go on,' Abbie said as she came into the kitchen. 'I told you you'd be sorry,' she added unkindly. 'I'll get you guys a cup of tea. Face it; you're too old to drink like that anymore.'

Libby looked out the window at the bleak day outside; a thick morning fog hung over the backyard cutting off the treetops and there was a steady drum of rain on the roof.

'I should introduce you to some artificial substances,' said Abbie, handing Libby a couple of Panadol. 'At least you'd still be cheerful the next day.'

'That's not even funny,' said Charlotte scowling at her. 'And look at you. All glossy hair, long legs and the face of a goddess. What would you know about anything? Just go back to bed and leave us to suffer in peace.'

'I think I'm beginning to settle down here,' Libby told Tom when he next phoned her. 'I'm feeling more my old self. '

'Really!' Tom said. 'That hasn't taken long.' He sounded disconcerted. 'Actually, I'm feeling different too. Maybe it was having those stents put in. It feels like a new beginning. The doctor said I was probably depressed because of the lack of oxygen getting through my system. It's as though I've been in a fog and I'm suddenly seeing clearly again. And you start to think about all the thoughtless things you've done in your life when you have an experience like that.'

'Oh spare me! Isn't that just a lazy excuse for bad behaviour? Lack of oxygen!' Then she added quickly, remembering Charlotte's advice. 'Well it's great that we are both feeling so much better isn't it. Right, I'd better get on as we're off for a walk. It's a fabulous day.'

'That's not what the weather forecast says,' said Tom. 'I check it every day. Who are you going with?' he asked.

'Oh just a friend,' Libby replied. 'You wouldn't know him,' she added unkindly.

'Mum, try to be kind to him,' Abbie said when she told her Tom wanted to come to see her. 'Dad's been through a lot too you know. 9/11 changed him forever. Let's face it. And shouldn't you remember how kind and understanding he was when Rose died? You were a mess then.'

'Rose!' said Libby. 'Since when have you called her that? You always called her Nonna.'

'Oh Mum. We'd called her Rose for ages. She asked us to. She said being called Nonna now seemed pretentious and made her feel old. And don't change the subject. You must know that we girls would all like nothing better than for you guys to get back together again. Even if Dad is a complete dickhead, he's *our* dickhead.'

20

After Rose died, Libby's heart rusted up like an old piece of neglected machinery. She didn't seem to be able to feel anything anymore.

'Do you think it's because I feel abandoned by her? *Again,*' she asked Tom.

'No of course not,' he said. 'It's natural. You have to shut up parts of yourself to get through grief. You have to learn to live with things, but the loss never actually goes away.'

And anyway, it was too late to make up for everything now Rose was dead. How beastly she'd been to her at times. Now she was often alone, with the girls gone, she realised how lonely her mother must have been when she, the youngest, left home. When the girls were little Rose would phone Libby every day and often Libby would find herself being short with her or listening to her chatter about the family at home only half-heartedly, wanting to get away so she could get on with her busy day. Her own bustling life in Hong Kong, with work, and the girls' activities and the endless round of dinner parties that went along with expat life in those days, made her so selfish, now she thinks back. Now she often wishes they hadn't spent all those years living overseas. Although she knows it is irrational, she blames Tom for this too. She has seen at firsthand how their

Chinese friends look after their aged parents and the extended family. This, surely, would have been a better way to live.

November in Hong Kong was the worst time in the first few years after Rose died. At that time of year – coming into winter – the skies were clear and the weather was generally settled. There was often a welcome chill in the air in the mornings and people donned heavy winter clothing far too early, so fed up were they with the unrelenting summer heat.

Grandparents arrived in preparation for Christmas and Libby felt a pang of grief every time she saw the extended families out at one of the local clubs having dinner, or mothers and daughters shopping together in one of the market streets running between Queens Road Central and Des Voeux Road, with their fake handbags, cheap outlet shops selling label clothing and kids' clothing shops.

And now everything she found as she cleared out Belle Maison reminded her of the past.

When she was going through the camphor wood chest on the landing, she found a piece of material left over from the beautiful pink dress her mother made her for her first proper dance. Rose would sit sewing in the sunroom in the early afternoon, after she'd done the lunch dishes, pins in mouth, working on her old Singer sewing machine and constantly popping her head out the French doors to cajole Libby to come in from 'play'. Children stayed children for longer then and Libby usually spent her afternoons after school outside, banging tennis balls against the shed door or lying on the back lawn, basically doing nothing. There were no after school activities and plenty of time for day-dreaming. What a luxury that had been.

The dress was a miraculous creation she now appreciated, and just as delicately and skilfully made as any dressmaker could make in Hong Kong. It had a halter neck and a Grecian type top gathered onto an empire line skirt. Yards and yards of pink pale chiffon were gathered over a silky lining of an even paler pink which rustled and swayed back and forth as Libby walked. Libby couldn't be bothered with the all the trying on her mother wanted her to do, but she fell in love with the dress at once when it was finished, ironed and hung ready to have the hem sewn. Where sewing was concerned Rose was a perfectionist and made Libby try the dress on again and again, making such small alterations with her pins that Libby wondered what on earth difference it could make. Then, when Rose was finally satisfied, she sat up late one night over-sewing the seams and finishing it off so when Libby tried it on the next day, she saw it had become the most wonderful dress in the world. Fit for a princess.

'You are going to be the most beautiful woman, Libby,' said Rose. Then, wistfully. 'Don't waste your beauty will you? So many women do. They think that is enough and get lazy. Then when their beauty is gone they have no resilience left. With you, your beauty is both inside and out.'

'Oh Mum. You do exaggerate,' said Libby turning away from the mirror. Then; suddenly shy at the thought of wearing such a sophisticated dress for the first time. 'Do you really think I look ok? I'm not sure what the other girls will be wearing.'

'You look better than ok. You will be the belle of the ball,' said Rose firmly. 'And you must learn to have your own style. Don't think you always have to dress like other people.'

'You never have, that's for sure,' said Libby. 'If I looked like you Mum, I wouldn't care what other people thought either. I really, really love it Mum,' she added, holding the skirt out and swirling it around her.

'Not only will you be the belle of the ball,' said Rose, standing behind her as Libby looked at herself in the full length mirror in their hallway. 'This will just be the beginning. All you children have that special something. It's called charisma.'

'Oh Mum. Don't be silly,' said Libby. 'You see us all through rose-tinted spectacles. Especially Edward. He's perfection in your eyes. Mine too come to think of it. *He's* the one with the star quality.'

They both laughed. It was a magic moment. Sam had cleaned the top hinged stained glass windows in the living room the weekend before and the rainbow of light cast into the hallway held Rose and Libby in thrall as they looked at Libby's reflection in the mirror.

'I've let you down in so many ways,' said Rose enigmatically. 'But I've sewed all my love for you into this dress. You can wear it like a magic cloak.'

21

'He's gone. He's dead!' Tom was shouting down the phone. He was in New York visiting his brother Charlie and they had planned to go by train to Washington that weekend. Charlie worked for Cantor Fitzgerald on the 102nd floor of One World Trade Centre.

Libby had watched the nightmare unfold at home in Hong Kong, sitting on the end of the bed, eating her breakfast cereal before she left for school. She had been idly watching CNN. At first she thought she must be watching a movie preview. She actually watched the second plane hit, live, and it was only then that it dawned on her that this was in real time.

Tom said he and Charlie were to meet for breakfast and Tom was half a block away when the first plane struck. He told her he waited with an army of ghosts; other relatives praying for miracles that never happened. He spoke to Charlie for a while on their mobiles but eventually he said, 'It's over Tom. There are people jumping all around me. I need to make a decision. I love you all.'

Libby often wondered whether it would have been better if Tom knew how Charlie had died. He told her once – in those early days before he stopped talking to them all about it – that the agony in his mind was like a physical thing: a broken record going round and round. He couldn't stop thinking about what the last few seconds must have been like for Charlie. 'If I could find someone who could operate on me to cut out the pain and my memories of that day I would. *That's* what I need to even begin to survive this. I don't want counselling,' he said dismissively when Libby suggested it. 'I get more comfort from talking about Charlie with his mates down at the pub when I go back to London than I do "working through it" with a stranger. I don't want to get over it. I want to carry the pain to my grave. It's the least I can do.'

And then, gradually, Tom began to distance himself from her and the girls. They tried to be understanding but he built a wall around him that they couldn't seem to breach. He threw himself into his work and took on an impossible caseload that involved working late and even on weekends he had conferences. And of course he always had a junior to help him with his cases. Usually Amy.

Libby held no truck with the apologists for the terrorists who said America had it coming. America! The buildings were full of young people from all over the world. She was incandescent with rage when people – her fellow teachers were the worst – talked endlessly and with little compassion about how Americans should have thought about their conduct, as the world's 'policemen,' in other countries. Her head of department, a self-published poet who read his own work to his students when he should be following the syllabus and teaching T.S. Eliot or Auden, even suggested, as he lounged back complacently in their next department meeting, that the terrorists were, in effect, 'soldiers.'

'Soldiers! Don't be so fucking stupid,' Libby said, shocking the old guard in the department who thought swearing unbefitting of a teacher of English literature. 'Soldiers fight wars, against other soldiers. It's not fighting any sort of war I've heard of to kill yourself by flying a commercial airliner into a building full of innocent citizens. Soldiers wear uniforms. Guerillas fight in their own countries. Terrorists are cowards.'

'You are wasting your time,' Tom said when she told him about it. 'People like that sicken me. I wouldn't even deign to speak to them about it.'

For a long time Tom often woke in the middle of the night panicking and gasping for breath. When Libby told him there was nothing he could have done to help Charlie because the plane had crashed into the tower well below his offices, he shook his head.

'The *firemen* weren't too frightened to go up, were they?' Then, apologetically, like a small boy. 'I *did* try, but they wouldn't let me into the building.'

'Yes and 347 of them didn't come down,' Libby said. She thought, in fact was sure, that he sometimes wished he had died there too. She read up about survivor guilt. This was a classic response. Tom had always protected his little brother from harm. That was what big brothers did.

22

'I can tell Charlotte thinks I should let Tom come down to see me to "talk",' said Libby. 'What do you think?'

Tilda stretched back in her chair and raised her face to the sun. It was a beautiful day and she and Libby were lunching in a café alongside the Avon.

'I thought we discussed this weeks ago,' she said reprovingly. 'I told you what *I* think. That it's not what Charlotte thinks about anything, or what *I* think, that matters. You have to learn to make decisions yourself, and then live with them. You can't keep just going round and round.'

'You seem preoccupied today,' said Libby. 'And *not* with *me*. Maybe all this analysis is getting to be a bit of a bore. Mind you; I wouldn't blame you,' she added hastily. 'It's a bit of a bore for me as you well know. But then making a decision like this isn't like deciding what flavour ice-cream to have when you go down to the corner shop is it?'

'I *know* that,' said Tilda, drawing out the word like a further reprimand. 'Look,' she said, sitting forward as though she'd had a sudden brainwave and smiling at her encouragingly. 'Let's suppose you tell him he can't come to see you in Akaroa and he accepts that. How do you think you will feel about that?'

'Sad, rejected, a little lonelier on those long Sunday afternoons that seem interminable, cowardly because I haven't given it a chance…..Oh I don't know! Oh why can't I be rational like you? My thoughts are always so complex. Muddled even.'

'You can say that again. It's a simple question. I just want to know if you'll be happy if there's no resolution. Has he ever had to forgive *you* for anything? I can see you don't want to go there', she said quickly as Libby held up both hands. 'Fair enough. That's fine. And if he does come to stay with you? How will you feel about that?'

'*Well*. I'll be apprehensive, maybe a little excited. Part of me – the lazy part that likes an easy life and is scared of change – will hope that he sweeps in in his usual confident manner and takes it all out of my hands. That is; that Tom will make the decision for me. He's far better at that. And he's big on forgiveness now that he realises he needs a large dose of it. Maybe he can talk me around.'

'Ah yes. Forgiveness. It is always vastly underrated,' said Tilda. 'Look at Dad. Aren't you happy that he was eventually able to forgive Mum after she left him; and then came back to him again? Don't you think that changed all our lives? For the better.'

'Of course. That goes without saying. Don't all kids like their parents to stay together? There'd be far more divorces I reckon if parents didn't take their kids into account.'

'Well maybe that's your answer when you think about giving Tom a chance to come and see you,' said Tilda. 'Not that I am telling you what to do,' she added hastily.

'Oh but I *want* you to tell me what to do. You're my big sister. Then I can blame you if it all goes wrong,' she added. But when they parted she said in a mock angry tone. 'Oh alright. I'll bloody well let him come.'

She was waiting at the airport for Tom when he arrived, despite telling Charlotte that he could jolly well find his own way to Akaroa. She had things to do in town so she had driven to Christchurch in the morning and it seemed churlish not to pick him up; she knew from experience how tiring the long journey was, with the inevitable long transit in Sydney. And then of course the plane was late.

When he finally appeared it was awkward. She hugged him, but with a calculated reserve and their conversation was stilted as they made their way through the outer suburbs.

'The city just keeps expanding,' he said. 'But outwards not upwards. I liked it better the way it was. Are you sure you don't want me to drive?'

'No,' said Libby firmly. 'Why do you always think you have to be in control? What's wrong with my driving anyway?'

'There's nothing wrong with it. It's just that you've never understood the road rules at roundabouts and it makes me nervous.'

'And anyway, why do you just keep making small talk?' she said as they left the outskirts of Christchurch behind and started to drive around Lake Ellesmere.

'Well now is hardly the time to get into a deep conversation,' said Tom. 'I'm not really up to it when I've been travelling for twelve hours. Or more.' He sighed wearily in an exaggerated fashion. 'Just concentrate on your driving.'

When they finally drove into the village, Libby keeping up a sulky silence, it was late afternoon.

'You'll be tired,' he said as they drew up outside the house.

'Are you being sarcastic?' said Libby, looking at him suspiciously. 'Shouldn't you be the one who is tired?'

'Let me get you a drink,' said Tom ignoring the question. 'And shall we just enjoy the evening and then I'll make us something easy for dinner.'

'A good choice of yours,' he said as he joined her on the terrace. 'A sauvignon blanc from Marlborough with just a hint of Kiwi fruit.'

'It's my sort of wine,' Libby agreed when she tasted it. 'Like syrup.' They sat in silence as they watched the sun go down. Tom handed her his fleecy to put around her shoulders as the evening grew chilly. The silence was deafening; even the bell birds that had been singing all day had fallen silent.

'I've been thinking a lot about Charlie,' said Libby eventually. 'I wondered whether all this started after he died. I know you were so angry.'

'What do you mean?'

'Oh you know. When people suffer an appalling tragedy like that they often re-evaluate their own lives. Not consciously of course. You became very distant with me and the girls. Not that I blame you for that,' Libby said hastily, putting her hand up as if to ward off a blow. 'It's a common thing with PTSD to feel resentment towards your "loved ones". God I hate that phrase,' she added. 'It's such a euphemism. Your *loved* ones. When did that stupid saying come into vogue?'

'I'm not sure about that,' said Tom. 'I don't *think* I blamed you. I know I couldn't talk about it to you, or anyone, for a long time. I've never talked to Amy about it, if that's any consolation. She didn't know him.'

'We all loved him too,' said Libby. 'The girls and I. He was so easy to love. But of course that is *nothing* to what you felt like losing your brother. None of us can even imagine what that is like.'

Tom got up from his chair and walked over to the wall where he stood looking out over the water. Without turning to look at her he said, 'I will never ever get over his death. I can put it out of my mind for hours, but I think about it every day. I feel as though I failed him. It's such an appalling waste. It eats away at me.'

'I know,' said Libby. 'I'm so, so, sorry.'

'Remember when I told you about my dog Basil dying when I was ten? I'm not comparing Charlie's death with that of course, but I told you I'd never get over that. And I never will. I had lots of dogs over the years, but none that I loved as much as him.'

'What about that story you told me: about your mother being so angry when you told her it hurt more when they had Basil put down than when your grandmother died. It's awful to think that we laughed about that.'

'I said that to hurt her, although actually it was true. For years I blamed my parents. They made me go to school that day and then took him to the vet. I never got to say goodbye. He was *my* dog. I should have been there for him. As I should have been for Charlie.'

He turned to look at her. 'You are probably right. I did shut you and the girls out when you tried to help me. I just wanted to change everything in my life. I hated everyone for being alive.' He sighed and shook his head. 'Even you and the girls.' He picked up the bottle of wine and refilled their glasses.

'You shouldn't blame yourself for that. It's natural to feel like that after such a trauma. Look, would it help you to write all this down? It's amazing how therapeutic it is once you get going. And it would make a nice change from writing lengthy submissions for the Court of Appeal judges. You can swear and rant and rave and be as angry as you like.'

'I think I prefer to write submissions. I like the order law imposes. Its logic. *And,*' he said laughing, 'I have juniors to do the research for me. What about you? Your novel? Have you decided on a protagonist?'

Libby rubbed her chin and pretended to think about it. 'Maybe I will use you as my model.'

'Me! You want a hero, not an anti-hero. If you write about me your protagonist will be pretty unsympathetic. He'll be grumpy, narcissistic, self-serving. According to your assessment of my character anyway.'

'I think I'll turn you into a very flawed but fundamentally likeable character. Your one real weakness will be women. I think I'll have you meeting up with a Russian "dancer" on one of your golfing trips to Macau and leaving me for her. She'll be tall and statuesque and sexy and she won't speak a word of English.'

'Talk about poetic license,' he laughed. 'I've only played golf in Macau once.'

'Never let the truth gets in the way of a good novel,' Libby said. 'You were the one who suggested I take bits and pieces of people we know and create characters from them. And we do know lots of people like that.'

'The men I know play golf in Macau. That's it,' he said. 'They don't all consort with Russian dancers.'

Libby held up her hand to interrupt him. 'And then, while you're still in thrall to her and have convinced yourself that that she loves you for who you are and not what you can offer her you'll take her down to New Zealand. She's read about Queenstown and she persuades you to buy her a vineyard. She thinks her life will all be mountains and après-ski parties and gorgeous ski instructors and rugby players with magnificent legs. But as sure as night follows day – because life is like that – after you get a passport for her and you're playing golf every day and she has tastelessly furnished the showy house she's persuaded you to buy, you'll grow tired of her.'

'Oh. How disappointing. She sounds such an alluring figment of your imagination. Why would I grow tired of her?'

'Because she's just too much damn trouble! She's so temperamental. She looked fabulous in Macau with her lush bright big red lips and her Russian hauteur and charming accent. And because she can't speak much English, you imagined in the beginning that everything she said was enthralling.

Unfortunately, when she does finally master the language she just turns out to not be very bright; in fact she has the mind of a proverbial Russian peasant. She has absolutely nothing to say but loves the sound of her own voice. She keeps interrupting when you are in the middle of an interesting conversation with friends. She likes expressing her opinion and doesn't like debate. She comes from a family where disagreements are traditionally settled by fists…or even guns.'

'I didn't realize you suffered from Russophobia. I'm sure she's a very nice girl with a profoundly poetic soul.'

'Yes. That is the crux of the problem. You think she has the poetic soul of a Russian beauty like Anna Karenina but she's actually just always depressed in a dreary sort of way. She is perpetually bad tempered. She's bored on the vineyard. She's bored in the dull village with the dull women with their iron grey hair cut in the ubiquitous bob and their chunky legs with no ankles. She was hoping to wear furs on a daily basis. She wants to shop and listen to hip-hop music. She's a child at heart. Also,' Libby paused theatrically, 'she owes money to the people who paid her fare to Macau and they come after her. You've stolen their possession.'

'What? Isn't that a step too far? To the remote South Island of New Zealand!'

'Well then,' said Libby, undeterred, 'Maybe she persuades you to bring all her ghastly extended family to New Zealand. They've all got bad teeth and her uncles chuck gallons of vodka down their throats every night and talk sadly of the wonderful country they've left, and cry. And then they get so drunk they all start fighting and whenever you get home after golf, they are all there, gathered in your kitchen. They are waiting for you to cook dinner, or better still, take them out to a restaurant so that they can continue to eat and drink at your expense.'

'It sounds like a winner to me – a work of extravagant fiction. I suspect there's an element of wishful thinking involved. Would you really like that to happen to me?' He laughs, but Libby notices he is rubbing the knee that has the old rugby injury – a sure sign he is feeling vulnerable.

'And then one day,' she continues, ignoring him, 'you'll see your ex-wife. It will be in Italy somewhere, maybe, because that is where ex-wives tend to go on holiday. You will be walking arm in arm with your Russian girl, because she always clings to you in public. You liked this at first, but now you feel like shrugging her off. And your ex looks ten years younger than when you last saw her. She's all animated and glowing. She's sitting in a chic café with a group of people. They look like an eclectic mixture of lawyers and politicians, actors and artists...'

Tom held up both hands like a man at war, about to surrender. 'Enough! I've got the message. The novel will be a best seller and probably be picked up by a movie producer. Go for it! Don't worry about my reputation.'

Libby smiled. 'Yes...I really think I'm onto something here. It will be a sort of Hans Christian Andersen morality tale for the 50 something's.'

'That's that then,' said Tom. 'All you have to do now is finish it, and write a very large disclaimer at the beginning stating that the characters bear no resemblance to any person living or dead. If you don't I may be forced to sue you. *Now,* can we have dinner?'

As Libby sat at the kitchen bench watching him beating eggs for an omelette, Tom suggested other outrageous embellishments she might make.

'None of those are any good,' Libby said, softening the remark with a smile. 'There's not an ounce of poetry in your soul I'm afraid to say.'

'I've always said it's you who should have been the barrister,' Tom said afterwards as he watched her stack the dishwasher. 'It's all about telling a good story. We make a good team,' he said. 'Maybe we can co-write the novel.'

'Get lost,' said Libby. 'You're too pragmatic to be a writer. Stick to the law!'

But the next morning the light-hearted mood of the night before had changed and Tom was silent as they ate breakfast. He picked up one of the photos Libby had arranged on the sideboard, of Sam with his regiment before they sailed off to war.

'I've never understood why you didn't like school,' he said abruptly. 'I loved being part of a community. I loved school. I loved boarding. Those were some of the best years of my life.'

Libby got up from her chair and walked to the window. With her back to him she said, 'That's where you and I are so different. It was a kind of hell as I recall. I was perfectly happy just being at home with Mum. It seemed an infringement of my rights to be dumped there every day. All those bossy teachers and those nasty girls who loved ganging up on you. It was like being in a prison. The innate cruelty of the playground world made my life a torture. You may think I'm being overly dramatic but I'm not. That's how I felt. Nothing gave me more joy than leaving school and becoming independent of all that. Remember that I was the baby of the family and although the others teased me and bossed me around, they also protected me. And I always felt there was a core of weakness in me even though I learnt to hide it. We're not all like you, Tom. Some of us hate restrictions and rules. In your job you abide by them. You love the rule of law.'

She swiftly changed the subject. 'Can you believe Charlotte showed me an article about Sophie in the latest *Tatler*. Remember her? The one who kept asking me to lunch after I had Abbie? She's so successful now and has her own dress label.'

Tom looked at her with his eyebrows raised. In his job he was used to dealing with clients who tried to distract him when he asked them searching questions. So many of their incoherent stories seemed to have no beginning and no end. And from years of experience he knows that Libby dislikes any form of deep analysis. Where she is concerned.

'And I could never fathom why she and Charlotte were good friends? They had nothing in common.' And here she came to the point of the story. 'But that's Hong Kong, isn't it? When we first went there you just had to make friends where you could and often with women you'd have nothing in common with back in your home country.'

'You sound bitter,' said Tom, reaching out to refill her glass.

'Do I?' said Libby, surprised. 'I thought we weren't being judgmental. But yes, now you mention it, maybe I am. Or maybe I'm just envious. I'm all over the place myself, and when I make a friend I tend to stick to them, even when we have drifted apart or I feel they've let me down. It's not really a strength on my part. Blind loyalty is a bit like modesty; it's not considered a virtue anymore.'

'So if you feel like that about loyalty, how do you think I felt when you fell in love with David? You seem to have conveniently forgotten that.'

'Oh but that was different,' Libby said hastily. 'The girls were young, we were both working too hard... and anyway, I didn't decide to leave you. I stayed. So I was loyal in my own way.'

'Maybe that was partly my fault looking back. I was so hurt and angry I couldn't even bring myself to talk about it. I cut myself off from you the way I did after 9/11.'

'It was my fault too. I was too ashamed and it was better just to let time heal things. And it did. Didn't it?'

'Did it?' said Tom. But he didn't sound convinced. 'Bitter memories die hard. Believe me. I wouldn't have any family law cases if that was true. '

23

'It might be time to get rid of some of this old stuff,' said Libby. Tom was sitting behind Sam's old English rosewood desk, writing a submission for an appeal he was working on. The desk had been moved to the Akaroa house as a sop to Sam when Rose wanted to get rid of it when they renovated their Christchurch villa. Sam was sentimental about old possessions and the brass Buddha head Libby had given him years ago still sat on top of its scratched green leather top. This morning the sunlight streaming through the windows fell on the Buddha's smiling face and illuminated his dusty bald head.

'Don't let me disturb you,' she said quickly. 'I'm just thinking aloud.'

'Family stuff,' Tom said, pushing some papers aside. 'Sam cherished all this stuff. I'm with him on that. You seem happier today.'

'It must be the weather. It's also good to have company. It's easy to become reclusive in a small town like this. And in the end you and I had sort of stopped talking about anything that matters, hadn't we? It's different here. We have more time. And,' she said grudgingly, 'I think I'm beginning to feel kindlier towards you.' She turned away and dusted the Buddha's head vigorously with the tea towel she was holding. 'But then I remember how badly you've behaved and I feel hostile again. I felt abandoned by you. Betrayed.'

'Like you did when your mother went to London?' said Tom. 'Do you think that made you particularly insecure? Other couples get through these things. I think what Rose did to you affected you all. It was bloody selfish to up and leave you kids like when you were so young. And Sam.'

'Oh don't you dare change the subject like that and criticise Mum,' said Libby fiercely. '*I* can of course. And the others. But you're not an immediate family member so you can't.'

'What is this? Some recent family law ruling I haven't heard about?' said Tom. But he was smiling.

Libby fiddled with her bracelets and looked out the window. 'But I must admit; you might have something there. And none of us ever talked about it. Maybe that's why I always feel the need to keep other people at arm's length if they try to get too close to me. So often people let you down. Isn't it ridiculous that I am so muddled up,' she added. 'At my age. Just as I was getting to the stage where I thought I knew myself, I've regressed. I'm just not sure about where I'm going any more. And there's no joy. Everyone gets on my nerves. Most of the time I prefer to be alone.'

'But at least you're beginning to talk to *me* about things,' said Tom. 'That's a good start.'

'I've thought a lot about loneliness since I came back. I even made a big effort with Nancy. I could tell you a few stories about that! But I don't think you ever feel lonely, do you? And of course you had Amy.'

'Oh you'd be surprised how lonely I've been at times,' he said. 'There's nothing lonelier than grief.'

'That was thoughtless of me, I'm sorry.'

But he shook his head and said, 'Go on.'

'You know how I made an effort to visit Nancy regularly after Mum died. Every time I came back. But I got so sick of the relentless digs she got in at every opportunity.' She mimicked Nancy's high whining voice, and Tom rewarded her with an amused smile.

"What do you do there all the time if you have help? You mean you never even have to make a meal? Or do the garden? What a hedonistic life people must lead there. Money isn't everything."

'On and on she would drone,' Libby said. 'All the usual garbage you get from people when you are an expat visiting home. But I kept going to see her because I knew how Mum always felt responsible for her as her baby sister. She forgave Nancy everything. Always.'

So, on this particular day Libby had purchased a large bottle of Gordon's gin in the bottle store nearby, and now, like a lamb to the slaughter, she followed the nurse aide along the corridor to Nancy's room.

How small Nancy's world had become now. Rose used to tell Libby bedtime stories about the sprawling houses they lived in as children, with bells in every room to summon the servants and colossal bedrooms with rimu wood tallboys, spacious armchairs and elaborate four poster beds. Now Nancy was confined each day to this tiny room, more like a box room than a bedroom and an ensuite that was optimistically called a bathroom, although there was barely room to sit comfortably on the toilet and certainly not enough room for all the pill bottles and accoutrements of old age which had gradually spilled out to all the surfaces in the living room. In the corner of the room was a small round table with a damask runner laid across it. On it were two photos, one of Normie and one of her grand-children. An old-fashioned clock, a small crystal vase and a cloisonné ginger jar rested on the narrow mantelpiece above the gas fire. These were the remnants of her life. Even the French doors opening onto a narrow balcony offered only a grim view of the gravel driveway lined with some papery hydrangeas and the rendered side of the next unit.

'Shoot me when life gets to that,' Charlotte said last time they had visited together. 'In the good old days, I used to bring the biggest bottle of gin I could find because I had to anaesthetize myself to get through the visit, but sadly I can only have the *one* now that my serious drinking days are over.'

And today Nancy had already had a couple of gins and was spoiling for a fight.

As soon as Libby closed the door behind her she said triumphantly, 'You've no doubt heard that Max died.'

'How on earth would I know that,' Libby replied. 'I haven't heard anything of Max for years and years.'

'Of course your silly mother fell passionately in love with him the moment she set eyes on him,' Nancy went on. '*Why* I don't know. I always thought him so shallow. *And* he drank too much.'

'You *all* drank too much,' said Libby.

'And he liked the sound of his own voice too much,' Nancy continued. 'It was that posh English accent. That's what she fell for.'

'And his charm,' said Libby. 'And Mum was lonely. Dad was always off delivering babies. You always resented her coming back, didn't you? And don't think I don't know why.'

She suddenly remembers a day when she was about eight and they were over at Akaroa for the school holidays. Forewarned that Sam was planning to attend church in the morning, the children had feigned sleep when he put his head around the door, but their ruse hadn't worked because when he tickled Libby she giggled and gave the show away, so they had reluctantly accompanied him to the small church on the seafront. Although he had rewarded them with an ice-cream afterwards, Libby, as the youngest, had grizzled as they walked back.

'Stop complaining,' Sam said, but he hoisted her onto his shoulders so that as they went in the gate she could see her mother and Max standing close together, by the mantelpiece, in the living room. Libby had wriggled down from her father's shoulders as they came through the front door and called out 'Mum, Mum,' in such an anxious voice that her mother had hurried into the hall and said,' What on earth is wrong?'

'It was a scandal,' Nancy added. 'None of us ever forgave her. It ruined the family.'

'Oh *really*? That's not how I remember it. I always thought Mum held the family together after she came back. And how good was she to you! All you ever did was complain but she never gave up on you. All those Christmases together. She made sure you were never on your own.'

'Oh yes. So charitable,' Nancy said sarcastically. 'Always so patronising and putting such a perfect face on things. And Sam was always so weak. Taking her back like that. She didn't deserve his forgiveness.'

'Why did you hate Mum so much?' Libby said shaking her head. 'Was it envy? And why do you lash out at us all like this? And Mum not even here to defend herself. Let's face it. You just can't bear it that we all loved her so much. *Everyone* loved her,' she added with emphasis. 'She had that effect on people. And yes, it was bad that she left us – but she never stopped trying to make up for it. And I know you don't like being reminded, because you hate other people being happy, but she and Dad *were* happy at the end.'

'How *dare* you speak to me like that,' Nancy yelled, her voice shaking with rage. 'And don't think I'll be going *anywhere* with you *madam*!' And then, very deliberately, she picked up one of her precious cut crystal glasses from the wooden trolley and poured a liberal dose of gin into it. 'You've always been a spoiled brat, she added contemptuously over her shoulder. 'Now get out!'

'Better than being a bitch,' Libby said. And then for good measure she added, 'And you can forget lunch. I wouldn't take you out anyway,' before she slammed the door behind her and dashed out to her car.

She had planned to drive Nancy out to New Brighton, so she went there anyway and found a café overlooking the pier where she sat staring at the angry sky and sea outside the full length plate glass windows. The waves were sloshing up against the piles of the pier, sending showers of white spray up into the air. A white carpet of frothy water rushed up the sand and just as quickly retreated. Three young girls were playing down on the beach; their father sat on one of the large rocky outcrops at the edge of the beach smoking and reading what looked like a racing magazine. He was marking things in it with a pen and only glanced up occasionally. The girls raced to and fro at the water's edge, breaking the foaming bubbles with their toes and trying to race the swirling water as the waves broke and rushed up the shore. They wore pretty pastel gingham dresses – now tucked into their pants – and appeared oblivious to the chilly wind.

She must be kinder to Nancy. That's what Rose would have wanted.

She sighed. Maybe she'd go back and try again tomorrow. That was the wonderful thing about age and drink. Nancy would have forgotten everything by then. They could start all over again.

But things didn't go according to plan, because when she went back the next day Nancy was still sulking and had taken herself off to the sunroom with her book. She wasn't reading though. She was sitting on a sofa beside her closest friend – a woman Nancy had been friendly with since her school days. You could hardly call them friends now, in the conventional sense, since Ingrid, once a well-respected GP, was now lost in a world of her own. She would smile when Libby said hullo but always looked past her, never at her, and Libby wondered whether she was searching in her mind's eye for a world lost to her, one not puzzling and frightening like this one where strangers kept talking to her and seemed to be expecting a reply to the many questions they threw at her like an interrogation. One day Libby had said, 'Do you know who I am, Ingrid?' and the reply had come smartly back, with a smile.

'Of *course* I do, Libby,' so there was something there, a semblance of memory.

Nancy looked startled when Libby appeared.

'You had an affair with Dad didn't you? When Mum went away.'

'And hullo to you too madam,' she said. Then, 'You must be mad! Where did you get that idea from?' She picked up her book sitting on the table beside her and threw it with surprising force across the room at Libby. It caught her on the cheek. 'And anyway, what if I did? She left him. She deserved it.'

'That hurt,' Libby said. She rubbed her cheek, picked the book up, put it back on the side table. 'It's the truth. I've known for years. But do you know what? I actually feel sorry for you. You were left with nothing. Nothing.'

'You're a nincompoop; you always were,' Nancy said as Libby went to leave the room. 'And look at you now; running away as always. You're no better than your mother,' she yelled as Libby – for the second time in two days – slammed the door behind her.

And of course Libby *had* known the truth all along. So had Charlotte and although she had never discussed it with Edward she suspected that he knew as well. They were the ones left at home when Rose went away. Tilda had been lucky enough to escape all that. She remembers Sam coming home later than usual, often smelling of drink and behaving in an uncharacteristic way, throwing Libby up in the air and tousling Edward's hair roughly, with a kind of anger, so that Edward would say, 'Ouch. Don't.' and go off to his room.

Like most memories there was no clear narrative in her mind, and no lightbulb moment of realisation. But Nancy would always be there, dressed to the nines and standing behind the children like a real mother would as their father came through the door. She always seemed to be hovering there, 'like a bad smell,' Edward said one night when he and Libby were in bed. 'Did you see her almost falling over herself to take his coat? And that 'would you like a drink Sam? Give me your coat Sam, shall I lick your boots Sam'….

But later, after she had been to the supermarket, Libby sat in her car in the carpark for a while thinking and then decided to try again. She found Nancy in the sunroom, nodding off in front of the television and something about seeing her there like that, just another old person slumped in an armchair in the late afternoon half-heartedly watching television, aroused such pity in her that she leant down, and said softly, 'I've come to say I'm sorry.'

Nancy, startled, looked up at her and Libby saw that she had tears in her eyes. She brushed them away impatiently. 'I don't know why I'm crying. Maybe it's because of the wretched thing on the TV about training sheepdogs. I think I dozed off and started dreaming about Rover and that set me off. Fancy crying about that bloody dog. All those years later and I still cry at the thought of him. That's why I never got another dog. I couldn't bear the loss. And that's what you and your silly brother and sister did to me. All your family have caused me so much pain.'

'You are right Nancy,' said Libby. 'We *were* thoughtless and uncaring and spoilt. I can see that now.'

She knelt down beside Nancy and straightened the rug covering her knees.

'You were just kids I suppose,' said Nancy grudgingly. Then she stroked Libby's hair back from her face, just as Rose used to do.

'Well that's all settled then,' she said, quite perkily. 'And tell Charlotte I expect to see her soon. My gin needs replenishing. Just because she has given up extravagant drinking doesn't mean that *I* have to!'

'I think it's good that you decided to make your peace with her,' said Tom, when Libby told him the story. 'After all; she's had a pretty disappointing life.'

'That's true. In the end nobody ended up really loving her. Not even Normie. Not the way we all loved Mum. And she was right in a way. I *did* used to be a spoiled brat. And yes, it must have been a thankless task at times, looking after the house and picking up the scraps of Dad's affection when he wasn't drunk, or morose, or both at the same time. But her own sister's husband! That's never going to end well is it? Mind you, we all know it takes two to tango, don't we?'

'We do,' said Tom wryly. 'We do.'

24

Libby found Sam's letters to Rose when she was starting to clear out the furniture before the new owners took possession. They were in the Chinese red lacquer cabinet set in the alcove at the top of the stairs. She had decided to clean it out because the sun was pouring onto the landing and it seemed a pleasant thing to do on a bitterly cold afternoon. Tom had offered to help her clear out the house and had just set off with a trailer load of junk to take to the local dump. Libby had been surprised to see that the chest was still there when she decided to stay at Belle Maison after Sam's funeral; it was the sort of treasure one might imagine Tilda spiriting away along with the Indian brass tray. Then again, it was so vibrant its absence would not go unnoticed by the others.

Libby had bought it for Rose when she was visiting Hong Kong in the early eighties; they were wandering up and down Queens Road East with its array of Chinese chest and rattan shops and Rose had fallen in love with it at first sight. Libby personally had thought it overly elaborate with its brightly painted butterflies on the cabinet doors and gold leaf borders but Rose was so enchanted by it that Libby had slipped out the next day and arranged to have it shipped home for her birthday. Although far from its origins, it always looked at home in the alcove there and the butterflies lit up spectacularly when the sun shone on their vibrant wings through the window above.

After Libby had dusted it she began emptying the shiny red lacquer shelves of the hand-embroidered table cloths and napkins she had sent Rose over the years; carefully ironed before Rose stored them, the folds were now yellowed with age. Nobody in the family would find any use for them now, but she would still soak them in Napisan and hang them out in the sunshine to revive them. She knew that's what Rose would have done. She sighed. Maybe then she could persuade Charlotte to lay claim to the chest and store the tablecloths until more time had passed and one of *her* children could put them on eBay or give them to a charity shop.

As she knelt on the floor, on a Panja dhurrie rug Rose had brought back from India, she smiled to herself in satisfaction. She hadn't felt angry or sad all afternoon. Perhaps all it took to find contentment was a hefty dose of housework and a good clear up.

There were two drawers at the top of the cabinet; one full of pins, safety pins, and paperclips, which she threw into the rubbish bag. Stuffed in the other, along with a bundle of some loose receipts, were some old letters, still in their envelopes, creamy with age now and tied together by a silk ribbon embossed with the traditional Christmas Hong Kong flower, the Poinsettia.

After making a cup of tea, Libby sat down on the floor and opened the first letter. Sam's writing – the ubiquitous doctors' scrawl that Rose had always complained about – meant that the letters did not make for easy reading. The first was dated October 8, 2000, the year before Rose had died. That year, Libby recalled, Sam had flown over to London to attend a reunion of the Obstetricians he had graduated with before returning to specialise in Christchurch. Surprisingly, Rose had decided at the last minute that she wouldn't go even though it would have meant she could spend time with Libby and the family in Hong Kong on their way over. Perhaps she was just too tired; but not diagnosed yet with the heart problem that would eventually kill her.

'My darling,' the letter began, I don't think I have used that endearment since I wrote to you from India, before you came out there to see me, all those years ago. It seems a lifetime ago now. It was such an elegant age when lovers wrote letters to one another wasn't it; it meant I could pour out my heart to you and express things I was far too shy to say to you when we were actually together. And I know it's sad that I find the word "darling" so hard to say. Or so our grandchildren tell me. Of course they use it effortlessly and far too freely if you ask me. (Along with all that incessant hugging they all do.) But here we are; apart for the first time in years and so I can put all the things I'd like to say to you down on paper once again. First things first. I want you to know that you are the love of my life. You always have been. Old age focusses the mind, and even more so when you go abroad at my age, as when you are alone in some unfamiliar hotel room, you find yourself getting into bed each night wondering whether you will be lucky enough to wake up in the morning! That may sound melodramatic but I look around at my old friends, many of who I haven't seen for decades, and I realize with a shock that we are now very old men. And although we enjoy a few whiskies together at night and laugh and reminisce about the past, invariably we end up becoming maudlin and talk about loneliness in old age and who wishes they had lived their lives differently. I find myself nodding along with them about what a ruddy nuisance old age is, but after I retire to bed, I lie there, and think how lucky I have been. Something magical happened as we got older, didn't it. For me anyway, these past years have been the happiest of my life. And to think that once, I came close to losing it all. I

know I haven't been an easy man to live with, I know I was often deliberately cruel to you after you came back from London. I know I drank too much and made life miserable for both of us.

But we made it and now I am missing you so much that all I want to do is get on the next plane home. I'm homesick and sad; like the little boy my mother dropped off at boarding school all those years ago, when she drove away with a wave of her gloved hand and not even a backward glance. At least if I was a boy again I could cry myself to sleep every night as most of us did in that wretched dormitory. But I am an old man and so I must grit my teeth and live for the moment I return to you.

There is something so nourishing about a marriage that endures. It's like building an everyday dry stone wall, searching to find the stones that fit into place and then finding – to your surprise – that you have somehow created a thing of beauty. I wish I was one for grand gestures, but I will be back with you soon and I will show you how much I love you in my own inimitable way; A cup of tea for you in bed "madam" in the morning and a brandy and dry every night. Believe me, I am living for those moments.'

Libby got to her feet and clumsily wiped her tears away with the dusting cloth. She imagined Rose, her glasses on the end of her nose, having to read the letters over and over again to decipher Sam's illegible handwriting.

Only then did she get the sense that someone had walked across the landing and down the stairs and she knew – without a doubt – that Sam was still around. Somewhere.

'It's as though I've found the answer to a riddle,' she told Tom when he called her for afternoon tea on the verandah. 'So, I was wrong about them. We were all wrong about them. They had far deeper feelings for one another than we realised. They weren't just two old people getting by together. Theirs was a real love story.'

'That shouldn't really surprise you,' he said. 'It seems to me that you've chosen to dwell on the past; to remember them when they were young, when their lives were unhappy and complicated, as though that was the only part of their lives that defined them. But there was so much more than that. Don't forget that their generation was different. They were made resilient by war. They didn't "share" every emotion, sometimes not even with one another and certainly not with their family and friends.' He sighed. 'Sometimes I listen to you on the phone to the girls and it sounds as though they share every fluctuating emotion with you .They don't have a filter.'

He frowned and Libby wondered, not for the first time, whether, like Sam, he might have preferred the brave old world, with all its stoicism.

'But look at all the cruel things they did to one another over the years. How did they get past that?'

'Look,' said Tom firmly. He sounded impatient. 'They just led ordinary lives. Nothing more, nothing less. Their families loved them despite all their faults. They loved their children. They did their best. You know what? Maybe you need to forgive your parents before you can forgive me,' he said, springing up from his desk eagerly as though he had just made a breakthrough. He picked up her empty cup.

'Want another one? That's what we are really talking about here isn't it. You, me and forgiveness.'

'Wait!' said Libby. 'You always walk away when a conversation gets too demanding. I know you think I'm unforgiving but I'm not like you. I can't just shrug things off. And I *know* I take everything too seriously. I want things to be perfect, especially love, and it's hard to forgive once trust has gone. And to me life is hard work. I'm so Presbyterian in that regard. It's not about having fun and going on endless holidays.

It's all about having meaningful work – that matters – and looking after your family. And romantic love of course. But maybe you are right. I think about things too much.'

'Have you ever thought that maybe the truth is sometimes out there all along,' said Tom. 'You don't have to always be searching for it. Life is beautiful in itself.'

Libby looked at him. "That is all ye know on earth and all ye need to know."

A pause. The day was so still outside they could hear the raspy chatter of the cheeky magpies trying to dislodge the rubbish bin lids outside the kitchen.

'Keats,' said Libby eventually. 'In case you didn't know.'

'Of course I knew,' said Tom. 'It's always Keats with you. Not that I understand a word of that quotation. Might be useful in court someday though,' he added.

'There you go. So, Keats is not completely wasted on you,' she said as he disappeared into the kitchen.

Late the next day, while Tom was on a conference call with a solicitor, she walked on the back roads up into the hills. The lanes there were lush and overgrown at this time of the year; redolent of the English lanes found in the crime dramas she watched obsessively on long solitary Sunday afternoons when she first moved into Belle Maison. She imagined they were much like the ones Rose walked along when she spent those dreary weekends in the countryside in England after everything with Max turned sour.

At the top of the first rise Libby paused, breathless from the climb, and looked back down the road to the township below. When she'd first come over here to live, she had found the charming French cottages sprawled everywhere irresistible, nostalgic of other, simpler days, with their eaves and the tiny attic rooms at the top of them. Now she was beginning to tire of them, the way one tires of anything if one has too much of it. It was just all too twee. What was wrong with her? One minute she loved the place; the next she hated it. Sometimes she found herself yearning for the chaos of Hong Kong; the soaring apartment blocks everywhere and the jostling crowds in central at midday.

She continued up the overgrown path; she liked the comforting familiarity that came with this walk and took the same route most days. Up the path, past the low wooden wool-sheds on her left that marked the edge of the farm which ran right up the hillside here, a brief stop at the top at the rocky outcrop marking the highest point of this walk and off across the low hillocks to the other side of the gully. There she would scramble through the blackberry bushes on an overgrown part of the path, nothing more than sheep tracks really, and clamber over the turnstile and through the cemetery before heading back down the track to the main road along the waterfront.

The cemetery was beautiful in its simplicity and symmetry. No manicured landscape here. The old, mostly untended and lop-sided French headstones in the 'old part' of the cemetery, a reminder that Akaroa was so nearly colonised by the French, were scattered in a haphazard fashion so that they looked now as though they were part of the original landscape, lying between the golden, weather-burnished tussock grass and various unkempt wild flowers and bushes. The wild hydrangeas on the edges of the graveyard grew extravagantly out of the rocky outcrops, their papery blooms rusty at this time of year, while the large creamy flower plumes of the toetoe grasses growing beside the barbed wire fence separating the graveyard from the farm next door rippled and swayed in the slightest breeze. The 'new part' with the gravestones, more often marking urns of ashes rather than the wooden coffins buried in the old area, marked the graves of people with more Anglo-Saxon names and were occasionally decorated with balloons, or children's plastic pinwheels, always in cheerful colours and fresh or often fake flowers arranged in the gravel beneath. Sometimes a solitary person or a group sat quietly on one of the simple wooden benches scattered throughout the cemetery. In winter it would become a gloomier place to walk through, when the sun went down early behind the hills, and then Libby would take a shortcut down to the waterfront on one of the back roads and join the tourists milling around the cafés or watching the fishing boats return from their day's work.

How different this was from the walk she used to do most days along Bowen Road in Hong Kong. She would set out early in the morning and even at that hour the area was a hive of industry, Filipino helpers calling to one another or giggling melodiously in groups of three and four as they walked their employers' dogs, the impatient bleat of car horns, the excited chatter of secondary school children on their way to the nearby school and always, the hum of the city below.

And then there was the passing parade of eccentric Hong Kong locals. You couldn't make it up if you tried. Just after she set out she would be passed by a young Chinese woman, running in short precise steps in her designer high heels and clutching her designer handbag. No backpack for her.

On the way back from her walk she would meet the elderly couple in matching tracksuits who walked one behind the other, in step to a whistle the wife blew on a piece of reed she plucked each morning from the side of the path where the road narrowed and was fringed by Bauhinia trees.

If she walked in the early evening, when she came to the elegant pagoda set in a small park she would hear the familiar sound of the middle-aged man, dapper and exaggeratedly gay, who, as night fell, sang Chinese opera along to his car radio, or danced to disco music under the trees surrounding the car park. There was something poignant about the solitary ritual; perhaps he lived with his elderly parents and an extended family in a typically tiny Hong Kong flat and this was his only sanctuary.

And always, as she neared home, she would encounter the old lady with the hunched back and the bowed legs who walked to the corner and back each night, always with a small smile on her face. She was delighted with the way her life had turned out; she lived in her own comfortable apartment now, provided for her by a grateful daughter, whom she had managed to send to university overseas. Familial sacrifices were always richly rewarded in Chinese culture.

After she had cut down through the steep lanes leading to the village Libby wandered along the wharf and sat on the end, dangling her legs over the side as she used to do when she was a child. The day was blustery now and the wind was getting up. A boat with a large sail on it advertising 'Dolphin Watching' went past, a scattering of people on the bow, clutching their windcheaters around them and looking miserable. The hills beyond, bleached by the long summer, were partly hidden by the huge cumulus clouds coming from the east. She could see a lone tractor trudging up the nearest hillside, the lean shape of a dog trailing behind it. She shivered. The easterly winds were bitter. They turned glorious summer days into cold biting ones, ruining plans for barbecues and sending people scurrying indoors for cardigans and jumpers. The waves were crashing on the mud-flats below, their creamy edges like dirty melting ice-cream, and the beach looked sad and cold and grey.

On the sea wall scanning the bay, a lone painter sat by his easel. He was wearing only a t-shirt and shorts, apparently impervious to the cold, and she shivered just to look at him. She watched as he languidly rolled himself a cigarette and then, lighting it, gazed out to sea as if he had all the time in the world to sit there thinking, as though it was a sunny 25 degrees and he was Monet surveying his waterlilies on a splendid Giverny day. Libby envied him his serenity.

25

Libby usually loved auctions. The anticipation, watching the prospective buyers pretending to be indifferent spectators, listening to the music of the auctioneer's patter. But she was overcome by nerves this time. She still hadn't decided whether she really wanted to bid for Belle Maison or not.

As usual, she had woken far too early that morning and in the cold early light of day, lying in an unprepossessing bed in a sparsely furnished motel in Papanui Road, the dream she had of living in a small seaside town suddenly seemed unrealistic. Tom had told her she was mad the night before when she told him she intended to put in a bid and could not bear seeing her parents' old home go to complete strangers.

'It just doesn't make any sense,' he said. 'If you'd wanted to buy the house you should have negotiated to buy it from the others *before* the auction.'

'They still treat me like the baby and never take me seriously,' said Libby. 'Tilda just set the whole thing in motion behind my back and the others are so lazy they just fell in with her. And don't worry.' She rolled her eyes theatrically. 'I can pay for it myself if that's what you are worried about.'

'It's not that I'm worried about whether you could afford it or not. I just think we need to sit down and think about what your options are. The girls will never get over to see you there; or at least not as frequently as you'd like them to. It doesn't have enough attractions for them and their families when they start to have children. By all means buy a bolt hole here in New Zealand but think carefully about where that might be.'

'You're probably right,' said Libby. 'It is an impractical idea but I am sick of not belonging anywhere. Don't you ever feel like that? I don't want to be an expat all my life.'

The auction took place mid-morning in a new building in the middle of town. This part of the city centre was deserted and since the earthquakes had flattened the area it had become a wasteland of carparks and half-completed commercial buildings. It was a Saturday and all the professionals and office workers and retailers had scurried back to the suburbs. In other cities this would be the heart of the city but now, even those people who had slowly returned as bookshops, cafés and department stores opened up again, escaped back to their suburbs on weekends. No doubt time would change that, but today only a few ubiquitous tourists, no doubt puzzled by the lack of activity, wandered aimlessly as they waited for the shops to open. A middle-aged group of Japanese huddled in one of the cafés under an outdoor heater, talked in subdued tones and gazed around them suspiciously as though they suspected the streets may have been cleared for some reason known only to the locals. Maybe a madman was loose? Maybe they were shooting a film set in a war-torn city? Maybe life would be restored when someone appeared with a megaphone and called 'action.'

A toddler was lurching up and down the aisles like a drunkard, while his grandparents followed nervously behind and his parents were in a huddle with a middle-aged man dressed in a suit. No doubt he was about to bid for them. There were also several people leaning nonchalantly at the back of the room – phone bidders no doubt. This was the trouble with globalism;

nothing was sacrosanct anymore. All the best kept secrets, those villages in previous generations known only to those who lived there, were now sought out by the new breed of multi-house owners. It was not enough anymore to possess only one home; most of Libby's friends in Hong Kong had at least two, often in places as far-flung as Phuket, France, Bali or Italy and always with a base in England or Australia or wherever they came from. When Tom and Libby first went to Hong Kong nobody they knew, at least none of their expatriate friends, owned apartments in Hong Kong and certainly never dreamed of retiring there, but all that had changed after the crash of 1997 and the (ironic) resurgence of optimism in Hong Kong as it became apparent that China would leave Hong Kong basically as it had been; the street names would stay the same, the army would not have an overt presence in the streets and common law would prevail. Well in the short term anyway. One just had to hope for the best.

The auction was about to begin. Thank goodness Charlotte had reluctantly agreed to come with her.

'You know I think you're mad, don't you?' she whispered to Libby as the auctioneer delivered the preamble. 'Let it all go. The house is in our past now and I think you're being overly sentimental. And houses really don't matter when all is said and done.'

And then, in an effort to lighten Libby's mood, she began to sing the refrain from the Abba song.

'When the summer's over and the dark clouds hide the sun
Neither you nor I'm to blame when all is said and done.'

'Shhh,' said Libby, frowning at her. 'The bidding is starting.'

226

26

The wooden bench that had been there for as long as Libby could remember still sat doggedly at the end of the garden. An apricot tree, planted as a sapling, had grown up behind it, the glossy leaves shading it in the afternoons and softening the solid paling fence between the house and the next-door neighbours. Libby sat down on it and lifted her face to the sun. The only sounds to be heard were of birds calling to one another in the trees on the hillside beyond and the distant throb of a motor boat crossing the bay.

'I want a chamomile lawn,' she said. 'I've always wanted one. Now I'll never have one. I wanted to buy the house so much it hurt.'

Tom sat down on the lawn beside her, looked thoughtfully around the garden like a man who knew what he was about and then scratched his head.

'That isn't as simple as it sounds. I think you need a well-drained acidic soil and it is difficult to mow if you have grass growing as well. What about a wildflower meadow? It would improve the garden's biodiversity and would only have to be mowed once or twice a year. I think I know a place down south where the soil would be perfect.'

Libby looked at him incredulously. 'And since when, may I ask, have you had all this information at your fingertips? What you know about horticulture could be written on the back of a stamp.'

Tom stretched out on his back on the grass with his hands behind his head and smiled up at her.

'Has it ever occurred to you that I may just have hidden talents you know nothing about?'

'No. It hasn't. I know you too well. You have lots of talents but none of a practical nature.'

He looked up at her with his eyebrows raised.

'Oh alright. I looked it up on Google actually. But you must admit that it is touching that I had the foresight to think of doing some research. And to remember how you have always wanted a chamomile lawn.'

'I suppose it *was* a little naive. I just pictured myself scattering seeds over a lawn and leaving it to grow wild. Maybe the meadow idea is better. And I wanted a very large Labrador. Or two.'

They sat in an easy silence, both looking out across the village to the bay and the hills beyond.

'Somehow I always thought of this as our house, just sleeping patiently, waiting for me to grow up, and return to look after it.'

'You called it "our house"?'

'Did I?' She paused. 'What was she like?'

'Who?'

'You know *who*. Don't make me keep saying her name. It gives her some sort of status. And I don't want to sound like her friend.'

'Like we all are when we are younger I suppose: energetic, flirtatious, and confident. She agreed with me on most subjects and was intensely interested in all my cases. In the beginning, she found everything I said very amusing too. That's always appealing isn't it? The way to a man's heart...'

'But I bet that adoration only lasted a few months. I hear she has no sense of irony.'

'Not like you,' he added consolingly. 'You have a great sense of humour. Most of the time.'

'Yes I *do,* don't I,' said Libby complacently. 'What else?'

'She was clever too.'

'What! Intellectually or did she just work hard?'

'Both I suppose. Her way of always looking for an angle or not caring about how she got a result, as long as it was the right one, got me down in the end. It's a big cultural difference. And her obsession with work.'

'What. And you're *not* obsessed with work?'

'Not to the extent that she was. No. She wasn't all bad, you know. She was careless about other people though. Cruel in that sense.'

'Why do you say that?'

'She didn't let anything stand in her way. At first I admired that in her. I suppose we were that generation that muddled our way through. We didn't plan our families or think about having time for ourselves. She was totally focused. Let me give you an example. If she wanted to get a case she'd do anything to get it, undercut all the other barristers, and court the solicitors.'

'Surely everyone does a bit of that?'

'Not in the same way. There is a code of honour at the Bar, believe it or not. When she was first made a QC she was prepared to charge the same per hour as middle ranking barristers. That's just not done. They'd never get any work if we all did that. We are just meant to do it hard for the first year or so after we take silk. She was too greedy.'

'Gosh. You *are* being honest. When did you start to be so critical?'

'Since we're speaking truthfully, predictably, when the passion died. About two years into the relationship.' He put his hands in a v shape over his nose as if he was thinking. 'Or was it 18 months?'

'Don't be flippant. It's not funny. Life is so disillusioning isn't it? All great love stories end in disappointment if they survive long enough for people to grow up. Or grow old.'

'Not all. Enduring love is probably the best of all. It's just different.'

'I love it too you know,' Libby said suddenly. 'Hong Kong I mean. It's not just *your* city. It's mine too. It's in my blood.'

'I know it is,' said Tom consolingly. 'Maybe we'll only feel ready to leave it permanently when the political situation changes and we don't have a choice. The young people there are already demanding more democracy and there's only one way that can go. '

'You look like Antheia,' said Libby admiringly, as she closed the gate behind them. She and Charlotte were setting out for a walk to the village to get a takeaway coffee. Charlotte had arrived first thing to help Tom tidy up the garden.

'With that hat and those trendy boots. Only you could look like that in your gardening clothes. You get more beautiful with age.'

'Oh stop it *"Rose"*, drawled Charlotte. '*You* get more like Mum every day you know. She was always telling us we were beautiful. Mind you I do miss her lavish compliments,' she added wistfully.

'Maybe you are looking radiant because you are happy,' said Libby suspiciously. 'Is it the same mysterious guy? Spill the beans. I promise I won't tell Tilda and Edward.'

'There's no secret about it. *You* would say that the gods have forgiven me my youthful hubris and so I can just get on with being happy. It's true that I was possibly excessively confident when I was young, but life soon knocks you about and sets you straight, doesn't it.'

'Sadly that is so,' said Libby. 'So who is it?'

'It's John. Remember him? From primary school. The skinny Maori boy with the mass of curly black hair, the birth mark on one side of his face and those thick glasses like the bottom of our school milk bottles. Edward used to call him four-eyes.'

'Oh *yes,*' said Libby. 'Of course I remember him. The teacher used to make him take his glasses off when we played rounders on Friday afternoons, which was ridiculous and cruel as he was as blind as a bat. Where on earth did you meet him again after all these years?'

'Would you believe it? On Facebook. We just got chatting as part of the group and then by the time we actually met up there was no awkwardness. We've both been on our own for far too long and we both agree that you take nothing for granted when you are older and know what loneliness can be like. He's a widower. He loved his wife, he loves his children. He's funny and lovely and very independent. Like me. He's perfect.'

'Oh that is *brilliant*,' said Libby. 'Brilliant. I know it's been hard for you, being on your own for so long, even though you never complain. And now I won't feel so bad if I decide to leave, although I have just *loved* living near you. You and I are not only sisters; we are kindred spirits.'

'You are not going to cry are you,' said Charlotte. 'There's no need for *that*.'

'Oh don't pretend to be heartless,' said Libby, smiling. 'It doesn't fool me anymore. I know you don't want me to go.'

'I'm not heartless, and of *course* I don't want you to go, but you *need* to leave here,' said Charlotte firmly. 'Sometimes big sisters have to tell you what to do. You can't dilly dally around forever.'

A morning dew lay on the grass even though it was mid-summer and most of the town appeared to be still asleep. A few lights shone half-heartedly from a couple of the cottages as Libby and Charlotte turned off the main street and made their way back up the hill, and Libby wondered idly what other people were doing up at that hour. In a cottage window she could see a woman in a short nightie doing something at the kitchen counter. The lights were on in the kitchen of the grand white house with the boutique vineyard sweeping up the hillside behind it. Nigel and Anna, who drove the sort of clean four wheel drive the locals scoffed at, were probably getting up to tend to the grapes, although Tom said that Nigel had confided in him over a beer in the pub one night that the whole 'bloody enterprise' was a financial disaster.

'When money goes out the door, so does love,' he had announced stoutly, in the sort of braying Canterbury Country accent that Tom said would not be out of place in the heart of the English counties. 'I told her from the start that you never make money out of grapes: I'm from a farming family; I would know. But Anna had read an article in one of those *House and Garden* magazines, with photos of glossy women who hardly ever eat wandering around with a couple of Labradors in tow and wanted to live the dream. Of course she can hardly tend a pot-plant, let alone get her hands dirty looking after grapes. We'll be back in the city in no time.' According to Tom he seemed exceedingly pleased with himself, as though to be proven right was far more important than watching all that money trampled underfoot.

'If you'll pardon the pun,' Tom said.

'Your puns are pathetic. How sad!' she said when Tom recounted their conversation to her. 'Can't dreams ever come true?'

'Only if you think them through carefully and do your sums,' Tom said. 'Just joking,' he'd added, tactfully.

As they walked up the hill some smoky grey clouds began to roll in over the summit and the tussocks that grew around the perimeters of the paddocks ahead of them began to sway back and forth in the freshening breeze.

'I can smell gravel,' Libby said. 'It must be all those new driveways. I love that smell.'

'*Gravel*?' said Charlotte. How can gravel smell appealing?'

'Well it *does,*' said Libby. 'It reminds me of summer days when we were kids. Kicking it as we ran along the drive, doing wheelies in it on our bikes, eating it.'

'Eating it!'

'Yes. I loved the taste. Mum was always taking it out of my mouth.'

'Honestly, I think you make things up. I have no recollection of that.'

'You were always too busy causing trouble to notice. And I don't make things up. Occasionally I may embellish them of course. If I could walk every day, just walk around the world, I would do,' she added.

'On holiday you mean?'

'Yes. Just set out every day. I love it. It brings meaning to life. And you feel you can eat a lot!'

'That's true.'

They walked in silence for a while. Libby noticed they were walking in complete rhythm. Left, right, left, right. For a tall woman, Charlotte took unusually small steps.

'I've noticed that Tom and I don't argue when we walk,' Libby said.

'I bet you do when you get lost.'

'Mm. Even then we get over it quickly. Maybe we could make a go of it if we just sold up everything and became nomadic.'

'I thought you hated planes.'

'True. But I think I might be over the whole "forever home" lark.'

'Maybe because you've found what you were looking for all along.'

'What do you mean?'

'The whole thing about Mum and Dad. It's like some sort of denouement….to find that they were actually as happy together at the end; in fact happier, than they were at the beginning. Or in the middle, which is the part you were obsessed with. Look how much you've learnt from finding out about them over the past few months. And now the letters. And you've sorted me out too. I've had the chance to be a big sister again. You've always had that ability. To create a sort of harmony in day to day living. It's a gift.'

She stopped and perched awkwardly on the top step of the stile opposite the house, leading into the field opposite. The sheep nearby raised their heads indifferently and then went back to chewing the grass.

'And think about the fine life Mum and Dad had together at the end. You and Tom can have that too. If you can bring yourself to forgive him. And he, you,' she added as an afterthought.

'Tom says that learning to forgive is the most important lesson of all. It bestows serenity on both parties.'

'Oh I loathe truisms,' said Charlotte dismissively. 'But in this case I think he's right. I don't think that is original though. It doesn't sound like Tom. I bet he got it out of a book or something.'

'Well at least he's trying to be sensitive I suppose,' Libby said, opening the gate. 'That's something. Don't worry, I'll think about what you've said.' She shook her head in mock disbelief. 'And by the way, since when did you become so wise?'

'Oh and did I tell you the others are coming over tonight,' said Charlotte. 'For the Last Supper.'

27

'You're just like Dad,' said Libby. 'You think every family gathering requires copious amounts of alcohol. It must be your Irish side coming out.'

'Family gatherings *do* require copious amounts of alcohol,' said Tom, as he set out glasses on the table and put several wine bottles into the fridge. 'Especially where your family is concerned.'

'I'm not sure Charlotte's idea is a good one,' said Libby, as she looked out to see Tilda and Hugo passing the kitchen window. 'We're all feeling pretty emotional about saying goodbye to the house.'

'Speak for yourself,' said Tom, rather smugly as he polished a wine glass on his t-shirt. 'The others will no doubt be very happy to get some money in their pockets.'

'I suppose you and Tom will just swan off into the night never to be seen again, now we've sold the house,' said Tilda. 'There'll be nothing to bring you back here now.'

Tom had been plying her with drinks since the minute she walked through the door and she was already slurring her words. When Hugo shook his head at her disapprovingly, she snapped; 'And *you* can keep out of this! It's *my* family and for once I'm going to say what I think. I'm sick of taking the blame for everything. Don't think I don't know how you talk about me behind my back. I've always been the family scapegoat.'

'Oh I wonder why that is,' said Charlotte. She was taking the last few books out of the bookcase and said over her shoulder. 'There is a history you know. We didn't just create the myth of you being the troublemaker out of nothing.'

'That is *so* unfair. Yes, I tend to speak my mind. What's wrong with that?'

'What's wrong with *that*,' said Charlotte, 'is that there is a big difference between speaking your mind and being outright nasty.'

'Oh you're ridiculous,' said Tilda. 'I can't say anything to you without you taking offence.'

'With good reason,' Charlotte said. 'You are always telling Libby and me how to lead our lives. You're so judgmental.'

'Oh *stop* it. Both of you,' said Libby, holding up her hand. 'But it's true that there's always an undercurrent of resentment where I'm concerned, Tilda. What have I ever done to you?'

'What haven't you done is more like it,' snapped Tilda. 'Living the dream while I had baby after baby, suffered years of post-natal depression and put up with a husband who was so concerned with making money he was never home. And I've always suspected he was shagging that ghastly secretary of his. And you were so wrapped up in your own life you never even noticed how sad I was.'

In the deafening silence that followed this announcement Hugo froze with a glass of wine half raised to his lips. It was the exaggerated posture of a man who knows he is in deep trouble.

'Hugo and his secretary?' Charlotte finally spluttered. 'You have to be joking. The one with boobs like a bookshelf?'

Libby found herself giggling uncontrollably. 'I'm sorry. That's a nervous giggle. It's just the look on your face Hugo. We all think of you as the model husband. And you Tilda.

You've always been so clever and accomplished. You're the typical eldest child. How earth were we meant to know what was going on if you never confided in us?'

'You forget that I was the oldest in this dysfunctional family,' said Tilda, rounding on her. 'I've always been the one who had to dissemble. I had to pretend everything was ok when Mum went away because you little ones were so sad. And so was Dad. So I took over and then I just became adept at keeping things to myself.'

'Oh Tilda, that's so awful,' said Libby. 'I wish we had understood more. We were just too young. I am *so* sorry.'

'And it's typical of this family,' Tilda continued. 'As soon as Tom goes off the rails you all rally around Libby. 'Oh *poor* little Libby. She needs us. She's not strong enough to cope on her own... It's pathetic. I've coped for years. Libby's not a baby. She chose to leave Tom. And we've never heard *your* side of the story Tom. There's always two sides.'

'But Tilda. What about when I came back from Hong Kong, crushed and beaten. A failure and a drunkard,' said Charlotte. 'You could have confided in me. I felt so inadequate because you were making a huge success of your life.'

'That was even worse,' said Tilda. 'You took up all Mum and Dad's energy. '*And* I never lived overseas. It's the one thing I always wanted to do.'

'But you never let on,' Libby interrupted. 'I just didn't know how you felt. I'm not a mind reader.'

'Didn't know? Or didn't care. You were always off somewhere exciting. Greece, Italy. You name it. You've got no idea what it was like to bring up kids back here. No maids like you and Charlotte had. All that bloody monotonous housework.'

'Hang on,' said Charlotte. 'You can't blame Libby for that. Her life wasn't perfect either you know. Nobody's is.'

'And Mum always loved you the best. Her "baby".'

'Oh don't be ridiculous Tilda,' said Charlotte. 'We mothers have a special place in our hearts for our youngest. It's only natural.'

'And you keep out of this,' said Tilda. 'It never occurred to you that my family was missing out when you came back. No more babysitting for my kids. Mum and Dad had yours to look after full time. You. No husband. Alcoholic. It's ironic because *my* kids were the ones who missed out. Not yours.'

'Ladies, ladies,' interrupted Edward. 'Do we need to turn this farewell soiree into something out of a bad soap opera? All this is in the past now. You've had a bloody good life Tilda. We all admire your success. And Hugo hasn't even been given a chance to defend himself. And let's face it; you are one of the most spoilt wives I know.'

'Oh don't be *cruel* Edward,' said Charlotte. 'Tilda is a fabulous wife and mother. Anyway, you are the one to talk about being spoilt! We all know Mum and Dad set you up financially. You had nothing when you came back from London.'

'Whoa. Steady on. Where did that come from?' said Edward.

'The wide boy who'd made a lot of money but didn't bother to save any of it,' Charlotte continued.

'And I know for a fact that they paid for your kitchen renovation,' added Tilda triumphantly. 'Not that you needed any help!'

'*Stop* it all of you,' Libby said. 'You know I hate it when you pick on Edward. And,' she added hastily, seeing their incredulous faces. 'Mum would hate to see us carrying on like this. On our last night in their house. I'm sorry you feel like that Tilda and I apologise. I love you. You're funny and smart and I've always thought you were so confident and contented. And remember that at the end of the day, like all other disappointed lovers; Hugo's stupid secretary will just be a footnote. You'll be on every page.'

Tilda shook her head in astonishment. 'That's the kindest thing you've ever said to me, Libby. Is that out of a book?'

'I have heard it somewhere before, now that you mention it,' said Libby.

'You need to be more open with one another,' Tom said suddenly, enunciating each word as though he was addressing a jury. He nodded, as though he'd just resolved a rather thorny legal problem and continued. 'I've always thought that was the trouble with your family. Everything unpleasant is swept under the rug. Maybe Tilda has a point. You never confront problems. Or talk them through.'

'Oh do *shut up* Tom,' said Charlotte. 'And don't be so patronising. And don't get me started on *you*. If its honesty you want I could tell you exactly what I think of *your* appalling behaviour. Did you "confront your problems" with Libby?'

'Yes *shut up* Tom,' said Libby. 'I would keep *very* quiet if I was you. You don't even know what it means to be honest and you are a great one to talk about talking problems through and "sharing".'

'Yes you've got off lightly so far mate,' said Hugo moving into the middle of the room and speaking with the enthusiasm of a man who finds himself with a last minute reprieve from the gallows. 'Let's talk about you.'

'No, let's not,' said Libby. 'None of this is getting us anywhere. We've gone far enough. I know what we can do for the last time in this house. We'll play the "Song" Game. You start Charlotte. Choose a song that defines a time or expresses how you feel about life.'

Tom gratefully smiled at her across the room. 'Phew,' he said, wiping his brow in an exaggerated fashion. 'Good idea Libby.'

'Ok,' said Charlotte. 'Hugo. You're in charge of playing the songs.'

He looked gratified. He liked nothing better than fiddling with his iPhone.

'Mine is '*I Will Survive*,' Charlotte announced. 'Gloria Gaynor.'

'Good choice,' said Hugo. '1978. Ranked at #2 in Rolling Stone's poll of the best disco songs of all time.'

'I really admire that about you Hugo,' said Tilda. 'You are a walking encyclopaedia about music. It's fantastic.'

The others stared at her in surprise.

'That's nice,' said Charlotte. 'That's a really nice thing to say.'

'I'm not all bad,' Tilda said. There was an awkward silence as the others digested this.

Finally Charlotte said, 'you next, Tom.'

'It's old. But good,' said Tom apologetically. '*Yesterday*. Charles Aznavour. The lyrics express how I feel about life.'

Libby raised her eyebrows. 'Really? It's such a sad poignant song. It's so *not* you!'

'Perhaps you don't really know me,' Tom said. 'Maybe this is me. Sharing.' But he softened the words with a smile.

They listened in silence as Charles Aznavour's gravelly voice filled the room.

"*The taste of life was sweet, as rain upon my tongue.*"

'I love that line,' Libby said as she got up from the sofa and went to stand behind Tom. 'Is that really how you feel?' She touched his shoulder, hesitantly. 'I wish I'd known.'

'I don't always feel like that,' said Tom, looking up at her and covering her hand with his. 'But always when I think of Charlie. I regret that I wasn't a better brother. And I have regrets about what I've done to you of course.'

'Oh I can't take any more of this introspection,' Hugo announced stoutly. 'I've never heard of Charles Aznavour. I'm off to bed. Are you coming?' he said to Tilda.

'Not before I've told Tom that I'm glad he chose that song. I reckon it sums up how we all feel about life at our age.'

'I think we're all agreed on that,' announced Charlotte. 'I'm off to bed too. But this has been *fabulous* don't you think everybody? Just like a scene from *The Big Chill*.'

'And no Parthian shots Tilda,' she said sternly over her shoulder as she left the room.

'She will look that up on Google the minute she gets into bed,' Libby whispered to Tom.

'There will be hell to pay in the morning.'

28

'We're going on a road trip,' Tom announced the next day. 'It will help you get over the disappointment of not getting the house. And your hangover.'

'I'll never get over the disappointment,' said Libby stubbornly. 'And I'll never forgive the others. What were they dreaming of, letting Tilda put it up for auction.'

'I think they could see that it would just never work out for you. You're too obsessed with the past. You have to let go and find somewhere of your own. And I think I've found just the place,' he added triumphantly.

'You've found Paradise? It doesn't exist,' Libby scoffed. She raised her eyebrows. 'Where?'

'Remember when you talked to me about your plans for your novel; about me and the Russian girl and Queenstown? It made me think about going to that part of the world. There's a place near there that is perfect for us all. Lakes, hills, rivers, mountains, skiing. We can create a "Belle Maison" of our own. It's great for the girls; just a short flight from Sydney. And you won't need to worry about whether they'll come to visit or not. They'll be falling over themselves to get there. It's got what I would call the X factor.'

'I'm not sure I can live in a small town all year round...'

'No, wait until you hear my plan,' said Tom impatiently. 'We can spend part of each year there. I'm not ready to live there all year round either, and I'm certainly not ready to retire. I don't think you are either. You'll have to have a project. Maybe we can grow grapes.'

'That might have been my dream once upon a time,' said Libby. 'But I'm world-weary now. And certainly too sensible to think about growing grapes; there's no money in it. Of course I *could* have those dogs I'm always going on about,' she continued. 'But then who would look after them when we weren't there?'

'You have to stop this,' said Tom, ruffling his hair in exasperation. 'Life just works itself out sometimes. You have to forge ahead, optimistically, taking risks sometimes, or you'd never do anything.'

'I'm not like you,' said Libby. 'I worry about things and just want to be settled somewhere. I hate all the coming and going of the expat life. I'm over it.'

'Why don't you give my idea a chance,' said Tom.' And give me a chance too.'

'I want to see Nancy before we leave,' said Libby.

She had said her goodbyes to Belle Maison the night before and in the morning they would drive south to Central Otago on a road trip Tom had planned for them in meticulous detail.

'Saying goodbye wasn't as hard as I thought it would be,' Libby told him the next day. 'You're right. It was always Mum and Dad's house. It's better that we leave it that way.'

'I'll be sorry to say goodbye to it too,' Tom said. He was standing with his back to her reaching for something on the desk and for one awful moment, when he turned around, she thought he had tears in his eyes.

'I think we should take this,' he said, handing her the old Buddha head. 'If that is ok with you? It will look good on my untidy desk in Chambers and I don't think anyone in the family will be fighting over it.'

Libby smiled. 'You are getting sentimental in your old age. But yes. Take it. I don't think even Tilda would covet *that*.'

When they got to Nancy's retirement home Tom leapt out of the car like an eager schoolboy.

'Let *me* handle her,' he said striding up the drive with a spring in his step. 'I'll show you how it's done.'

Libby smiled at him encouragingly, but muttered under her breath. 'Good luck with that.'

'Ah. A *proper* label I see,' said Nancy when she opened the door and Tom handed her the largest bottle of Hendricks's gin he had been able to find. 'You've always known the way to a girl's heart, Tom. Welcome to my humble abode,' she said, ushering him in with no sign of the lack of enthusiasm Libby had grown accustomed to when visiting. Libby was amused to see that she glanced into the mirror by the door and patted her hair into place as though she was young again and welcoming a new suitor into her boudoir. Libby's presence was only acknowledged with a careless nod.

'Sit ye here Tom,' Nancy said, fluffing up the cushion on the only armchair in the room, while Libby found herself perching diffidently on the end of the bed and wondering why on earth Nancy was speaking in such an affected manner.

'Oh do tell all about your latest case.' Now she was practically purring like a cat. 'The law has *always* held a fascination for me. I have a particular interest in your sort of practice, involving prominent clients and complex points of law.'

Libby caught Tom's eye and shook her head, raising her eyes to the ceiling in disbelief.

Later, as they got back into the car, she said, 'You could charm the birds out of the trees. It's bloody ridiculous. And I swear she was actually *flirting* with you.'

'She's not *that* bad,' Tom replied.

'Are you gloating?'

'Of course not. I don't know why you find her so difficult. She's always struck me as being a very intelligent woman. It was just unfortunate that she was born out of her time and the frustration of not reaching her potential made her bitter. And *then* when your mother came back from England and she ended up alone again, she never got over it. You just have to get her onto the right subjects,' he added as though lecturing a child. 'Don't allow her to wallow in the past. She loves politics and rugby. And avoid talking about your family at all costs. Oh,' he added as an afterthought. 'And always tell her that her hair looks nice and she looks incredibly young for her age. She *loves* that.'

'You really are the limit,' said Libby. 'Sometimes you sound like a life skills coach. But you know what? I am actually *happy* that you made her happy. And after all; she and I sort of made up in the end. Charlotte said she was proud of me.'

'Sometimes Charlotte sounds like a counsellor, not a sister,' said Tom. But then he added, smiling. 'I'm proud of you too. You've been so patient with Nancy, despite the way she carries on.'

'I'm not sure why we are doing this road trip,' said Libby crossly. 'This isn't even our part of the country. It would have been warmer going north.'

They hadn't stopped for lunch because Tom said he wanted to press on and get there before nightfall and she was tired, hungry and badly in need of a bath and a wine.

'But we can *make* it our part of the country,' said Tom. He was squinting into the late afternoon sun as they drove into Tekapo and Libby thought about how long ago it seemed – a lifetime – since she and Charlotte had visited the crematorium and giggled like school girls as they followed Mr. Farrell down the hallway past the photos of the tiny chapel on the lake and the two boys sitting on the wharf at Queenstown.

When they turned off the main highway to make their way inland the plains gave way to lush rolling farmland and the riverbeds and lakes were lined with waves of pink and purple lupins. Further on, as they came out of the last winding pass before their destination, they were surrounded by bald sturdy hills, scattered with feathery toe-toes and tussock grasses until the road swept through a valley of vineyards rolling up the hillsides in perfect symmetry, each row of vines punctuated with red roses at both ends.

'I love this part of the drive, don't you?' said Tom. 'We're nearly there now.'

'I must admit that it really is enchanting,' Libby agreed. 'We haven't been down south for so long that I'd forgotten how dramatic the landscape is. It's so rugged and beautiful. So tell me. What *is* your cunning plan?'

The 'For Auction' sign was in a prominent place on the corner as they went for a walk after breakfast the next morning. And set behind an old stone wall, right next to the tiny Presbyterian Church, was a vast grassy field, right in the middle of the village.

'I told you I'd find something special for you,' said Tom. 'If we built a house here, you could clamber over the stile to walk through the church grounds into the village. And wake up on Sundays to the sound of the church bells.'

The stile – a few pieces of rough planks nailed onto a basic frame – sat half way along the rabbit proof fence erected between the church and the open land.

'The setting *is* quite perfect I must admit,' said Libby. 'Only a minute's walk to the nearest café. I like that. And yet it feels rural, with the park opposite and the hills all around.'

'So you *like* it?' said Tom. 'Well that's a start.'

'Yes but it's just an ordinary piece of bare land you know,' said Libby. 'You haven't exactly discovered the New World! You look so pleased with yourself. Like Stout Cortez. "Silent, upon a peak in Darien." You don't know what I'm talking about do you?'

'Keats,' said the man who had been pacing up and down between the pegs dividing the sections to be sold. Dressed like a gentleman farmer, he wore immaculate moleskin trousers and a sky blue and white checked shirt. His snow white hair was brushed sleekly back from his face and – incongruously – he had a flattened nose that suggested he may have been at the bottom of a few rugby scrums in his time.

'Sorry. I couldn't help but overhear you talking about the sections. Anyone in his right mind would buy these two sections next to the church yard. Now *then y*ou could build a house. He gestured in a theatrical fashion to the church, the trees and the hills behind as if they would be part of the whole package.

'Now that's a good idea,' said Tom. 'That way you'd get the best aspect looking up to the mountains.'

'But that would be mad,' said Libby, shaking her head at him. 'If we bought two sections you'd have to build a huge house. We don't need that at our age.'

'No,' said the man, looking at her sternly over his spectacles. 'You wouldn't build a huge house in this area. A large cottage would be the appropriate construction here. You'd build the house facing north-east to take advantage of these views over the park opposite. Simon Spencer,' he announced, handing Tom a name card. 'Architect.'

'Well Simon, this *is* serendipitous,' said Tom. 'If we went ahead and purchased one of these we'd be looking for a local architect.'

Simon Spencer folded his arms and appeared to be lost in thought. 'I only take on compatible clients nowadays,' he said eventually. 'I interview people before I agree to work with them. Let me know what you decide to do and I'll give it some thought though.'

'Can you believe the man?' said Libby, shaking her head in disbelief as they watched him climb into his Range Rover and wave imperiously before driving off. 'And are you trying to tell me this is all just a coincidence? You must think I'm stupid. An architect who just happened to be on site when you bring me here. And he's clearly a mate of Nigel's, judging by the pooh-bah accent. There's only one school in the country that turns out people who speak like that and believe me; they both went there. I bet Nigel put you onto him.'

'What do you mean,' said Tom in mock indignation. 'Do you think it was a set up?'

'I *know* it was a setup,' said Libby. But she took his hand as they walked down the road. 'It *is* touching that you've gone to all that trouble. But can you imagine me trying to cope with someone like him. I can tell already that he's eccentric and arrogant and will always want to get his own way. Come to think of it….'

'He knows this part of the world like the back of his hand,' Tom said quickly. '

'And you know that because…' said Libby suspiciously.

'Oh and don't worry. He will do the bidding for us too,' said Tom confidently.

'And you just happen to know that too, do you? What are you. Telepathic?'

'But really. Tell me. What could be better than this,' said Tom later, taking off his sunglasses and polishing them on his t-shirt. They had adjourned to the local pub for lunch, and were sitting outside in the courtyard.

'Maybe this is as good as it gets. The sun on our shoulders, good fresh simple food, a magnificent mountain background, and a bloody awful, but enthusiastic local band. If we decide to build ourselves a home here,' he said, warming to his theme, 'there will be a pleasing rhythm to our days. Each morning we will start the day with a walk, and just before sunset I'll go outside to water the garden. After I've cleared up the kitchen of course! Then I'll linger outside our "large cottage", watching the way the light falls in folds on the hillside behind the village. I'll spend time thinking up a fresh platitude to describe the sun going down. You'll groan when I describe it to you, appalled as usual by my high-flown prose.'

Libby took off her sunglasses and smiled at him. 'And I'll worry about what the weather is going to be like tomorrow. We all spend our time worrying about the weather in this country. You'll have to get used to it. It's not exactly the stuff novels are made of though, is it?'

'But that's the whole point. It *is*.'

Libby leaned down to stroke the golden lab that had given up hanging around the couple at the next table and now settled at her feet, looking up at her hopefully. 'Dogs always know when you have a soft spot for them,' she said, giving him a piece of bread from her plate. 'I want two dogs you know, not just one.'

'Your wish is my command, madam,' said Tom, but she noticed he was rubbing his arthritic knee nervously as he spoke. 'Although two *does* seem a little excessive!'

Then he said, nodding slowly. 'Two dogs it is.'

'That's non-negotiable,' said Libby. 'And we must bring Carmen out for a holiday every year too. I insist on that.'

'I like it when you're decisive,' Tom said. 'It's very attractive.'

'Now let's talk about our house. Then tomorrow we'll head for Riverton. You'll like it there. It's got everything you love. A fishing harbour, long sandy beaches and a lagoon.'

29

'You look very cheerful today,' Tom said as he came into the kitchenette the following morning. After a long drive they had spent the night in one of the abundant no-nonsense motels scattered around the area.

The misty morning rain had cleared and they took their coffee out onto a wide terrace overlooking the beach below. Seagulls strutted along a shore strewn with seaweed and a group of surfers lay indolently on their surfboards waiting for the next rolling swell to carry them into shore.

'Do you think you could be enthusiastic about building a holiday house for us, and the girls?' he asked, standing with his back to her and looking out to sea. 'If we do this it's got to be a new beginning.'

'I'm not sure,' said Libby. 'Sometimes I feel I'm too jaded to be enthusiastic about anything anymore. Do you think that happens as you get older? You just run out of steam. So for a while, remember, we were captivated by all those Nordic Noir TV series and also decided we liked the elegant minimalism of Scandinavian furniture. And then we visited Denmark and Sweden and found the people weren't nearly as interesting as the characters in the TV series. In fact they were cold and unfriendly. And although we still like the Scandinavian style, our apartment is becoming more cluttered and homely again. I'm sick of minimalism.'

'*You* liked the Nordic Noir series,' Tom reminded her, laughing. 'They were always too dark for me. We could end up like your parents, you know,' he said. 'Look how happy they were at the end.'

'*Really*. And how do *you* know that? You hardly saw them in their last few years. It was just me and the girls.'

'Is it really useful to throw in those snide remarks?' Tom said, shrugging and turning to go back inside.

Then, as he stood in the doorway. 'I came down here as much as I was able. *Someone* had to pay the bills after you left teaching. Sorry. I take that back. That's what I mean about snide remarks. They get you nowhere. Think about your parents and how forgiving *they* had to be. And they were together for over 50 years.'

'If you think it's so jolly marvellous to have a long marriage, why didn't you try harder? Why haven't we lived our lives with such resilience?'

'Because we're living in a different world,' he replied in exasperation. 'Look; I'm not saying I wouldn't like to end up like them. But we have to be practical. I can't just give up everything and move down here because you had a sudden romantic notion that you wanted to live in the old family holiday house. You can be so unrealistic sometimes.'

Later Libby sat sulking on the back lawn. The sun had moved around to the bottom of the garden overlooking the lagoon and although the grass was still damp she laid her cardigan on it and leaned against the old dry stone wall, enjoying the warmth of it against her back.

'Do you want another coffee?' Tom called from the kitchenette window.

'Yes,' she muttered ungraciously, and then under her breath, 'Dickhead.'

'Sorry? What was that?' She could hear him chuckling; how infuriating he could be.

He came out with a mug, but when she reached up to take it, smiled, held onto it and said, 'Thank you?' as if speaking to an ill-mannered child.

'Thank you,' she said, but didn't look up at him.

'You know you're a control freak, don't you,' he said gently. 'You want to stage manage your life. But you can't control everything that happens and certainly not the people around you. People sometimes just do what they do. They go through crises; it's all part of the human condition.'

'Is that meant to be an excuse for your bad behaviour? Can't you see that I *do* want to be forgiving? But somewhere along the way I've forgotten what it's like to live life passionately. Everything is better if it's black and white to me now; it's safer that way. And I've become so *anxious*. I feel as though I'm on the edge of a precipice all the time. I desperately want to get the girls' lives in order – and ours. If I can't do that I'm scared the whole world will fall apart.'

'It's not all bad,' Tom said, sitting down on the wooden bench beside her. 'You're good at creating order. It's what you do best. But you'll go mad if you think life is like a house you can tidy up; where everything will stay in place, just as you like it. You need to relax sometimes and not take life so seriously.'

Libby scrambled to her feet and stood with her hands on her hips glaring down at him. 'What do you expect after what you've put me through? I can't trust anyone again. I can't afford to let my guard down; it's all I've got between me and chaos.'

Tom patted the seat beside him. 'I'm here, aren't I? Isn't that enough for now? Nothing is forever.'

'No it's certainly *not* enough,' Libby said. 'Sometimes you're so insensitive I want to stamp my foot like a child. Don't you understand that I *want* forever? It's essential to me. I don't get it that you don't seem to care about the girls now they're older, or worry about them all the time like I do. Are they lonely? Are they happy? Will they be lonely for a lifetime if they never meet anyone who will love them? I couldn't bear that. I want to sort out the future for them. I want to take the future by the horns and put it firmly in its place.'

'But that's exactly what I've been trying to tell you. That way lies madness. You *have* to let go. Did your parents put the effort into you that you've put into your children?'

'No. But that was different.'

'*Why* was it any different?'

'Because *we're* different. Our generation. Women in Mum's time had the war, and big families, and wringer washing machines and not as many choices. They didn't have *time to* think about whether their kids were happy or lonely or unfulfilled. And I don't care what you say; our generation think they are responsible for their children's happiness, even when the children are adults. That's just the way it is,' she added firmly. 'But *you* don't. That's what I don't get. I'll never understand you.'

'Nor I you,' said Tom. 'But we can keep trying. Don't give up on me. Anyway,' he said, taking the mug from her. 'Let's just forget all this for a couple of hours shall we?'

Libby was still feeling out of sorts when they walked down to the beach. When they got there they crossed the road and walked across the strip of grass beside the local store, an old weatherboard building, its walls in need of a paint, cracked by the sunlight and sea salt. Tom stood, gazing out into the bay.

'What lousy surf,' said Libby. 'And it's so cold when the sun goes behind a cloud.'

'You're behaving like a moody teenager,' Tom said. 'Let's walk along to the lagoon.'

The lagoon lay at the end of the bay. A deep green in the morning sunlight, flashes of silver, like shards of glass, spun and swirled across it as tiny slices of breeze ruffled its surface.

Suddenly a woman with pure white hair, as long as a young girl's, ran out from one of the sand dunes ahead of them. She was stark naked, with a body straight out of a Ruben's painting: a plump bottom and generous sagging breasts that swung to and fro as she ran. She held a bright blue shirt above her head and they could hear her laughter as she splashed into the shallow water and then fell theatrically under a wave. Behind her a lanky male figure, also naked, appeared, running towards the water. His penis, no prize winner, bounced up and down cheerfully.

Libby turned and smiled at Tom.

'What are they like?' she said, shaking her head

The woman was wading clumsily into the lagoon now, floating the shirt out behind her like a sail and swirling it in the water. Spirals of spray rose glistening in the sunlight as she dipped it and then flung it up to catch it. Her arms rose in the air and her breasts, suddenly uplifted, were a startling white against the weathered brown of her body. The simplicity of the gesture and the ease of those hefty limbs marching through in the water lent the scene a sort of pagan beauty.

Now the man joined her in the water, belly flopping in through a breaking wave and then disappearing beneath the surface before suddenly reappearing beside her. She shrieked as he dragged her under and they splashed and gambolled in the mid-morning sun, the spray rising and their voices clear and shrill, like birds calling to one another.

'It's lovely really, isn't it,' said Libby. 'The dead opposite of those stupid adverts you see with ridiculously beautiful models lying beside an infinity pool or something. These are real people, warts and all. They don't care what they look like. They are just happy in the moment. I envy them,' she added wistfully. 'I really do.'

Tom turned around and looked at her. 'That's just what I was trying to tell you,' he said, nodding his head. 'Real life has warts all over it, but it doesn't mean it's not beautiful.'

Libby sat down on the sand right at the edge of the dunes and dug her hands into the cold of the sand beneath the surface. She let it dribble through her fingers. Tom continued on to the water's edge, head down, shoes off, dragging his feet. He looked despondent and Libby felt a pang of compassion for him, like a sudden cramp in her heart.

'*Watch me,*' he called suddenly and started taking his clothes off in huge exaggerated gestures, tossing them aside provocatively like a stripper. His t-shirt was followed by his shorts, then his boxer shorts. Libby noticed he was limping slightly – an old rugby injury – and his nudity made him look vulnerable. Old and slightly worn; not the virile young man Libby had fallen for all those years ago. She smiled and shook her head. Maybe that's what mature love was all about. The joy of familiarity.

Tom was showing off now. He picked up his boxer shorts, and waved them around his head before throwing them aside and running into the water.

'Come on in,' he called over his shoulder as he dived beneath a wave and reappeared on the other side.

'It's too cold,' she called to him, but she started slowly for the water's edge.

'Don't be a wimp.'

She imitated him, drew her t-shirt provocatively over her head, peeled off her bra, wriggled out of her jeans, and rushed headlong into the surf in her knickers.

The cold took her breath away. She felt the butterflies in her stomach that she always got in cold water.

'Keep your shoulders under.'

She dived under a wave and then gasping, swam hard out into the bay, diving under the waves as they broke until she was beyond the breaking line and only the swell of the waves indicated their passing. She turned and floated on her back.

Tom swam out and trod water beside her.

'Cheat. No clothes allowed.' He suddenly duck-dived so that his luminously white bottom popped up out of the water.

'I'm allowed to cheat,' said Libby, laughing. 'You look ridiculous.'

'There,' he said. 'See. That's how simple happiness can be. Live for the moment.'

Libby rolled over and floated on her back, kicking to stay afloat. The sky like a comforting ceiling lay above her, blue as a robin's egg with lashing of white creamy clouds.

'Maybe,' she said.

Now they both lay on their backs, looking up at the sky.

'*My* problem,' said Libby, watching a flock of seagulls circling above them. 'Is that at the end of the day I can't leave anyone or anywhere. I'm a coward. I can't face change. I can't leave you and I can't leave Hong Kong. Not for good anyway.'

'We'll have to leave it one day,' said Tom. 'We'll never get over it, but at least let's never get over it together. Can't we try to do that? Please.'

'All things considered,' Libby said, 'I think we can.'

Then, slowly, they began to swim back to shore. Half way back, Libby stopped to let Tom catch up to her.

'We'll never swim in perfect harmony will we? Probably because I'm a better swimmer than you. But maybe that's good enough for us.'

'I reckon it is,' said Tom. 'I reckon it's more than good enough.'

The End

About the Author

Diana Duncan lived in Hong Kong for many years, teaching English literature in an international secondary school.

She has had several short stories published and was a finalist in short story competions run by the South China Morning Post and the BBC World Service.

She has also won several Festival Recommendations for the eleven Children's Rhyming books she has written. (*hugothewinner. com*)

Diana, a New Zealander, now lives in Arrowtown and Sydney.